She wants this,

Garth thought incredu

He gave a soft moan as she returned the kiss and let him taste her, the way he'd wanted to for a long time. A long time.

God, Jenna, he thought, perhaps said.

She leaned into him, and a warm, urgent pleasure suffused his body.

Jenna had forgotten; now she remembered—all at the same time. A man's touch. A man's smell. She'd been alone too long. She wanted to weep. She wanted . . .

"Garth, no!" She tried to break away. "Garth. I don't want this." Her voice was barely a whisper.

He leaned back to look at her, his eyes searching hers.

"You're a liar, Mrs. Gallagher."

Dear Reader,

The Silhouette **Special Edition** selection has seldom been more satisfying than it is this month. For starters, beloved **Nora Roberts** delivers her long-awaited fourth volume of THE O'HURLEYS! *Without a Trace* joins its "sister" books, the first three O'Hurley stories, all now reissued with a distinctive new cover look. Award-winning novelist **Cheryl Reavis** also graces the Silhouette **Special Edition** list with a gritty, witty look into the ironclad heart of one of romance's most memorable heroes as he reluctantly pursues *Patrick Gallagher's Widow*. Another award-winner, **Mary Kirk**, returns with a unique twist on a universal theme drawn from the very furthest reaches of human experience in *Miracles*, while ever-popular **Debbie Macomber** brings her endearing characteristic touch to a wonderfully infuriating traditional male in *The Cowboy's Lady*. Well-known historical and contemporary writer **Victoria Pade** pulls out all the stops (including the f-stop) to get your heart *Out on a Limb*, and stylish, sophisticated **Brooke Hastings** gives new meaning to continental charm in an unforgettable *Seduction*. I hope you'll agree that, this month, these six stellar Silhouette authors bring new meaning to the words **Special Edition**!

Our best wishes,

Leslie Kazanjian
Senior Editor

CHERYL REAVIS
Patrick Gallagher's Widow

Silhouette Special Edition
Published by Silhouette Books New York
America's Publisher of Contemporary Romance

To Leslie Kazanjian,
for helping me fly

SILHOUETTE BOOKS
300 East 42nd St., New York, N.Y. 10017

ISBN: 0-373-09627-5

First Silhouette Books printing October 1990

Printed in the U.S.A.

Books by Cheryl Reavis

Silhouette Special Edition

A Crime of the Heart #487
Patrick Gallagher's Widow #627

CHERYL REAVIS,

public health nurse, short-story author and award-winning romance novelist who also writes under the name of Cinda Richards, says she is a writer of emotions. "I want to feel all the joys and the sorrows and everything in between. Then, with just the right word, the right turn of phrase, I hope to take the reader by the hand and make her feel them, too." Her last Silhouette Special Edition novel, *A Crime of the Heart*, reached millions of readers in *Good Housekeeping* magazine. Cheryl currently makes her home in North Carolina with her husband and teenage son.

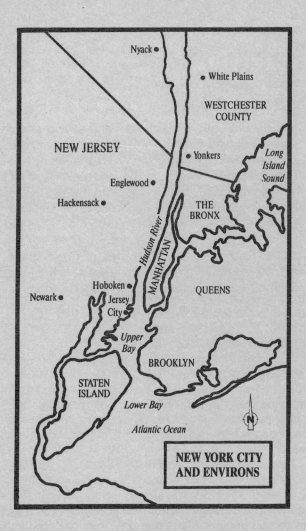

NEW YORK CITY
AND ENVIRONS

Chapter One

The widow Gallagher wanted to dance.

Johnson Garth stood on the other side of the room and watched her, moving whenever someone in the crowd got in his way so he could keep her in view. He suspected that she simply liked the music—Bob Seger and The Silver Bullet Band's rendition of "Old Time Rock and Roll"—and that there was nothing of the "merry widow" about her. If anything, she was trying *not* to respond to the hard, driving beat, and she seemed to be listening intently to the young woman talking to her, oblivious to the partying, off-duty police personnel around her. But he knew that she secretly had one toe tapping, regardless of her apparent attentiveness.

The music was loud, and his head pounded with the bass notes because he'd had too much squad room coffee and too little sleep. The house was already jammed with invited and uninvited guests, and the doorbell kept ringing with late arrivals. All the downstairs rooms were filled with the boisterous laughter and double entendres of wet law enforcement people who had braved the rain to get here. The air hung heavy with cigarette smoke, and past it he could smell wet leather and the aroma of lasagna, pan after pan of it being heated up in the kitchen.

Allegedly, he had come tonight because the party was for some patrolman who'd just made detective and been transferred into the precinct. Garth was one of the few in the Detective Squad without a partner. He liked it that way, but he always seemed to get stuck with the new ones when they first came in—which was surprising to him, considering that he was usually in hot water with the lieutenant for making somewhat liberal interpretations of the *Patrol Guide*. It was true that he did want to see the new man up close. He hated unknowns, and if he had to have a partner, he preferred somebody who was a quick learner, somebody he could depend on to keep his eyes open and his mouth shut. He had no intention of being paired with a dumb kid who thought everything had to be done exactly by the book and who would get on his nerves or get him killed, or both.

But the reason he'd come tonight was Jenna Gallagher. He thought that the new detective must be well connected to get the Gallagher woman out and about. Garth had done the legwork on the investigation of Patrick Gallagher's murder, because he knew the streets and because he had reliable contacts. But he hadn't been able to talk to Mrs. Gallagher, even in an official capacity. The word had come down from the top that Patrolman Gallagher's widow was not to be bothered. All inquiries were to be made through her brother-in-law, Detective Sergeant Hugh Gallagher— which was a joke. Garth didn't trust Hugh to tell him the right time of day, much less something he needed in a murder investigation.

Garth didn't really know Jenna. He hadn't seen her in almost a year, and that had been at Patrick's funeral. He was willing to admit that perhaps she shouldn't have been "bothered" then. He remembered what she'd been like. Pale. Too dazed by the horror of her husband's death to weep, even for the television cameras that dogged her every step.

But he had come to believe that there had been no reason for her to be widowed so young—unless Patrick Gallagher, on this one occasion, had been a fool. The circumstances of Gallagher's death still puzzled him. He had marked Gallagher down as a good cop—not as good a cop as his being killed in the line of duty had made him, but a more than adequate third-generation member of New York's finest, one with a good deal more sense than he'd evidently shown on the day he was killed. Supposedly Gallagher had walked up to a teenage boy who was behaving suspiciously in Central Park. He hadn't bothered to wait for his partner or even to let the man know what he was doing; he hadn't drawn his service revolver—because, his fellow officers surmised, he was Patrick Gallagher, and Patrick Gallagher *cared*. It was true that Gallagher's caring for his fellow man was legendary—particularly now that he was dead—but he had apparently assumed that anyone he encountered would know that, and that colossal stupidity had cost him his life.

Except that Patrick Gallagher wasn't stupid. There was a reason for his behavior that day; there was *always* a reason for people doing what they did. It didn't matter to Garth that the alleged perpetrator had been caught. It didn't matter to him that the case was closed, that Internal Affairs and the police commissioner and Patrick's brother, Hugh, were all satisfied that justice had been done. Garth wasn't satisfied. He didn't necessarily think that Gallagher had knowingly gotten himself into something dirty—it didn't matter now, anyway. It was just that Garth didn't like loose ends, particularly if there was a dead cop on the end of one of them. What he did like was poking his nose into things that made people nervous; more often than not, you came up with answers that way. And in this particular instance, the person who was most nervous was Patrick's brother, Hugh.

Garth didn't like Hugh Gallagher, and the feeling was mutual. Even in the academy they hadn't liked each other. Hugh had moved up fast, making detective long before Garth had, and he had the arrogance that came from belonging to a long line of honored New York policemen. Garth understood Hugh's air of superiority; he was arrogant himself. But his own arrogance had been fostered by the early disadvantages of being poor and fatherless and having a mother who refused to acknowledge the reality of either, not from belonging to an established law enforcement family and, therefore, knowing all the right moves in the unspoken etiquette of the brotherhood in blue. Garth had never really belonged to anything, and he had envied Hugh his inherited expertise in their chosen profession. Hugh had an easy acceptance of the inner workings of "The Job" that often left Garth frustrated and angry. Garth had always been outspoken. He said what he meant and he meant what he said, and somehow that never seemed to work with the police hierarchy. One had to play the game of favors done and paybacks, a game whose existence Garth acknowledged but whose unwritten rules left him more than a little irritated, because he hated having to keep up with who owed whom what.

But there was more than just professional jealousy on his part when it came to Hugh Gallagher. There was a certain wariness between them now—not his, but Hugh's. He worried Hugh. He had ever since Patrick had been killed and he had caught the case. He still worried him, and with a little luck, he'd find out why. That was where the widow Gallagher came in. It was time to bother her.

Garth worked his way through the crowd to get closer to Jenna. She was a pretty woman, he thought. He liked her hair—not quite red and not quite blond, and long and curly and a bit disheveled, as if she'd just gotten out of bed. When he'd seen her at the funeral, she'd been wearing black. The dress she had on tonight was a pale pink. Something soft and clinging, outlining her breasts and the swell of her hips. It was definitely an improvement. She was a pretty woman, he thought again, and he liked pretty women, particularly when they might have information he needed. It made a generally dull and routine part of The Job a little more enjoyable, and he was looking forward to this encounter.

Jenna Gallagher abruptly stopped talking, looking deliberately at the man who stood staring at her from the other side of the room. He'd been looking ever since he arrived, and there was nothing subtle about it. He held her eyes now, refusing to look away simply because she'd caught him doing whatever it was he was doing. In the first few months after Patrick died, she had, by necessity, grown accustomed to being looked at. It was one of the few things that had penetrated her grief. She hadn't been able to go anywhere people knew her without feeling their stares. Some of the looks were kind, sympathetic; most were filled with a kind of morbid curiosity, the same kind of expressions she assumed people wore when they gawked at the scene of an accident.

This man's was neither. His look was filled with determination and frank sexual interest, and in spite of herself, she felt compelled to look back. She assumed he was a cop. He looked like a cop, one of the rogue detectives who did undercover work in Narcotics and who had to dress the part. He wasn't wearing a suit or a tie. He had on jeans. And a white shirt and a zippered jacket. He stood with his hands jammed in the pockets, and he needed a haircut and a shave, and probably a bath.

But he didn't participate in the braggadocio that was so evident in the room. He was very quiet, the way Patrick had always been quiet, standing apart, tolerating the cockiness that some cops assumed as if it were as much a part of The

Job as their service revolvers and their shields. Lord, how the loud and often vulgar machismo of policemen had embarrassed her when she'd first married Patrick. She had been young and abruptly thrust into this strange, always potentially violent world of big-city law enforcement, and she'd spent nearly the first year of her marriage being essentially mortified. She had grown up in a small town on the Susquehanna River, and nothing in her staunch, middle-class upbringing had prepared her for the raucousness of people who had to put their lives on the line every day. Except Patrick. Gentle, understanding, teasing Patrick.

She smiled, remembering, then abruptly suppressed it and looked away. It was good that she could think of Patrick without such pain now, but she didn't want the man on the other side of the room to think the smile was for him.

"Debbie, who is that?" she asked the young woman with her. Debbie was barely five feet tall and had to stand on tiptoe to see.

"Oh, no!" she said immediately. "Why didn't you tell me he was here?"

"Because I don't know who he is."

"Johnson Garth," Debbie said worriedly.

Ah, Jenna thought, recognizing the name. So that was the notorious Detective Garth. She had never met him, but she had certainly heard of him. He had caused a good deal of comment in the Gallagher family a few years ago when he had some kind of public disagreement with Hugh. Garth had subsequently punched him in the nose, and not only had he done it while they were both on duty, but he hadn't been disciplined for it. Or if he *had* been disciplined, the punishment hadn't been harsh enough to satisfy the Gallaghers.

"What is he doing here?" Debbie said, obviously still worrying. "He never comes to these things—oh, my Lord, you don't think he's after Hugh again, do you?"

"I doubt he was 'after' Hugh the first time." Hugh wasn't the most tactful man in the world.

"Oh, my Lord! He's coming this way! What should I say to him? Jenna, don't go!"

But Jenna had every intention of going—not because she had the "hostess jitters" like Debbie, but because she suddenly didn't want to encounter this man. She found his overt interest disturbing. If she stayed, she had the overwhelming feeling that she would have to deal with him on a man-to-woman basis. There would be no quiet respect for her bereavement on his part, and no hiding behind widow's weeds on hers. She wasn't prepared to deal with that, not because she was still grieving, but perhaps because she wasn't.

Yet she looked into his eyes as he approached, sad eyes, compelling eyes. She felt awkward and uncertain. She shouldn't have smiled the way she had. He must think she'd sent him some kind of invitation.

She was being ridiculous. He was someone who knew Patrick. He'd offer his condolences, and that would be the end of it.

But he had to cross Hugh's path to get to her, and when he did, Hugh grabbed him roughly by the arm. Beside her, Debbie gave a high-pitched squeak of protest, reminding Jenna of a traumatized mouse.

Garth heard the peculiar noise the young woman with Jenna Gallagher made, but he looked around into Hugh Gallagher's eyes.

"Stay away from Jenna," Hugh said, his grip tightening on Garth's arm. Garth looked down at the offending hand, then back into Hugh's eyes. "Jenna who?" he said lightly.

"Listen, you son of a—"

"Excuse me, gentlemen!"

They both looked around. Jenna stepped closer. "I need to borrow Detective Garth a minute, Hugh," she said. "The two of you will have to talk shop later."

She linked her arm through Garth's, and he had the distinct impression that she'd had to dig deep to find the courage to do it. She pulled him away with her through the crowd as if it were a perfectly natural thing she did all the time. It wasn't that he minded going. She was a better-than-average-looking woman, and he wanted to ask her a few questions—he'd go anywhere with her. It was just that he didn't understand. She let go of his arm almost immediately, but he still followed her. The music abruptly changed to something slow and mellow and '50s. The Diamonds, his brain identified automatically, because, like Bob Seger and his Silver Bullets, he, too, liked the old-time rock and roll, and he knew most of the titles and the groups by heart.

"Where are we going?" he asked.

"Nowhere," she said over her shoulder. "I've done my good deed."

"What good deed is that?" he persisted, trying to catch up with her.

She kept going, and she didn't answer him.

"Mrs. Gallagher," he called, because there was no need to pretend that he didn't know who she was. "Would you like to dance?" It was a long shot, but it certainly got her attention.

She turned around, her expression, if he had had to describe it, completely incredulous. "What I would like, Detective Garth, is for you to behave."

It became clear to him then that incredulity must be catching. "Behave? Me?"

"Yes, you."

"What have *I* done?"

He thought Hugh was the one she should talk to about behaving, but he didn't say so. He looked over his shoulder, expecting the man to be coming after them. But Hugh was standing in the same spot—trying to remove himself from the clutches of some woman with big breasts who wanted him to dance. She was all over him, and she kept calling him "Hughie." Garth smiled. If Hugh's wife was here, that little scene had the potential for requiring a very lengthy explanation on Hugh's part.

"Driven your hostess to tears, for one thing."

"My hostess?" He bumped into an overweight patrolman with a huge plate of lasagna.

"Watch it, Garth! Can't you see I'm trying to feed my face here?"

"Yeah, Norm, I can see that. Why don't you let that 'face' of yours take a break? Leave some for the rest of us, will you? What hostess?" he added to Jenna Gallagher. He was beginning to feel a little desperate, because he'd gotten a real opportunity here, and she had clearly finished with him.

She stopped walking—or trying to. They were in a bottleneck of people trying to balance plates of lasagna and hold on to their beers.

"Debbie Carver," she explained patiently. "The wife of the new detective, Alden Carver. The person who is giving this party?"

"Never heard of her," he said in all truthfulness. "So why is she in tears?"

"Because you were going to punch Hugh in the nose. Again."

"No, I wasn't—at least I don't think I was. You didn't give me time to find out. So why should she care if I punch your brother-in-law?"

"Under the circumstances, the explanation was rather rushed, but I gather that her husband admires you. If you punched Hugh, he'd be on your side. He's got a wife, and he can't afford to ruin his career by trying to help you out when he's only been a detective for three days."

"You think helping me out would ruin his career?"

"Yes," she said evenly, and he smiled.

He rubbed his hand over the stubble on his chin, thinking that he probably should have shaved. "So would you like to dance?"

She looked into his eyes. "You don't even know who he is, do you?"

"Who?"

"Detective Carver!" she said in exasperation.

He gave a small shrug. "No. I don't."

She pressed her lips together, and she took him by the arm again, pulling him along with her toward the kitchen. "He's in there," she said, pointing to a fresh-faced, preppie-looking young man with a makeshift towel-apron around his waist. He was taking yet another pan of lasagna from the oven, and he paused long enough to kiss the young woman Jenna had been talking to earlier.

Garth glanced at Jenna Gallagher. "The kid admires me, huh? What do you know about that?"

He was being facetious, and she knew it—but she wasn't going to put up with it.

"Do you want to be introduced?"

He looked back at the kid with the towel around his waist. He didn't want to annoy Jenna Gallagher; he wanted to talk to her. "What's his name again? Carver?"

"Yes. His wife is—"

"Debbie," he supplied. "Debbie and—" He looked to her for help.

"Alden."

"Alden?"

"Skip—to his friends," Jenna added pointedly.

He looked back at Alden "Skip" Carver. He was in the kid's house, and he intended to eat his lasagna and drink his beer, and he wanted to pacify Jenna Gallagher. Those were good enough reasons to walk over there and wish him well.

But someone called Jenna away, and he stared after her, fighting down the urge to follow her. Well, what the hell, he thought. He had his toe in the door, and the few brownie

points he might earn by congratulating the Carver kid
wouldn't hurt. Apparently Jenna Gallagher was big on that
kind of thing—*behaving*.

A couple danced slow and close just inside the kitchen
doorway. He pushed his way farther into the room. He
should come to parties more often, he decided; otherwise he
was never going to get used to seeing two uniformed police
officers dancing together, even if one of them *was* a woman.

He sighed and turned his attention to Skip Carver, who
was shoveling lasagna into a line of heavy-duty paper plates
on the counter.

"Nice going, Carver," he said to make the new detective
look up. "Congratulations." He extended his hand, and
Alden Carver was so taken aback that he nearly stuck the
lasagna-covered spatula into it.

"Garth! I mean Detective Garth!" he said, trying to re-
cover. He laughed and shifted the spatula to his other hand.
"Debbie! Debbie, come here! This is Detective Johnson
Garth—I told you about him—this is my wife Debbie, sir."
He shook Garth's hand vigorously.

It was clear from the look on Debbie Carver's face that
her husband had indeed told her about him. It was also clear
that she'd been crying and might, Garth thought, start again
with very little provocation. "Garth," he said to her, still
trying to get his hand away from her husband. "Just call me
Garth. Everybody does. Nice party," he added.

"Is it?" she said worriedly, and he couldn't decide
whether she didn't believe him or didn't believe the fact that
he, of all people, the potential puncher of noses, would actually extend her a compliment.

He smiled. "Yes. It is. It's a good way to get to know the
people your husband will be working with." It was a good
way, but he wasn't so sure it was a good idea. The police
brotherhood in this precinct was very closed, and sometimes it didn't sit well for a young cop to try too hard to fit
in.

But wide-eyed little Debbie Carver didn't have to know that. Everybody seemed to be having a good time, and the lasagna certainly smelled good.

"I hear you might be Skip's partner," Debbie said.

"Well, who knows? Nobody knows what the brass is going to do until they do it."

Impulsively she gave him a hug. "Don't be mad because I sent Jenna after you," she whispered. "Please. And don't tell Skip," she added sotto voce.

"No, hey," he said, laughing because she'd taken him by surprise. "Mrs. Carver, I won't."

"What's going on?" Skip asked, looking up from the lasagna to glance from one of them to the other.

"Nothing, kid," Garth answered. "Keep going with the lasagna. You got a lot of hungry people out there." He smiled at Debbie and moved out of the way of another wave of starving guests. To his surprise, Jenna was standing just inside the kitchen doorway. Nice body, he thought as he approached her. Nice eyes. Blue eyes. He liked looking into her blue eyes. And he liked that pink dress.

Now, if she just stayed put.

She didn't run off again. She stood by the doorway, watching him, as if she were waiting for him to get to her.

"That was very kind," she began when he was close enough to hear her. "Talking to Debbie—"

"It wasn't *kind*," he interrupted almost harshly, because, for some reason he couldn't have explained, he didn't want her thinking he was something he was not—not when he was about to put everything he had into getting whatever information he could get out of her about Patrick and Hugh. In his life, in his work, he'd been called a lot of things, but rarely *kind*.

They stood there in the crowded kitchen, her eyes probing his, until, unsettled by the assessment he felt she was making, he suddenly smiled.

"So," he said, bending low so she could hear him, "do you want to dance or not?" He realized immediately that under the din of conversation and laughter the music had stopped.

A smile worked at the corners of her mouth. "Actually, Detective Garth, I'd rather eat. If you'll excuse me—" She put her hand lightly on his arm to get by, but he didn't move out of the way.

"I'll get it for you," he said. "Wait right here."

He didn't give her a chance to protest, plunging back through the crowd toward Skip and Debbie. He was counting on the fact that Jenna Gallagher was probably too polite to walk away.

"Skip!" he yelled over the heads of the people in front of him—because he was tall enough to do it, and if he was going to be somebody's hero, he might as well get some benefit from it. "Two!" He held up two fingers in case the kid had trouble hearing him.

"You got it, sir!"

Skip Carver passed him two well-laden plates and two plastic forks wrapped in yellow paper napkins.

"Skip!" Garth called again. "Don't call me sir!"

Carver grinned and saluted with the lasagna spatula.

Garth made his way back toward where Jenna had been standing, carrying the plates of lasagna high over his head. "Coming through," he said to the people in his way, but he didn't see Jenna anywhere.

Damn, he thought.

The music was playing again—The Drifters. "This Magic Moment." There was nothing magic about his being left holding two plates of lasagna.

Someone was poking him in the shoulder. "What!" he snapped.

"That way, Garth," a patrolman said, pointing across the living room. Jenna Gallagher stood in the foyer, motioning for him to come there.

Well, what do you know, he thought. Hugh was definitely not going to like this.

He made his way there without difficulty.

"I found a place to sit," Jenna said, taking one of the plates.

"I'll get the beer."

"No, I've got it," she said, leading the way.

Damn, he thought again.

The place she'd found was halfway up the stairs to the second story of the narrow house. He had to stand back for a moment to let some people come down the steps, one of them Rosie Madden, his partner for a time when she'd first made detective. He'd found her tough and smart and as outspoken as he was himself—which worried him now. God only knew what she'd say if she picked up on the fact that he was about to eat lasagna in the dark with Jenna Gallagher. Rosie had her hair in as many long braids as her head would hold, and as she passed by, she lifted up one of them and waggled it at him the way Oliver Hardy would have waggled his tie. Her eyes cut to the two plates of lasagna he was holding, and then to the widow Gallagher.

"You devil, you" was all she said, and thankfully that was in a whisper, which Jenna seemed not to hear.

Jenna sat down on the stairs. He took a step higher than hers so they wouldn't entirely block the way and so he could look at her without difficulty. He had to be able to see her so he'd know the right time to ask what he wanted to ask.

"Here you go," he said, giving her one of the wrapped forks from out of his shirt pocket. She handed him a beer in exchange.

He stared at her shamelessly, trying to decide how he was going to handle this. Sitting in the dim light on the stairs, she had become very quiet suddenly, as if she'd had to put on a front when she was out there in the middle of everything, but now that she was more or less out of sight, she was letting her guard down.

No more cheerful Mrs. Gallagher, he noted.

He kept watching her. She wasn't eating, but she didn't want to talk, either. Her job, evidently, was keeping the peace, one she'd accepted, albeit reluctantly.

She looked down at the people milling around below them. From time to time she smiled a bit at some overheard remark, because they had a bird's-eye view of all the social interactions going on—the budding relationships, the illicit assignations, the police wives like little Debbie Carver trying to keep things going smoothly for the sake of their husbands.

But he had to get the ball rolling.

"Nice song," he said when The Drifters' music ended.

"Yes," she said. Period.

Great, he thought. She was nothing if not succinct. He was going to have to try thinking of this as sitting in the dark with a pretty woman instead of interrogating a witness. Build your rapport, Garth. Then . . .

"The Drifters," he offered in an effort at rapport-building. "They don't have good groups like The Drifters anymore."

She looked at him quizzically. He thought that she wasn't dumb by a long shot, and he'd do well to remember that.

"No," she said, looking down at her plate and worrying a chunk of lasagna with her fork. "You like the oldies, then," she added quietly, carefully, as if her small response might be misconstrued on his part. What could he think from a halfhearted question like that? That she was being disrespectful to Patrick's memory? Disloyal to Hugh?

"Yeah, I like them," he said. "They don't remind me of anything."

She looked at him again—as if she considered that a peculiar reason for liking a certain kind of music but wouldn't say so.

"So what kind of music do you like?" he asked, because she'd given him an opening.

"Jazz."

"Yeah? That random . . . noodling stuff with no beginning or middle or end, or the quiet kind that makes you want to sit in the dark and chain smoke and feel sorry for yourself?"

"Both," she said. "But I've never thought of it quite like that."

"And you like Bob Seger and The Silver Bullet Band," he said, because he wanted her to think he'd noticed something specific about her—which he had.

"Yes," she said, obviously surprised.

"I thought so."

She smiled. She had a nice smile. Very natural. Warm. Real.

"Why?" she asked.

"I just did." He took a few bites of lasagna, wondering how long Hugh was going to let him get away with this. Hugh had spotted them sitting on the stairs, but so far he was limiting himself to killer looks. If Jenna noticed him at all, it didn't show. "This is good lasagna," he suggested, getting on with the rapport-building.

"Thank you," she said, smiling again.

"You made this?"

"Most of it. Debbie and I worked all day getting it ready."

"You should open a restaurant." It wasn't brilliant, but it was the best he could do—Hugh was coming closer. Jenna saw him, and an expression passed over her face he couldn't identify.

"Are you okay?" he asked.

"Yes, I'm fine."

"Are you worried about Hugh?"

She looked at him. "Are you?" she countered.

"No. I never worry about Hugh."

"Neither do I," she said. He believed her, but that stressed look was still there.

"Is this the first party you've been to since Patrick died?" he asked bluntly.

"I...yes. I've been out to dinner with friends, things like that. But this is the first time I—" She broke off and looked away again, sighing heavily. "I never liked these parties much even before Patrick died, but I..." She trailed off, and he didn't press it.

"You don't have to stay if you don't want to. If you want to go home, I'll take you."

"I wasn't trying to pick you up, Detective."

"I didn't think you were, Mrs. Gallagher." He grinned. "Even if you did drag me all around the ground floor here."

She laughed softly.

Bingo, he thought. Instant rapport.

"So tell me about...Skip Carver," he said. He wanted to ask about Patrick, about his state of mind before he'd been killed, but he suddenly found that he also wanted to be tactful. The truth of it was that he liked sitting here with her on the dark stairs, and it wasn't just because it was creating a buzz in the room. He could smell her fragrance. The scent was soft and womanly—like she was. Citrus, he thought. No, lavender, maybe.

"You're his hero," she said, and he laughed.

"The kid is hard up for heroes. Did Patrick know him?"

"Patrick? No, I don't think so."

"Hugh?"

"I couldn't say."

"Anything else?"

"Anything else?" she repeated, clearly puzzled.

He took a bite of lasagna. "About the Carver kid," he said, gesturing with his fork.

She looked at him thoughtfully. "His mother didn't want him to be a cop."

"Yeah, well, I can relate to that. *My* mother took to her bed for a week—until I told her I might be able to save some rich woman's life if I was one of New York's finest."

"I don't understand."

"See, the Garths don't have much, Mrs. Gallagher. Never have had. Never will. My mother lives in this fantasy from a '40s movie where her poor but handsome son will marry 'up' and change both our lives. She'd like me to marry somebody from the Upper East Side with blue blood and a lot of bucks. Or if I can't do that, somebody without blue blood with a lot of bucks."

"I'm sorry," she said.

He made a gesture of dismissal. "Don't be sorry, Mrs. Gallagher. It's not that bad. I made Hazel sound like some kind of gold digger. She isn't. She's eccentric as hell, but she's a good woman who's worked hard all her life. We all got to have our dreams, you know?"

He looked into her eyes. She did know, but she wasn't going to admit it to him.

"Your mother—Hazel—is she still working?"

"Oh, yeah. She's a waitress in this hole-in-the-wall restaurant in Brooklyn. The Humoresque. How do you like that for a name? Half the people who go in there can't even pronounce it. She's been there forty years. She's the life of the place, you know? Knows all the regulars. Pokes her nose into all their personal business—drags me into it if she things they need a cop. They love it. The place would probably shut down if she retired."

The conversation lagged. He could feel the interest in the room spreading; people kept wandering by: *Yes, by God, Jenna Gallagher is sitting up there with Garth.*

"You and Skip have a lot in common," she said after a time. "Only he's trying to get *away* from the blue blood and the money."

"Yeah? The kid's rich, you mean?"

"His family is. He's wanted to be a cop for as long as he can remember. *His* mother sent him for a psychiatric evaluation when he decided to join the force. And then he married Debbie. Her father's a cop, so she's supposed to be all wrong for him. Debbie's afraid she'll do something that will ruin Skip's career, and his mother will say 'I told you so' on both counts. That's why she was so worried about you. She panicked when she saw both you and Hugh were here."

"And you volunteered to save the day."

"Not exactly. It's hard to say no to Debbie when she's literally pushing you in the direction she wants you to go."

"People do a lot of that, do they? Push you into places you don't want to go."

"Since Patrick died they do," she said candidly.

"Why is that?"

"They think I have the Police Commissioner's ear. Or the Mayor's."

"And do you?"

"Let's just say if there's a neighborhood protest for better police protection in a park or a playground, they'd rather not see Patrick Gallagher's widow carrying a sign in a picket line on the six-o'clock news."

He smiled. She was the widow of a martyr, a real, media-approved hero. An entire city had mourned with her. He imagined she could make it hot for certain public officials if she wanted to. "So people just come right out and ask you to present their cases to the powers that be."

"Something like that."

"And you do it."

"Most of the time."

"Why?"

She looked at him thoughtfully. "Because I can. Because I don't want Patrick's death to have been for nothing. If it gives me an edge when something needs to be done, I use it."

Like baby-sitting me so I don't get into any trouble with Hugh and ruin Debbie Carver's party, he thought.

"I could use a raise," he hinted.

"Even *I* couldn't manage that," she said dryly.

She was polite, just the way he thought, but she had a bit of the devil in her, too. He found that interesting. And he found that he had a sudden, irresistible urge, not to annoy precisely, but to tease her a little. "Why not?" he asked to put her on the spot.

She only smiled.

"I didn't think my differences with Hugh were *that* notorious."

"Word travels."

"Yeah? What word?"

"The word that you hit him once when you were both on duty. It caused a lot of comment around the Gallagher dinner table."

"I can imagine. Everybody want me hanged?"

"No, I believe they were all leaning toward drawing and quartering. Except for Patrick."

"Yeah? What did Patrick want?"

"Amnesty, I think. He said Hugh probably deserved it, or else the disciplinary action wouldn't have been so hush-hush. He said one day you were going to clean Hugh's clock for him."

He laughed out loud. That sounded like Patrick. "You know, I always liked Patrick Gallagher."

She looked into his eyes. "So did I," she said quietly.

"Yeah? So why weren't you and Patrick getting along before he got shot?"

Chapter Two

Jenna stood up. Her face felt flushed. She was still looking into Johnson Garth's eyes, and she realized that the remark wasn't the result of blundering social ineptitude on his part. It was callous and deliberate. He knew exactly what he was doing. She didn't say anything to him; she moved quickly down the stairs, leaving her plate of lasagna, and she didn't look back. She was halfway to the kitchen before he caught up with her.

"Mrs. Gallagher—"

He put his hand on her shoulder to make her stop. "Mrs. Gallagher, I . . . I think you misunderstood."

She looked around at him, and she moved out from under the warmth of his hand on her shoulder. She hadn't misunderstood, and they both knew it. "No, I don't think so. I don't know why you would ask me something like that, and I'm trying not to think you're as rude as people say you are. What I do think is that it would be best if you go annoy someone else. Good night, Detective Garth."

She walked away from him, but he still followed.

"Mrs. Gallagher—"

She turned on him when he would have touched her again. "*Don't* push your luck, Detective!" she said, her eyes locked with his. Her knees were trembling. She felt cornered, trapped; she had to get out.

She didn't bother saying goodbye to Debbie. She didn't even look for her. She slipped away through the kitchen to the Carvers' glassed-in back porch where she'd left her coat and purse in a corner among Debbie's potted plants. Her car was parked in the small yard behind the house by a chainlink fence that separated the Carvers' yard from the property next door. It was raining still, and she ran the last few steps to the car. She didn't have her keys out, and she had to fumble in her purse for them. The rain was cold, and she couldn't keep from shivering. She could hear her heart pounding in her ears.

When she was about to get into the car, Johnson Garth called her from the back porch steps. She could not believe this man! She hurried to get inside the car.

"Mrs. Gallagher!" he called again as she reached to close the car door. "I had a reason—"

She slammed the door hard. Whatever he had to say, she didn't want to hear it. Incredibly she was close to tears—when she had thought she was all right now. She had thought she had her guilt in perspective, that the persistent physical response to it was now under control and she could get on with her life.

"So why weren't you and Patrick getting along before he got shot?"

That one question had brought it all back again—all the pain, all the regrets. She didn't care about Johnson Garth's reason for asking. Reasons didn't matter. Reasons never changed the final outcome of things. She had had her reasons for making Patrick so unhappy those last few months. She had had her reasons for sitting with Johnson Garth on the stairs—ostensibly because Debbie had forced her into it. If there was anything she hated more than the loneliness of her widowhood, it was the assumption people made that not only could she somehow take care of their problems, but that she would *want* to do it. She had always been happy on the fringes of life, yet since Patrick had died, she kept letting herself be pushed right into the fray. Tonight, she'd suddenly found herself in the position of having to intervene in a long-standing feud between two hotheaded detectives who would be better off if they settled their differences once and for all. It was nothing to her that they were at odds with each other, except that she liked Debbie, and she didn't want her to be so upset.

"You do a lot of that, do you? Let people push you into places you don't want to go?"

"Yes, Detective Garth, I do."

And because she did, she was going to have to deal with the Gallaghers, too. Hugh hadn't liked her interference. And Mamie—Patrick and Hugh's mother—would like it even less when Hugh told her about her daughter-in-law's improper behavior. Jenna had spent a long time sitting on a dark stairs with Johnson Garth. The reasons wouldn't matter.

You don't have to justify it, she thought. She had been married to Patrick—not to the police department and not to the Gallagher family.

In truth, she wouldn't even have considered having to justify her behavior—if she hadn't been enjoying herself. For the first time in a very long while, she had actually *enjoyed* herself, with no thought of Hugh and Mamie Gallagher and how things might look. After the initial awkwardness, she'd found Johnson Garth easy to talk to, and he'd made her laugh. He hadn't been loud; he hadn't been drunk. He had needed a shave, but he hadn't needed a bath. And until he'd asked his too-personal question, he hadn't been anything but quietly friendly in a way that reminded her all too much of Patrick.

And she wasn't quite sure why. He didn't look like Patrick. He wasn't handsome in the way Patrick had been. Johnson Garth had a kind of youthful, boyish look about him, but his eyes were very old; old and tired and sad, she supposed, from seeing whatever he'd seen, doing whatever he'd done. All too many of the men on the force had eyes like that. It had made her want to comfort him, when she knew personally how difficult it was to do that—comfort a cop. They didn't want it, no matter how much they needed it—not from the women in their lives. They didn't want to talk about the problems of The Job. Baring their souls they saved for their fellow police at the precinct watering holes, so that they worked an eight-hour tour and then spent another two—or more—winding down, and the women who cared about them sat alone and waited. She had always hated it, the collective assumption that civilians in general and women in particular either couldn't understand or had to be protected from the realities of police work. Patrick had been a good and caring man, but he was a cop, and he'd shut her out when he'd needed her. And, in spite of all that, she had been on the verge just now of letting herself become attracted to another one. She had let herself become all too aware of Johnson Garth, of his nearness, the warmth of his body, and his masculine scent, of his strong-looking hands and the small scar over his left eyebrow.

You've been alone too long, Mrs. Gallagher, she thought wryly. That had to be the problem when someone like Garth appealed to her.

She took a long, deep breath and tried to force his image from her mind. She didn't want to think about him staring at her from across the room, or sitting in the dark with her on the stairs, or standing on the porch steps in the rain.

She knew what was expected of her. She was expected to preserve Patrick's memory; she was expected to do exactly what she'd told Johnson Garth to do—behave.

The shaky feeling, the pounding heart, was passing. She switched on the car radio and turned the dial until she found one of the public radio stations. At least for the duration of the drive home there would be nothing in her thoughts but windshield wipers and oncoming headlights in the rainy night. And back-to-back sorrowful jazz.

What were you going to say, idiot? Garth thought. *I didn't mean it? I thought you might know something you aren't telling about your husband's death?*

He had meant it—and she knew it. He stood on the steps and watched her drive away. He just hadn't meant to upset her that much. She looked so pale, the way she'd looked at Gallagher's funeral.

He gave a one-word assessment of the way the evening had gone and walked to his car, his mind replaying his conversation with Jenna Gallagher over and over on the way home. He turned down the street of old two-story buildings where he lived, driving slowly, as if he were still in uniform and on patrol. Time and the weather meant nothing in this neighborhood. People still milled around in the streets, regardless of the late hour, regardless of the rain. But he had no difficulty finding a parking place. There was an asphalt parking lot next to the brick building that housed the small family restaurant where Hazel worked, and he pulled into it, the beams from his headlights bouncing over the wet pavement. He could get to his apartment through The Humoresque when it was open, but when it was closed or when it suited him, he entered using the metal fire escape that zigzagged up the side of the building to a second-story door.

He parked close to the building in case he had to leave in a hurry or in case somebody tried to strip his car.

"Good evening office-r-r-r-r," a group of boys standing in the doorways on the other side of the parking lot sang in falsetto voices as he climbed the metal steps.

He gave them his approximation of what they should go do with themselves in concise street terms, but he did so without malice. Since he'd begun living over the restaurant, they'd developed a kind of symbiosis. They knew what he did for a living; he knew what they did for sport, but they'd all come from the same place, and they took great satisfaction in hurling pseudoinsults at each other. He made no effort to try to establish any kind of rapport with them— if tonight was any kind of example, he was no good at it, anyway. All he wanted was for them to understand that when they needed rousting, he'd roust them. Or if they needed help, he'd do that, too, if he could. There was no need for any kind of personal relationships. He was from the streets himself. He knew what a delinquent kid thought of a cop with a social conscience. That kind of law enforcement officer was right up there with Santa Claus and the Easter Bunny—only worse, because nine times out of ten, he wanted something in return.

He worked his key into the lock, listening intently as he opened the door slightly. Then he pushed the door back until it was flat against the inner wall and he knew no one was hiding behind it. His eyes scanned the huge loft for anything amiss, but he saw nothing. There was no place for anyone to hide, really, except the bathroom, and that door opened outward, and he always left it ajar and the light on so he could see into it when he came home. He could also see into the galley, and the iron support posts that ran in two rows the length of the place were too narrow for anyone to hide behind. The sofa and the one matching chair were turned so that he could see all but the far ends. He supposed that someone could be hiding under the bed, but he hadn't yet grown that cautious.

He closed the door behind him and double-locked it. He understood those boys down below, but he didn't trust any of them. He'd once been just like them, and since he'd become a cop, he had seen too often what some punk kind with the wrong mind-set and an illegal weapon could do.

His mind went again to Jenna Gallagher. Supposedly she knew, too—*if* the boy charged with Patrick's murder was guilty. Maybe he was; maybe he wasn't. The kid had been one of Patrick's pet projects. Patrick's partner, people on the street, said the two got along well together. Why would the kid just up and shoot him?

Now Garth also knew that there had been some kind of problem between Patrick and Jenna. He'd gone on a hunch, and the stricken look she'd given him when he asked about it, and her reaction afterward, confirmed it. But how bad was it? *She* thought it was bad, apparently, but how had it affected her husband? Garth had seen men so emotionally traumatized by their personal problems, by the breakup of a marriage, for example, that they carelessly put themselves in harm's way—sometimes, he felt, not so much carelessly as deliberately. But if something *had* been wrong with the Gallagher marriage, it still didn't explain this nervousness of Hugh's. Unless there was some kind of triangle going on.

He shook his head. Patrick and Jenna and Hugh? He didn't believe that that was the case, but he wasn't quite sure why he didn't—except that he didn't *want* it to be. He had liked Jenna Gallagher, and he couldn't see her letting herself get involved with a self-serving bastard like Hugh. She wasn't Hugh's type. He liked the rowdy, big-breasted ones like the woman who'd tried to get him to dance with her tonight. Jenna Gallagher was quiet and a little shy—except when he'd upset her with his tactless question and when she'd had to come put herself between him and Hugh. She had guts, and he liked that. She'd let people push her around for a good cause, but she had her limit.

He sighed heavily. He was tired. He took a long, hot shower and put on a pair of sweatpants and a T-shirt. He wasn't sleepy, for all his tiredness. He kept thinking about Jenna. He walked around barefoot on the hardwood floor, roaming into the galley for a beer and to the "conversation area," as his mother called it, to turn off lights.

Conversation area. He didn't need a conversation area. Who the hell did he ever talk to? Certainly not to the few women he'd brought here. He didn't like bringing women into his home, and when he had, it hadn't been so they could talk. He'd brought them here because he needed a quick fix for the emptiness he felt almost all the time. They were always women he liked but not ones who would make any demands on him. They were women who understood that he was committed to no one and nothing but The Job.

He reached to pick up a framed photograph sitting on the telephone table. It was one of the few he had in the apartment, a picture from the old neighborhood he kept to remind him of why he was a cop. He stared at the young, smiling faces—his, Roy Lee Anderson's, Mary Zaccato's—the three of them standing arm in arm with Buono's Fish Market in the background. Smiling. All of them smiling. He couldn't remember why. He knew only that none of them was smiling now. Mary was gone, and Roy Lee was aimlessly wandering the streets somewhere, his life essentially wasted. Garth had cared about these two people; he had loved Mary—almost as much as he'd hated her brother Tony. Good old Tony, who had made Garth's life a living hell from grammar school on, beating him up for his lunch money when they were kids, keeping him away from Mary when he was a man. He sighed heavily. He was a cop because of Tony Zaccato, because he didn't think the Tony Zaccatos of the world should always win. It was wrong to be victimized because one was too young or too old or too poor or didn't understand.

Blessed are the meek, he thought. Maybe so. But the strong like Tony Zaccato ate them alive if somebody didn't try to stop them.

He set the picture down and picked up the phone book. Jenna Gallagher's number was still listed in Patrick's name. He dialed it quickly, before he changed his mind, but there was no answer. He had the sudden mental picture of Jenna staring at the ringing telephone and knowing it was probably him.

He walked to the big double-arched windows that reached nearly floor to ceiling at the end of the loft. The windows looked out on the street below, and the apartment suddenly smelled too strongly of fried food—onions—from the restaurant kitchen below. The onion smell had been the reason he'd been able to get the loft in the first place. The owner of the restaurant downstairs had lived here for years—until he made enough money to be able to afford to let the smell of fried onions offend him. He'd moved to a renovated brownstone in Park Slope—and Hazel had gone to work on him. How would he like to rent his place and get a certain amount of on-the-premises police protection all at the same time, cheap? Garth smiled to himself. Luckily for him, onions or not, the man had liked the proposition. Now Garth had more room than he knew what to do with, but the downside of that was that he kept meeting his loneliness head-on.

He pushed open the upper half of one of the windows to let in some air. It was raining still, and the air that came in was damp and cold. It would be winter soon. He hated winter. Winter was the time of dead things, dead trees and grass, dead memories.

Again he thought of Mary.

Maybe that was why he was so down tonight. Maybe he was about to do it again—let himself become personally involved with someone he needed for a case. He had loved Mary, but there had still been his need to finally, *finally*, get

Tony. But for the accident of their environments, he mused, Hugh Gallagher and Tony Zaccato were a lot alike. Maybe he'd transferred his obsession for one to the other. Maybe—

He swore out loud. He wasn't going to worry about this. He'd do whatever he had to do; he always did. He popped the top on a can of beer he didn't really want and walked to the radio, flipping around the dial until he found some music. Jazz. Nobody seemed to play golden oldies at one o'clock in the morning, and he didn't want to hear the usual contemporary rock stuff.

He walked back to the window, sliding a folding, corduroy-covered lounge he liked close to the windows. As he sat down and propped up his feet, a woman on the radio began to sing. He could hear the rain, the voices carrying up from the street below. The loft filled with the soft strumming of a jazz guitar and her husky, poignant voice. She made promises. You're my man, she sang. And she made him believe it. He closed his eyes, and in his mind, with no thought as to how it came to be, he made exquisite love to Jenna Gallagher.

Chapter Three

He awoke with a start, trying to identify the sudden noise from the outside. Gunshot? The noise came again. No. Firecrackers. Somebody was celebrating the Fourth of July nine months early.

He was cold and damp, and he had a crick in his neck. He got up from the chair and closed the window, then carried the half-drunk can of beer back into the galley.

"Here's to you, Mrs. Gallagher," he said, and he poured the beer down the sink.

He glanced at one of the several clocks on the nearest wall. He felt like hell, and he had the day watch, and there wasn't enough time to go back to sleep. He had to start taking better care of himself. Eat better. Exercise. Sleep more. The mere thought of all that healthy living made him groan.

He looked out the arched windows. The rain was gone, and the sun was just coming up. The street was already alive with its legitimate and not so legitimate doings. An old man was sweeping the water off the steps of the A.M.E. Zion

Church just down the block, the broom worn down on one side and curling on the other, his breath coming out in white puffs in the chill morning air. The "fences," with everything from hot watches to temporary oblivion, were out and ready to haggle, drawing small, interested groups of men into some of the doorways. It didn't matter whether they had any money or not. It didn't cost anything to look.

He wondered how Jenna Gallagher was feeling this morning. Better than he did, he hoped. In the cold light of day, he knew that he wouldn't have done anything any differently. He had asked her exactly what he meant to ask her. Only it was the cop who had asked it, letting the question zing her in an almost automatic response to her increasing vulnerability. It was the man who couldn't forget the way she'd looked. He hadn't wanted to hurt her, but he'd done it, and he had no idea why it should matter to him. He was going to have to do something about her today, and he wasn't quite sure what.

He started to make coffee, then changed his mind. For the first time in a very long while, he dressed and went downstairs to the restaurant for breakfast.

"My God, if it's not my only son, the detective," Hazel announced to the clientele when he walked in. She was wearing her usual hair net and a green cotton smock with a plastic "Hazel" name tag pinned to it. Not that everybody didn't know her name already. The place probably hadn't had a new customer in years.

"Don't do that, Ma," he said, dutifully giving her a kiss on the cheek. "What if I'm undercover?"

"Undercover or not, there ain't nobody in here that don't know you're a cop already. Am I right?" Hazel asked the crowd. "All of you know he's a flatfoot, right?"

They all mumbled and nodded.

"See?" she said. "So what'll it be? You come to eat or what?"

"To eat. Give me some oatmeal."

"Oatmeal!" his mother and the counterman, Luigi Lufrano, said in unison.

He sat down on one of the stools at the counter. "Didn't I say that? I want oatmeal. It's good for you—lowers your cholesterol and stuff like that."

"What's the matter?" Hazel asked suspiciously. "You sick?"

"No, Ma. I'm not sick. I *like* oatmeal."

"You haven't eaten oatmeal in twenty-five years," she said, unconvinced.

"Look, have you got oatmeal or not?"

"Yeah, we got it. We keep it for the old guys with the ulcers."

"Well, am I going to get any, or do I have to go down the street?"

His mother threw up her hands. "Coming up. Luigi, what do you think of this? Oatmeal, yet!"

"I think we give him some nice peaches with it, he'll like it even better," Luigi said, giving Garth a big wink.

Garth grinned in return. He couldn't remember when he didn't know Luigi Lufrano. Luigi was the closest thing to a father he'd ever had. And the old man was right. The peaches were just the right touch. He ate two bowls. Oatmeal. Peaches. Real cream. So much for lowering cholesterol.

Hazel was watching every spoonful.

"So how come you're eating breakfast?" she persisted.

"I was hungry?" he suggested.

"When you're hungry, you eat junk. You always did. You're sure you're not sick? You can tell me—I'm your mother."

"Ma, I'm not sick, okay? Quit worrying, will you? I've got to go."

"Okay," Hazel said. She suddenly smiled. "Hey, you. You got a new girlfriend? Some woman's making you do this—making you take care of yourself, right?"

"No, Ma! Jeez! Eat a little oatmeal and look what I have to put up with."

"So why not? You need somebody to take care of you—somebody with a little money..."

"That's it!" he said, kissing her on the cheek again. "Goodbye! The oatmeal was great, Luigi!" he called to the old man as he went out.

He smiled to himself on the way to the station house. Hazel should have been the detective in the family. She had the instinct for it, and she probably had more contacts in the street that he did. As he drove past the building that housed the patrol precinct to which he had the dubious privilege of being assigned, he thought he saw Jenna Gallagher on the front steps, but by the time he'd parked the car in the basement parking garage, she'd gone—to lodge a formal complaint, no doubt. The lieutenant would just love this. One of his detectives harassing Patrick Gallagher's widow at a party.

"Garth!" the desk sergeant called to him as he passed by—an ominous sign.

"Yeah, Sidney, what?"

"Himself is looking for you, lad. Were it me, I'd be getting my tail into the Detective Division with the utmost haste."

"What does he want?"

"He didn't say, and what he *did* say wouldn't bear repeating."

"Great," Garth said, more to himself than to Sidney. He headed for the lieutenant's office, encountering Hugh along the way. Hugh had his morning coffee in his hand, but it was obvious that it had done nothing for his disposition. Garth looked past him for Jenna, but he didn't see her.

"Good morning, Hugh," he said to annoy him. His good wishes went ignored, and if looks could kill, Garth would have been on his way to the city morgue.

"Garth! Get in here!" the lieutenant yelled out his door.

Garth went, but no faster than he would have under normal circumstances. As far as he knew, circumstances *were* normal, and he'd learned in grammar school not to act guilty until he was caught. "Good morning, sir," he said as he came in. "Nice morning, after the rain."

"If I want the weather report, Garth, I'll watch Channel Nine. And don't call me sir. We both know you don't mean it, and it just pisses me off. Shut the door!"

Garth shut it. Oddly enough, when Garth called the lieutenant "sir," he did mean it. The lieutenant was an old street cop, and he knew his business. He was one of the few men around for whom Garth had enough respect to show it. That wasn't to say that they didn't have their differences.

He waited to see if the lieutenant wanted him to close the blinds. There were certain detectives in the squad room proper who could teach lipreading for a living, and the lieutenant knew it. The seriousness of this meeting would be indicated by whether or not he wanted the blinds left open or closed.

Open—this time.

The lieutenant leaned back at his desk and belched loudly.

"You ever have trouble with your gut, Garth?" the lieutenant asked, his face screwed up as if belching had only compounded his misery.

"Ah, no, I don't."

"No, you wouldn't, would you? You *give* ulcers, you don't get them. You do whatever the hell you please, and to hell with it. Well, some of us can't do that, Garth, you know what I mean?"

"Not exactly."

"This new kid—Carver. I got people all over me about him. His old man's got clout with the big boys downtown—they play squash together or some kind of ball us poor working stiffs never heard of. *I've* been playing 'Yes, sir, yes, sir, three bagsful' ever since I got here this morning. Now, I'm giving the kid to you, and I don't want him shot up his first day out, you got me?'' He eyed Garth closely. ''You got something to say here? Keeping in mind, of course, that with my gut the way it is, I'm in no mood for rebuttals.''

''I was just wondering—''

But Garth lost his train of thought, because Jenna was standing out in the squad room with Hugh. She was wearing a black coat—something left over from her mourning, maybe—but the severity of the coat was relieved by a black-and-gold striped scarf. She looked in his direction, her eyes catching his, and she didn't look away.

''Am I boring you, Garth?'' the lieutenant barked.

''No, sir. I was just wondering why Carver's not at Midtown,'' he said forcing his eyes away from the window. ''He wouldn't get his hands dirty there.''

''Because he asked to be put where he was 'needed,' even if it's someplace like here. The kid's got a bad case of the noblesse oblige—only Mummy and Daddy don't like it too much, see?''

''So what am I supposed to do with him if it looks like we're going to get into something?''

''Listen!'' the lieutenant said, jabbing his finger in the air. ''You do your job! The kid's been through the academy. He's supposed to know how to handle himself. And he was a good patrolman from what I hear. Just don't go running around kicking ass with him along—at least not until my stomach settles down. I don't need any new aggravation, you hear?''

Garth glanced out the window. Jenna was still talking to Hugh, and Skip Carver had joined them. ''Anything else, Lieutenant?'' he asked. He moved a little closer to the window, and Jenna turned and walked away.

''You catching a plane, Garth? When I'm done, you'll be the first to know.'' The lieutenant got up from his desk and opened the door. ''Carver!'' he yelled with his usual aplomb. The kid was standing with his back turned, but he didn't jump. When he turned around, Garth could see the edge of anxiety in his face, but he was trying hard not to show it.

Not bad, he thought. The kid had a handle on it.

"You called me, sir?" Carver asked with just the barest edge of amusement—as if there could be any doubt in a three-block radius that the lieutenant had.

"Meet your new partner," the lieutenant said. "Detective Johnson Garth."

"We've met," Garth said, extending his hand.

"Garth here'll show you the ropes. I expect good work from the two of yous. If there happens to be some personality conflict between yous, feel free to settle it yourselves, because I don't want to hear about it, understood? Now get out of here. I got work to do."

"Does he always yell like that?" Skip asked when they were out in the squad room.

"Nah. He's a little under the weather today. His volume's way off," Garth said, scanning the area to see if Jenna was still on the premises. He walked toward the hallway, and Skip trailed along after him.

"She's gone," Skip said.

Garth stopped looking. "Who's gone?" he said, annoyed that Carver had second-guessed him.

"I thought you were looking for Jenna."

"Now, why would you think that?"

"I thought something happened between the two of you last night—or Debbie did."

"Well, you and Debbie thought wrong."

"She was here to—"

"Did I ask you why she was here?"

"Sorry," Skip said. "I thought maybe you were interested."

"I'm not interested."

"My mistake then."

They stared at each other. Garth turned and walked back to his desk.

"So why aren't you interested?" Skip asked, tagging behind him. "She's a nice person. She's intelligent. She's pretty. Of course, she's not feeling up to par this morning, and that takes away some of her usual vivaciousness."

Garth picked up a folder on his desk and shuffled some papers in it. Skip Carver waited. He didn't presume. He wasn't impatient. He just stood there.

Garth suddenly snapped the folder shut. "So what's wrong with her?"

"Who?" Skip said obtusely.

"Jenna Gallagher!"

"Oh. She was at the hospital most of the night."

"Why?" Garth asked abruptly, and from the look Carver gave him, he realized he wasn't exactly being nonchalant.

"She was with a rape victim."

"Why?"

Skip Carver took a deep breath. "Because," he said, patiently, "she does volunteer work with the Family Crisis Council. She got a call from them last night after she got home from the party."

"I thought she just championed losing causes before the community relations board."

"Yes, she does that, and she substitute teaches at Saint Xavier's with Debbie."

"Anything to stay busy," Garth said to get a rise out of Skip. Not that he wasn't familiar with the work cure. The busier you were, the less time you had to think. He could feel Skip looking at him. "What?"

"I admire her," Skip said a little testily.

"Yeah?" he said, feigning disinterest by shuffling papers in the folder again.

"It's not easy for her to go into a hospital."

"Why not?"

"Because she—it's a problem she's had since Patrick was killed. He was still alive when she got to the emergency room that afternoon—she could hear him calling her, but they wouldn't let her in to see him. And then it was too late. Sometimes she has acute anxiety attacks when she has to go into a hospital now—especially Bellevue. She told Debbie the smells, the hospital noises, anything she associates with that day, bring it on."

"What kind of anxiety attacks?"

"Palpitations, the shakes—you know."

"Then why the hell does she do it?" Garth barked.

"I imagine because she needs to prove something to herself."

"Are you going to go around like that?" Garth asked abruptly, because the expensive suit Carver was wearing suddenly registered and because he didn't want to know any more personal information about Jenna Gallagher. It made her too real, made him too much at fault for her abrupt departure last night. He looked Skip up and down, realizing that he was going to have to spend his working days with somebody who looked like a Ken doll—or an undertaker.

"Are *you*?" Skip countered, returning the inspection. Garth was wearing his usual—jeans, shirt with no tie, a jacket that zipped up the front.

"Yeah. I am."

"Me, too," Skip said mildly.

"I don't know how the hell you think you can work with me dressed like that."

"Oh, no problem. They told us in the academy that men from the affluent part of Manhattan sometimes go into the rough neighborhoods—purchasing pleasure, as it were. I expect I'll look like a customer."

"*Whose* customer?"

"Yours."

"Mine. And what am I supposed to be selling—just in case somebody should ask?"

"Oh, about anything, I guess."

"You guess? Carver, this is not some kind of police academy role play here. This is the real thing."

"Oh, I know that, sir. So what should I do first?"

"First? First, you stop calling me *sir*."

"Right. What else can I do?"

"You can invite me to your house for dinner. And you can make sure Jenna Gallagher is there."

Chapter Four

I...I think I've found out why Garth hit Hugh that time,"
Debbie said.

Jenna looked at her sharply but didn't comment. She had
had nearly a week of Debbie's campaigning to get her to
come to dinner. Debbie had made no secret of the fact that
the invitation was at Johnson Garth's request, and thus far
she had covered everything from Garth's brilliant, if somewhat checkered, career, to his flaming youth, to his apparent availability, as evidenced by his total lack of a social life.
Jenna had been expecting yet another pitch, but this approach was a little different. And the worst part was that she
was interested. She had been interested from the first, or
perhaps *intrigued* was a better word. She and Garth had
certainly not parted on the best of terms, and yet he'd elicited Debbie and Skip's help to mend his fences. If that was
what he was doing. She really didn't know what he was
doing, and she constantly puzzled over possible reasons for
his wanting to see her.

"It wasn't easy," Debbie continued. "I had to name-drop— Everybody line up for hand washing!" she called to the five-year-olds who milled around them.

"Whose name?"

"Yours, silly. I told my dad Garth wanted to have dinner with you, but you were worried about whatever that thing was between him and Hugh— Hand washing!" Debbie called again as the children more or less got into line. "Hernando! Leave that lumber alone! Jenna, if we don't get all that stuff for the new cubbyholes out of here, Hernando's going to either set fire to it or sell it."

But Jenna wasn't concerned about the disposition of the precut lumber. "Debbie, I wish you wouldn't go around letting people think I'm somehow involved with Johnson Garth."

"The man wants to have dinner with you, Jenna. If you know some of the particulars about him, you can make up your mind better."

"I've made up my mind."

"Hernando! Leave the gerbil alone! What did you do with the soap! Oh, Lord, Jenna—you can't make a gerbil eat soap, can you? You take him this time. I'm liable to pinch his little head off."

Knowing that it was Hernando Cooley, the "old man" of Saint Xavier's kindergarten class, whose head was in danger and not the gerbil's, Jenna went to frisk him. Hernando was almost six, and he was one of Sister Mary John's finds, a little boy who was learning-deprived in every area except how to survive on the streets. Jenna doubted that he'd ever been a child, and the fact that he tried so hard to hide how much he wanted to be one made him all the more endearing. He was completely fascinated by the simplest of things—crayons, coloring books, wild animal pictures—when he wasn't causing complete chaos. In the past few days she had begun to think of him as an early version of Johnson Garth, and it was becoming apparent to her that something needed to be done about both of them.

"Hernando, why did you put it in your pocket?" Jenna said, trying to scrape the wet, slimy clumps of soap out.

"'Cause you find it everyplace else," Hernando said matter-of-factly. He gave her a charming grin. "You're smart, Miss Jenna. I didn't think you'd ever find it in there."

"Yes, well, lucky me," Jenna said, looking for something to do with it now that she'd retrieved it.

"I don't like washing my hands," Hernando said, watching her try to press the soap back into shape. "That's all you do—make peoples wash their hands."

"Washing your hands will help keep you from catching a cold."

"I ain't washing mine no more," he informed her.

"Fine," Jenna said. "It's up to you. No clean hands, no cookies."

He thought this over. "You mean everybody else gets a cookie and not me?" he asked, apparently to make sure he understood all the particulars of her pronouncement. "Just because my hands ain't washed?"

"You got it," Jenna said.

"You're crazy," he informed her further.

She smiled. "Give me a hug anyway."

He hesitated only a moment, then flung himself into her arms. There was progress in that direction, at least. Hernando was learning to accept affection from her and Debbie both, even if clean hands were sometimes the price.

"How come you ain't mad at me?" he asked.

"Crazy, I guess. Go wash your hands."

"You ain't got no soap no more," he said.

"You wish," Jenna advised him, pressing a small blob of what used to be the bar of Ivory into his palm. "Use that."

"Do you want to know what I found out or not?" Debbie said when Jenna had Hernando pointed in the right direction and the hand-washing line was moving again.

"Tell me," Jenna said in spite of herself. She couldn't have dinner with Johnson Garth, but Debbie was right about one thing: she might as well know as much as she could.

"Well, it's just a rumor Sidney, the desk sergeant at the precinct, told my dad. I don't think anybody knows for sure except Garth and Hugh—and probably the lieutenant. I don't know if it got to Internal Affairs or not." Debbie paused long enough to check on the progress of the hand washers. "Anyway, there was this kid from Tennessee— Juanita something. She'd hitchhiked all the way to New York looking for her boyfriend. He was supposed to send her the bus fare, but he never did, so she came anyway. Can you imagine that? Some kid from Tennessee trying to find a guy who probably didn't want to be found—in New York City—with no friends and no money? She ended up on the streets, of course, and it didn't take her long to get into harm's way. Sidney said he remembered her because she had the saddest eyes he'd ever seen. He said she reminded him of a little sparrow someone had deliberately stepped on. Anyway, Hugh and Garth caught the case. When they were questioning her, trying to find out about the men who had—" She broke off.

"Go on," Jenna said.

"I'm sorry, Jenna. I know Hugh's your brother-in-law."

"Go on, Debbie."

"Hugh asked her if she'd enjoyed it. And Garth hit him. It would have been worse if Sidney and some of the others hadn't broken it up. I...don't think it's just a rumor. I think it's the truth."

Jenna stood watching the children waiting to wash their hands. She thought it was the truth, too. She was a part of a volunteer support team for women who were victims of

violent crimes. She knew the harassment they sometimes still
had to endure from investigating officers, regardless of the
efforts toward more humane treatment for the victim. And
she knew Hugh Gallagher. She had no trouble imagining it,
Hugh with his arrogance, and his perfectly barbered little
blond mustache, and his piercingly cold blue eyes. How he
must have scared a little girl from Tennessee.

"What?" Jenna asked, because Debbie had said something.

"I said I think he's a very complicated man. I tried to find
out this business about his name, but Skip doesn't know.
Even Sidney doesn't know about that."

"Who are we talking about?"

"Garth, Jenna. His first name is Johnson. Everybody
knows that, but nobody calls him by it. They don't call him
Johnson, or John, or Johnny. Nothing except Garth. That's
what he said to me in the kitchen: 'Just call me Garth.' I
think— Hernando! Leave that lumber alone!"

The kindergartners, Hernando notwithstanding, were
getting too restless for their just-before-going-home cookie
and milk for Debbie to go on. It was standard practice to
give the children something to eat before they left for the
day, because it was a long time before dinner for many of
them—if they got dinner. Jenna wasn't at all certain Hernando was fed anything after he left here. She didn't think
he would have washed his hands for the cookie otherwise.

"I think—" Debbie began again as soon as the last of the
peanut butter cookies were given out.

"That I ought to come to your house for dinner," Jenna
finished for her.

"Well, I do. You ought to at least *talk* to him. You aren't
going to find out what he's up to any other way. Lord
knows, Skip can't find out, and he's tried. He thinks Garth
likes you."

Jenna laughed.

"Well, he does. Why don't you come to dinner tonight, Jenna? Let me tell Skip to bring Garth home and—"

"No."

"For the love of Pete, why not? For curiosity's sake, if nothing else."

"Because," Jenna said firmly, "I have something else in mind."

Garth had been waiting all day to hear whether Jenna had changed her mind about coming to dinner. He hadn't asked because he didn't want to seem too eager. He didn't need word getting back to Hugh that he was hotly pursuing his sister-in-law.

Skip waited until they were in the middle of a traffic jam to tell him.

"Debbie said Jenna couldn't make it."

"Couldn't?" Garth asked offhandedly.

"Wouldn't," Skip answered. That was one thing about Skip. Garth could trust him to tell the truth. There was no denying the pang of disappointment he felt, just as there was no denying that he was beginning to dwell less and less on his original reason for wanting to talk to Jenna Gallagher in the first place and more and more on the woman herself. He found himself thinking about her at odd times of the day, remembering the way she had looked and the way she'd smelled. There was a lot to be said for a woman who took the trouble to smell nice—not loud, but nice. Soft and womanly. Of course, that could be false advertising on her part. This particular woman was turning out to be anything but soft. When she said no dice, she apparently meant it.

"Did she say why?"

"No. Do you want to come to dinner anyway?" Skip said.

"Why?"

"Why? Because you're my partner and Debbie told me to ask you to come anyway."

"Why?" he said again.

"I just told you why. Debbie thought you might like a hot meal. Look, if you don't want to come, just say so. I can tell Debbie I asked you, and you said no. No problem!"

"Skip—"

"It doesn't matter that she's been knocking herself out trying to be your go-between with Jenna. It doesn't matter that she's been practicing on *me* so she can cook something she thinks is good enough to feed *you*. It's nothing to you. It's important to her, Garth, but trust me, the Carvers will survive your absence."

"Skip!"

"What!"

"Did I say I didn't want to come?"

"You don't have to. I'm not *that* dense."

"Since when?" Garth asked mildly. The kid had made a few mistakes in the last few days—not bad ones, but bad enough that Garth wanted to keep him from thinking he was Super Detective.

"I'm ignorant about some things, Garth. Ignorant, not stupid."

"If you say so. You're the one with the big Harvard education."

"Princeton. It's Princeton. And I do say so. I'll just tell Debbie you don't want to come."

"Hey—I want to come, okay?"

"Don't do us any favors, Garth."

"What is it with you, today? I'm not doing you any favors!" And he wasn't. He liked Debbie and Skip, even if he did overdo it with the Bill Blass suits. "You can tell Debbie I'll be there!"

Skip kept cutting looks at him as they inched along.

"What?" Garth said in exasperation. "What!"

"Okay, I'll tell you 'what.' I want to know what it is with you and Jenna. Debbie's all worried about her. It's the first thing I hear when I get home—'What is it with Jenna and Garth?' It's the last thing I hear before I go to bed. And when I'm at work, you're working me over about her, too. I want to know why."

"It's nothing— watch where you're going!"

"Watch where I'm *going*? I'm not going anywhere, Garth. There's a bus in front of us and cabs everywhere else. You're changing the subject."

"I'm not."

"Yes, you are! I'm your partner. If you're up to something that's going to get both our butts kicked, I want to know what it is. What do you want to talk to her about?"

"It's personal."

"Personal? Have you got the hots for her or something like that?"

"Yeah, something like that— watch the bus!"

Skip slammed on brakes just short of a rear-end collision.

"Look, Garth, Jenna is a friend of ours. I'm not going to help you get her in the sack."

"Skip, I just want to get to know the lady. That's all."

"Maybe so, but there is no way in hell she's coming to dinner if she knows you're going to be there."

"Thanks a lot, Skip. Why don't you build up my social confidence here."

They sat in silence, waiting for the traffic to move, ignoring the free-lance pedestrian windshield washers who ran around the car spraying and wiping and making a pitch for a "donation."

Garth suddenly rolled down the window on his side, because he recognized one of them. The wind was blowing, and the shadows were deep. It was cold on the street today. Very cold.

"Roy Lee!" he yelled, and the man he recognized came trotting over. "Get in," he said, unlocking the back door.

Roy Lee hesitated, bending low so he could see into the car and hugging himself to stay warm. His rheumy eyes darted around as if he expected something worse than passing conversation.

"Get in," Garth said again, and Roy Lee suddenly smiled.

"Garth! What's happening?" he asked as he crawled into the back seat. His voice was hoarse. He tried to clear his throat, but it didn't help. That it had been a long time between baths for Roy Lee became rapidly apparent in the small confines of the car.

"I've been looking for you, Roy Lee," Garth said mildly, and he left the window down.

With his usual reluctance to play stool pigeon, Roy Lee feigned surprise. "Yeah? I been around, Garth. You know I ain't going noplace."

"What have you got for me?"

"Nothing, Garth."

The old familiar holding-out pattern. Garth turned around in the seat. "Don't you start with me, Roy Lee. I'm not in the mood. Am I, Skip?"

"No," Skip said with great sincerity, and Garth smiled.

"This is my new partner, Roy Lee. His name is Skip. Skip's caught all kinds of hell today because I couldn't find you. I can do that, see, because I'm the top dog. I can take out all my annoyance on him. Can't I, Skip?"

"Damn right," Skip said on cue.

Roy Lee tried to clear his throat again. "No, hey, Garth, I been working for you. I said I would. You know I don't lie."

"You owe me, Roy Lee. Cut the crap and tell me what you've got."

"I got—I got a message for you, Garth. From Tony—Tony Zaccato," Roy Lee offered. Clearly Roy Lee was going to try to fob him off with some useless piece of information about Tony Zaccato, but Garth played the game anyway.

"Tony's out of the country, Roy Lee."

"No! No, he's back, Garth! He said if I saw you I was to tell you that."

"Roy Lee, what is this?"

"I don't know, Garth. It's just what he said."

"Here," Garth said, digging into his shirt pocket for the bills he'd gotten back when he paid for a hot dog at lunch. "Go buy yourself some thermal underwear, man." He slapped the money into Roy Lee's hand without counting it. "Now beat it. Get off the street before you catch pneumonia."

Roy Lee looked down at the money in his hand, and for a brief moment Garth thought he was going to cry.

"Beat it," Garth said again, and Roy Lee opened the door.

"Garth," he said before he got out. "That cop that got whacked—Gallagher. It's still the same. Nobody's talking."

"Yeah, yeah, you told me. See you around, Roy Lee."

"You know what that means, Garth," he said anxiously.

"Yeah, I know, Roy Lee. It means somebody doesn't like me asking about it."

"It means that cop was doing just like you—poking his nose where people didn't want it. You better take it easy, Garth."

"I always do that, Roy Lee. Tell Tony I'm glad he's back. Tell him the three of us will get together sometime—for old times' sake."

"No—Garth—you watch your back. I mean it. It ain't just Tony you got to worry about. Hugh—"

"What do you know about Hugh Gallagher, Roy Lee?"

"He knows you're still asking about his brother. He don't like it."

"Good. You make sure he keeps on knowing it."

"Garth . . ."

"Beat it, Roy Lee. I got things to do."

Traffic was finally moving, and they left Roy Lee standing on the windy street. Skip was very quiet. Garth could almost feel him weighing information.

"You know what Roy Lee's going to do with that money," Skip said after a long time.

"Yeah," Garth said absently, his own mind once again working on how to see Jenna, apologize after a fashion and get her to talk about Patrick.

"He's not going to buy underwear," Skip persisted.

"Skip, I know what he's going to do with it!"

"Then why did you give it to him? He didn't tell you anything. We already know about Zaccato."

"Because we go back a long way, okay? Roy Lee and Zaccato and I, we all go back a long way."

"So what do they have to do with Patrick Gallagher?"

"Nothing, as far as I know."

"But you think they might."

"Why do you say that?"

"Because all three names *and* Hugh's came up in the same conversation, and because you're acting as if it's not important. That's the way you work, Garth. The more important it is, the more you behave as if it's not."

Garth gave an indulgent smile. "If you say so, Detective."

"You think Patrick was a dirty cop?"

"If he was or wasn't, it doesn't matter now."

"I'm beginning to see what you want with Jenna."

"No, you don't."

"Yes, Garth, I do. Hugh doesn't want you asking questions about Patrick. The only reason I can think of is that one or both of them was dirty, right? Right?" Skip insisted. "You've got a score to settle with Hugh, and you think poking into Patrick's death for something is the way to do it."

Garth didn't answer.

"Look! I told you before if you're doing something that's going to get both our butts kicked, I want to know about it!"

"Skip, will you take it easy? This has got nothing to do with you, okay? Nothing. Just ... don't say anything to Jenna about it. Or Debbie."

"Yeah, right."

"I mean it."

"I know you do. That's what worries me."

They rode the rest of the way back to the station house in silence.

"I understand why you'd want to take Hugh down if he's into something," Skip said when they were in the parking garage. "What I don't see is why you have to use Jenna to do it."

"I'm not using Jenna. I told you before, Skip. I like her."

"Yes. *That* worries me, too."

The shifts were changing, and inside the building was the usual madhouse.

"Garth!" Sidney called over the heads of several patrolmen hanging around his desk. He had a bunch of pink slips in his hand. "You're popular today, lad. Several calls from the D.A.'s office. And two from a Mrs. Gallagher."

"Thanks, Sid," Garth said, reaching for the slips and shuffling through them until he found the two that interested him. But they only had the CALLED box checked, and there was no return telephone number on them. "What Mrs. Gallagher is this, Sidney?"

"Now, how would I be knowing that, lad? She said what she said, and what she said is on them pink slips."

"This doesn't tell me anything."

"Ah, well," Sidney said philosophically. "Perhaps she'll be calling you again."

Garth looked down at the slips. The only Mrs. Gallagher he knew was Jenna, but she wouldn't call him. Would she? Twice?

Frowning, he walked to his desk.

"Garth!" Sidney called after him. "Line one! I believe it's the lady again!"

Garth looked at the telephone on his desk. Only line three was blinking, but knowing that Sidney refused to be intimidated by a multiline telephone system, he answered it. Everything to Sidney was generally "line one," and when one answered the telephone in this station house, one took one's chances.

"Detective Garth," he said into the receiver, feeling Skip's undivided interest. No one responded, but he could hear background noise on the line. It sounded like a bunch of children. "Detective Garth," he said again.

"Oh," a woman's voice said. "I'm sorry. I thought I'd be on hold longer. Sidney must be getting better. This is Jenna Gallagher."

He glanced at Skip, who suddenly got busy shuffling papers, but who was still listening.

"Yes," Garth said noncommittally, because he couldn't think of anything else.

"Is this a bad time?" she asked. "I can call back later."

"No, now is fine."

"I was wondering if you would consider doing some volunteer work. I know tomorrow is your regular day off—Debbie told me. Do you think you might have several hours free?"

She was short and to the point. He waited before he answered, glancing again at Skip.

"Detective Garth?" Jenna said.

"Sorry," Garth said, making up his mind quickly. "Tomorrow? I could manage a few hours tomorrow."

"Could you come to Saint Xavier's, to the school—Skip can tell you how to get there—around ten o'clock?"

"Yes, I could do that."

"Good. You'll need to wear old clothes. And could you bring a hammer?"

"A hammer? Yeah, I've got one." Somewhere.

"Good," she said. "Ten o'clock then."

"Jenna, wait—" he said just as she hung up. He sat for a moment pondering this unlikely situation, wondering if she'd noticed that he'd been so agreeable he hadn't asked for any details. *Come to the school. Bring a hammer. Anything you say, Mrs. Gallagher.*

Skip was fidgeting.

Garth looked up at him. He was not about to discuss the phone call, and he meant it.

Skip's eyes shifted sharply to the right—where Hugh was standing.

Chapter Five

Garth stayed too long after dinner at the Carvers, over-sleeping the next morning in spite of his numerous clocks. He was nearly an hour and a half late when he arrived at Saint Xavier's. There was a locked car with the engine running in the parking lot. He thought it belonged to Debbie Carver, but he wasn't certain. He assumed there was a good reason for burning up a tank of gasoline like that, but none came to mind. It was cold today, but not that cold.

He crossed the lot to the old brick building behind the church itself and tried the first door he came to. It, too, was locked. When he turned to leave, the door suddenly opened, bumping him hard on the shoulder.

"Oh! Garth! I'm sorry!" Debbie Carver said. "You can come in this way." She stood back to let him inside, but the little girl with her didn't. The child was carrying a huge plastic bag with what looked like a winter coat in it; the bag was nearly as big as she was. "Let Detective Garth inside, Becca," Debbie said, maneuvering the child out of the way.

"You know your car's running?" Garth said. Debbie seemed a little high-strung to him, and he thought he'd better mention it.

But then, as he stepped inside the building, he was distracted from the gasoline issue. He suddenly understood Jenna Gallagher's difficulty in going into Bellevue Hospital—that the smell and feel of a place could bring back a flood of memories. Saint Xavier's had several annexes, but this wing appeared to be the oldest. It smelled of books and mimeograph fluid and creaking, varnished wood. It smelled of his own school days, and for a brief, painful moment, he was the Garth in the picture on the telephone table, young and smiling and in love with Mary Zaccato. It took a conscious effort on his part to thrust the sudden attack of nostalgia aside.

"Oh, yes," Debbie was saying. "I've got to take Becca home. The Phantom Coat Flusher's struck again, and I had to get the car warm."

"The what?"

"The car."

Garth frowned. "No. I mean the other thing. The phantom?"

"The Phantom Coat Flusher," Debbie said. "Jenna will explain it. You're late, by the way. We'd given up on you— are you all right this morning?"

"Yes, I'm all right. Why?" He was late not just because he'd overslept, but because he'd had to go buy a hammer. He didn't want to tell Debbie that. He'd bought wine to impress a woman before, flowers even. Never a hammer.

"Well," she said, taking the little girl by the hand, "with my cooking, you never know. See you!"

Garth laughed and held open the door for her. "How many times do I have to tell you, Mrs. Carver? The dinner was fine. You want me to carry the coat?" he called after her because Becca wasn't doing too well, and Debbie didn't seem to notice.

"No, thanks. Becca's coat is new, and she's very territorial. Jenna's inside. Just go straight down the hall to the end."

The Phantom Coat Flusher? Garth thought as he firmly shut the outside door. He started down the long hallway, once again fighting down the feeling of déjà vu. And he halfway expected to meet Hugh somewhere along the way. Hugh must have known he was talking to Jenna yesterday, and sooner or later Garth expected him to do something about it—a little "friendly advice" on Hugh's part, prompted by his concern over the vulnerability of his brother's widow, no doubt. Or maybe he'd just cut the crap and get right down to it. It would, Garth supposed, depend on how nervous he was getting.

The cafeteria was somewhere close and in high gear. He could smell something cinnamon baking. He saw no one, and he kept walking. There were classrooms along the way, but they all had their doors shut.

"And just who are you?" someone said sharply as he walked by the one door that was open.

He backed up. A diminutive nun sat behind a desk in the room he'd just passed. Saint Xavier's certainly had a penchant for undertall staff people, he thought. Jenna only came to his shoulder, and she was the tallest he'd met so far. If this little person's feet touched the floor at all behind the desk, it was just barely.

"Detective Garth, Sister. NYPD," he said.

"Jenna's policeman?" she inquired, trying to get him in the right place in her bifocals. Apparently she couldn't, because she pulled them off and put them aside.

"Yes," Garth said. He supposed he was that.

"You don't look like a detective."

"I do the best I can, Sister," he said without apology.

The sister smiled. She had a beautiful smile, and very dark, merry brown eyes.

"Oh, but, you see, that's exactly what we want, Detective Garth. We want someone who doesn't look like what most of these children are used to seeing. You look very...suburban and leisurely. Very Saturday morning. And you have your hammer, of course?"

"Of course," he said, showing her where he had it stashed in an inside pocket of his jacket. She was clearly delighted.

"Excellent, Detective Garth! This is going to be so wonderful!"

"I . . . certainly hope so," he said vaguely.

"Now. There are several things I insist upon while you're here. You will be under the most exacting scrutiny. You must not swear under any circumstances. You must not smoke on the premises. And at lunchtime, you *will* drink your milk, won't you?"

He opened his mouth to say, but she didn't let him.

"Well, run along, Detective Garth. The children are waiting for you."

"The children?"

"Yes, Detective Garth. That way!"

She shooed him; he went, thinking that the time to bail out of this thing was now. He didn't like milk, and he backslid and had a cigarette now and again, and he had certainly been known to swear. If a conversation with Jenna Gallagher hadn't been the prize, he doubted that this— whatever this experience was—would be worth the aggravation.

Ah, well, he decided as he continued down the hall. If he ran into The Phantom, at least he had a hammer.

He could hear voices coming from the last door on the left, but the long hallway gave them a hollow, echoed sound. He couldn't tell if it was Jenna he heard or not.

She came out of the door just before he got there, and he was infinitely aware of his own response. He was glad to see her—and not just because she was the possible means to an end. Yes, he wanted to rattle Hugh's cage as much as humanly possible. But no, that wasn't the reason he felt the way he did now. It was difficult to describe. There was sexual attraction certainly; she was a good-looking woman. Her hair was tied back in a black ribbon, and she was dressed in dark green today—a soft-looking sweater he immediately wanted to put his hands on, and a long wool skirt.

But he also wanted to sit down and talk with her. He wanted to explain about the other night—as much of an explanation as he could give, at any rate. He wanted to know about the anxiety attacks and what she was doing about them. He wanted to know how she was today. He wanted . . . everything.

It may have been that she was a little glad to see him, too—until she remembered herself.

"Detective Garth," she said, her eyes reserved but looking directly into his.

He smiled. "Don't look like that, Mrs. Gallagher. I'm supposed to be here."

She didn't return the smile. He was late, and she had nearly given up on seeing him. She wasn't looking forward to explaining why she'd asked him to come, the official reason or the real one. Her eyes scanned over him. He looked . . . himself. He dressed the same for a kindergarten visit as he did for a party, but he had shaved, and that was something, she supposed. She was worried that he was going to immediately insist on talking about her declining his invitations for dinner, or that he'd want to launch into some explanation as to why he'd made such a prying remark about her relationship with Patrick.

But he didn't. He merely stared back at her. And that was more flustering for her than his questions or apologies would have been.

She took a deep breath. She was in control of this situation. It was she who had initiated it, and for no other reason, she wanted to assure herself, than to relieve Debbie and Skip of the obligation Skip felt toward his new partner.

They both took Johnson Garth too seriously; they were too career conscious not to. But they were in no way accountable for her refusals to join him at the Carvers for dinner— *he* was. And before the day was over, she intended that he understand that. She also intended that, from now on, she would be able to get through an entire day without being bombarded by thirdhand dinner invitations.

She looked into his eyes, hazel eyes with thick dark lashes. She *wanted* to assure herself. But she couldn't. There was still the other thing. Insensitive or not, enemy of the Gallagher family or not, Garth had stayed on her mind. All morning she'd been thinking about him and about some lines of dialogue, something she remembered from a movie she'd seen when she was a girl growing up by the Susquehanna River. Joanne Woodward and Thelma Ritter perhaps. She didn't think she had ever really understood the emotion involved until now:

"What's his name?"
"I don't know."
"What does he want?"
"I don't know."
"Is he coming back?"
"I don't know! *I just know if I don't see him again I'll die."*

She had wanted to see Johnson Garth again, and there was no use pretending otherwise. There was something about him, some sadness that she could feel when she looked at him. And she thought that he knew she felt it, and that he let her empathy draw him to her in spite of himself.

"Yes, well," she said. "I think I need to explain a few things to you."

"That would be good. Belated, but good."

"Belated?"

"I just had a very puzzling conversation with a little nun about so high." He held out his hand to show her how high he thought the nun would have been if she'd stood up.

"Puzzling?"

"Yeah. Something about children and a hammer?"

"Oh, yes, it's very simple. Sister Mary John—"

"The short one," he interrupted, because he sensed her nervousness and because, once again, he had an irrepressible urge to tease her. She was already angry with him. It couldn't hurt.

"Yes. She's—"

"She's even shorter than Debbie."

"Right. She—"

"She didn't tell me who she was."

"Sister Mary John," Jenna repeated, and she paused in case he had yet another two cents he wanted to put in. His eyes were full of mischief, and she tried her best to ignore it.

"Go on," he prompted.

"Sister Mary John," Jenna said carefully, "saw a television special about Scotland Yard. It dealt with the Golden Thread."

"What Golden Thread?"

"The policy Scotland Yard has for dealing with the public is called the Golden Thread. The Golden Thread is Courtesy, Compassion, and something else—I've forgotten what. Anyway, Sister Mary John said they lost it in the '60s because they stopped having their police officers walk a beat. But then they realized how important it was for a policeman to know his people and for them to know him."

"Go on," he said again.

"Especially the children. This one bobby knew all the children in a school on his beat by name. So, Sister decided yesterday that she wanted a police officer to come spend the day with the kindergarten—because you need to start young. And she didn't want him to *look* like a policeman. And she didn't want a policewoman because more of the children don't have fathers than don't have mothers, and she thought they'd benefit more from a male role model."

"Is that what I have to be? A father figure?"

"In a manner of speaking, yes. I don't think it will be too difficult. The only one who may be a problem is Hernando Cooley."

"Tough guy, huh?"

"Well, he's five going on thirty. Yesterday he tried to start a game of strip poker."

Garth smiled again, and this time she smiled with him. Not much, but a little.

"And what did Sister Mary John have to say about that?"

"Some things, Detective Garth, are better kept from Sister. You know what I mean?"

His smile broadened. "Yeah, I know what you mean. I'm just surprised that you do."

"Are you going to stay?" She tried to sound neutral, but she was very well aware of how much she wanted him to.

"That depends."

"On what?"

"On what I have to do with the hammer. Or is it for protection?" *That's more like it,* he thought. She smiled genuinely this time, no holding back, no trying not to give him an opening because she thought he was going to presume.

"The hammer is so you can put the cubbyholes together. We've run out of space for the children to keep their things. One of the parishioners donated the lumber. It's already precut and grooved, so it's just a matter of putting it together—I knew you'd hate it," she finished abruptly.

"I don't hate it, Mrs. Gallagher. If I hated it, you'd know before we got this far."

He was looking into her eyes. She glanced away, and he waited for her to look back again.

"It beats the hell out of sleeping till noon," he said when she did. "What with The Phantom Coat Flusher and everything."

"How did you know about that?"

"I met Debbie on my way in. So why isn't Skip in on this? It's his regular day off, too."

"Skip went to Southampton. He was summoned to the palatial estate. Debbie thinks it's the family's formal announcement that he's been cut out of the will."

"I don't think he'll care, do you?"

"Not a bit. Are you ready to meet the children?"

"Not until I find out about The Phantom."

She gave a small shrug. "Somebody—one of the children—keeps trying to flush coats down the toilet."

"You have an idea who it is?" he asked, thinking that this was one problem he'd never run across before.

"Of sorts. But we can't catch him at it. The Phantom is very diabolical."

"You don't need a carpenter, ma'am. You need a detective."

"Does that mean you're staying?"

He was still looking into her eyes—as much as she'd let him—and enjoying every minute of it, because she was still trying not to smile. "Oh, yeah," he said. "Just watch where you hang my coat, okay?"

She smiled after all, a warm smile that made him glad he'd come.

"Boys and girls," Jenna said to the small upturned faces. "This is—" She was all set to say Johnson Garth, but he cleared his throat sharply to interrupt her. She glanced at him, and he mouthed the word "Garth."

"This is Garth," she continued, and he nodded. "Garth is a police detective."

"He don't look like no police detective," Hernando said immediately. "Where's his gun?"

"Detective Garth is going to build the new cubbyholes for us today. He doesn't need a gun. He has a hammer." She looked at Garth, who dutifully produced the hammer from inside his coat and held it up as if he were a letter-turner on a television game show.

"How old is he?" Hernando said suspiciously, looking Garth up and down. Jenna had no idea what that had to do with anything, but apparently, to Hernando, it signified.

"I don't know," Jenna said. "Why don't you ask him?"

"How old are you, man?" Hernando said without compunction.

Garth scratched the side of his face with one finger. "Um . . . thirty-five."

"You're *old*, man."

"Yeah, well, I used to be just *plain* five," Garth said ominously. "Like you."

"Now," Jenna said, trying to regain some control here. "I want all of you to get your name necklaces out and put them on so Detective Garth will know who you are."

"I don't want him to know who *I* am," Hernando said, folding his arms.

"I already know," Garth advised him.

"Do not."

"Do, too."

"Oh, yeah? Who?"

"Hernando Cooley. Himself."

Jenna tried not to smile at Hernando's incredulous look. She waited while the children shuffled through the stacks of papers on the tables in front of them, looking for the laminated circles of construction paper that had been threaded onto long pieces of yarn. She glanced at Garth, who grinned and raised and lowered his eyebrows once.

"What is it, Mallory?" she said to the little girl who was pulling desperately on her skirt.

"I can't find my name necklace, Miss Jenna," Mallory said. "It's all lost!" Everything was a major crisis to Mallory, and she was very near tears.

"Don't worry. I'll help you find it."

"But—but what if we *can't*!" Mallory wailed.

"Then I'll make you another one. It'll be all right. Let's go look."

"You're not going far, are you?" Garth asked when she took Mallory by the hand.

"Don't worry," Jenna said to him, too. "You've got the hammer."

"Yes, but I'm seriously outnumbered."

She smiled and went to help Mallory find her necklace, feeling Garth's eyes on her as she bent over the low table. She was certain that nothing was showing, no cleavage, no lace on her underwear. Her skirt was too long to do anything but hide the backs of her legs, and yet she felt as if he could see *something*, something he rather liked, and the feeling made her want to pull at her sweater and fuss with her hair. She glanced back at him. He looked entirely innocent—rather like Hernando with the missing soap in his pocket.

"I'll take your jacket," she said when she came back.

He gave it to her, but with some reluctance.

"Do *not* let The Phantom get that," he said as he handed it over.

"I'll do my best," she promised.

She took it and hung it with her coat in the small closet at the back of the room. When she returned, Garth had taken matters into his own hands. He was reading the name necklaces and having the children "give him five," all except Mallory, who was afraid to do it.

"Come here, Hernando, my man," Garth said. "Show Mallory how."

Hernando slapped Garth's open hand with his—hard.

"Way to go, Hernando!" Garth said. "Now tell Mallory what that means."

"It means you're cool, man," Hernando said. "It means you're cool and *I'm* cool."

"Right," Garth said. "Come on, Mallory. Let's see you be cool."

She stood hesitantly with one finger in her mouth and tentatively slapped his hand. "Good, Mallory! One more time!"

This time she struck harder.

"All right, Mallory!" Garth praised. "Now a 'high five' like the Jets do—all right!"

Mallory was beaming, and Garth moved on to the next child, who had definitely been inspired by Mallory's success. Jenna could only hope that Garth's hand held out through the rest of them.

But, not only did it hold out, he had enough left to insist that she "high five," too.

"Okay, Miss Jenna," he said, holding his hand up and giving her a mischievous grin.

Jenna slapped his palm.

"You call that a high five? Come here, Mallory. You show her."

Mallory was on the scene in an instant, slapping Garth's hand like a pro.

"See, Miss Jenna?" Garth said. "Like Mallory does it—all right!"

Jenna's palm stung from "high fiving." She looked into his eyes too long, and they both glanced away. He *was* kind, she thought, regardless of his apparent aversion to the term. There was a kindness, a gentleness, evident in him in spite of what he might intend.

And there was a part of him that was not so kind, too. She'd already had experience with that.

She looked at her watch.

"What's the matter?" he asked. "Have I worn out my welcome already?"

"No, I was just wondering what was keeping Debbie. We'd planned to keep the children out of your way for a while so you could hammer in peace."

He looked at her, but he didn't comment on the obvious: She hadn't planned to have to deal with him alone.

"It won't bother me if they watch," he said.

"Are you sure?"

"I'm sure. I might need a couple of helpers. How about you, Hernando? You want to be my Main Man?" As he said it, he caught a glimpse of Mallory's crestfallen face. "And you, too, Mallory."

"Both of us can't be no Main Mans," Hernando said, a small frown between his eyes that Jenna recognized immediately. Illogically she felt as if it were a kind of caste mark—not of his birth, but of his environment—a symbol of frustrated anger she'd come to associate with violent and potentially violent young men. It was the same expression the boy who had shot Patrick wore.

"Yeah, you can," Garth said. "Miss Jenna, too. You want to be a Main Man, too, Miss Jenna?"

"Yes," she said after a moment, realizing that Garth was looking at her with some concern. But he didn't say anything. He started on the cubbyholes instead, and he was a whiz at organizing. He assigned her to be the Main Man With The Official Lumber Loaders, who put cubbyhole pieces into the red wagon that was part of the kindergarten play equipment. Then there were The Official Wagon Escorters, who pulled or walked alongside the wagon until it reached its destination—Garth. He supervised The Official Lumber Unloaders and fitted the pieces together with the help of Mallory, who held the bag of nails, and Hernando, who stood by with the hammer.

Amazingly enough, with Jenna on one end of the operation and Garth on the other, it worked, though Jenna was filled with misgivings about giving Hernando anything so lethal as a hammer.

But Garth seemed to know how to handle him, and in a short time it became apparent that Hernando liked his job as one of the three "Main Mans" and intended to stick to Garth no matter what.

Now and then, Jenna could hear bits of their conversation.

"You have to be smart, Hernando. Everybody gets ticked off. Everybody. But when you get mad, you got to put it someplace where it does some good. Like out this hammer and into this nail, see? You want the nail in the wood, right? And that's a good thing. It's going to hold these shelves together. When you're ticked off, you put it where it doesn't hurt you and it doesn't hurt anybody else—then you're a smart guy. Now hit that sucker! Harder!"

When they stopped for lunch, the cubbyholes were almost finished. Garth was escorted royally to the cafeteria by his adoring new friends, and he seemed to enjoy the attention. Because they all wanted to sit at his table, seating arrangements precipitated a small riot, one Jenna averted by pushing two tables together.

"Be strong," she told him when he looked down at his plate—chicken and noodles, carrot sticks, cinnamon pumpkin cookies with raisins, and milk.

"This is not bad," he said a little too earnestly after a bite or two.

"I'm glad you think that. Sister Mary John is very big on setting an example."

"Is that why I have to drink my milk?"

"That's why."

"Well, here goes," he said, picking up his milk carton and clicking it against hers—which led to having to toast everybody else's as well. "I keep forgetting you have to do everything here in twenties," he said to Jenna. "To your very good health," he said to the children. "Now you say that back to me—To your very good health!"

They said it with enthusiasm, and he tipped back the carton and drank. "Okay, who's got to burp?" he asked when he'd downed the last of the milk.

"Detective Garth!" Jenna said.

"Miss Jenna, you stay out of this. We're going to burp really loud—and then we'll be good, won't we?" he asked the group. But most of them were already warming up and, therefore, too busy to answer.

Jenna sat surrounded by giggles and rude table noises. "Sister Mary John is coming," she nonchalantly advised them when the school's principal appeared in the doorway.

Garth desperately tried to shush everybody, but he had started this impromptu concert, and he was about to find that five-year-olds were nothing if not difficult to de-program.

"Aren't you going to help me?" he whispered frantically to Jenna as the noise escalated.

"No way," she whispered back. "I've never seen any of you people before in my life."

"Ah! Detective Garth!" Sister Mary John said, coming over immediately. Every child at the table had the giggles. Garth had Hernando's head in a combination hug and hammerlock in an effort to keep him from really letting one rip. He smiled broadly, but he didn't let Hernando go.

Sister Mary John looked from Garth to the top of Hernando's head and back again. "Having a nice lunch?" she wondered.

"Oh, yes, Sister," Garth assured her. "Very nice."

"And you, Hernando?"

"Yeah!" came the muffled reply, punctuated by a giggle.

"What about you, Jenna?" Sister Mary John inquired.

"Oh, I don't know when I've had a lunch like this," Jenna assured her.

"Good. Very good," Sister Mary John said. She wandered away, and Garth released Hernando. He came up grinning.

"I wasn't going to do nothing!" he said.

"The he-heck you weren't," Garth said.

Mallory put her hands on her hips. "Garth! I thought you were going to say a *bad* word!"

"Who me? Mallory thought I was going to say a bad word," he said to Jenna.

"She's not the only one," Jenna assured him, and he grinned. He was a rascal all right; she had no doubts about that. And the children loved him.

"You've got to loosen up, Miss Jenna," he had the nerve to suggest.

"No, thank you. I don't have the stamina for it. And I'm supposed to be in charge here. Could we go now, or do you have some other totally gross thing in mind?"

"How would you feel about a food fight?" he asked, clearly still trying to annoy her.

"Are you the target?" she countered, and they both laughed.

But he could tell the very instant Jenna Gallagher remembered that she intended to handle him, not enjoy him, and her smile slid away.

"So what's next?" he asked to cover the moment.

She stood up and began getting the children into line. "It's time for them to go outside."

He got up from his chair. "Can I come along?"

He was standing too close to her—much too close. "I think we've taken up enough of your time."

"It's my time, Miss Jenna. I haven't finished the cubbyholes yet, and I'm supposed to get to know the children, right? I'll come along."

He went with her to take the children out to the playground—because there was no way to stop him, and because, she reasoned, Debbie still hadn't gotten back, and she needed the help. Fortunately The Phantom hadn't struck again, and dressing for the outing went smoothly. No one had misplaced anything, not even Mallory, though it took a while to retie all the shoes that had come untied. Even the children with Velcro fasteners wanted help—if Garth was the one helping. He sat patiently on the floor, surrounded by small lifted feet.

The group opted for the sliding board, with Garth supervising the climb up the ladder and Jenna catching at the bottom. The sun was bright, but the wind was brisk, and she huddled in her coat, watching him furtively. He was certainly good with the children, and he seemed to know all their names now without having to refer to the necklaces. Sister Mary John should be pleased. As for herself, she was acquiring a grudging respect for him, one that conflicted strongly with her need to be left alone. He didn't behave like Patrick and yet he...

She didn't know what he did—except disrupt everything. Her hard-won serenity. Her emotions. Her life.

He caught her looking at him, and she glanced away. She couldn't escape the fact that she was glad that she'd asked him and glad that he'd come, even if she hadn't addressed any of the reasons behind it. But when they got back inside, she tried once again to release him of his obligation to the class if he needed to go. Talking to him about his unwanted dinner invitations would be awkward at best.

"They'll be taking naps now, so you can't hammer any—" she began.

"I'll wait until they're awake," he interrupted. He looked into her eyes, giving her the opportunity to tell him the real reason she was so determined for him to leave.

But she didn't press for his departure, and he walked away to supervise hanging up coats on the pegs along the back wall of the classroom and to get down the sleeping mats, letting Mallory and Hernando show him exactly what he was supposed to do. Then he helped tuck all the children in, covering them with the beach towels they'd brought from home. Jenna might have worried about the logo on Hernando's towel if kindergartners could read. CERTIFIED BEACH DOCTOR, it said. FREE CHEST EXAMINATIONS GIVEN

HERE. She saw Garth smile when he read it and pat Hernando on the head.

"Go to sleep, man," he told him. "You've worked hard today. You deserve a good nap."

Jenna turned off the overhead lights and closed the blinds, then sat down on one of the two adult-size chairs to watch over the room. Everyone grew quiet, and after a moment Garth dragged up the other chair and sat down close to her.

"My God," he whispered. "They're actually going to sleep. I didn't think they ever wound down."

"Amazing, isn't it?" She looked at him. "Tell me, how is the investigation coming?"

"Investigation?" he asked, a bit taken aback.

"The Phantom Coat Flusher," she said.

He looked out over the sleeping children. "You've only got one slick enough, angry enough, to do it."

"Hernando," she said without hesitation, and he nodded.

"Why would he do that, do you think?" He had been very close to Hernando all day, and she found that she wanted his opinion.

"Well, one good thing about a Catholic school is the uniforms. Everybody dresses alike. Theoretically, nobody gets the business about what they wear. Except they aren't alike when it comes to their coats. That's the one place you can tell a difference in them. Hernando's wearing a third hand-me-down ghetto kid special, and he knows it. It's adequate, it keeps out the cold, but it's got 'Poor Kid' stamped all over it."

"I don't think any of the children have said anything."

"They don't have to. *He* knows it."

"I'll talk to Sister Mary John."

"If you don't mind, I'd like to take care of it. If Sister Mary John or the school arranges a new coat for him, it'll make him feel worse, see?"

"Not exactly."

"The coat he's wearing now is a kind of symbol to him—of what he is and what he hasn't got. He already knows he's different, and if you single him out with a new coat, he'll know it all the more. Understand?"

She didn't precisely. "Won't your getting him a new coat make him feel bad, too?"

"Nah," he said blithely. "I'll think of something." He yawned and stretched his arms over his head. She was so aware of his body suddenly, of his strength and his masculinity, that she shifted in her chair. She had been alone for nearly a year, but no one had made her feel her aloneness as much as he did with that simple gesture.

"I could use a nap myself," he said.

"I could use the official kindergarten teacher for this class," Jenna said to take her mind off his physical presence. "I wonder where Debbie is?"

"Are you worried?"

"Yes and no. She was only going a few blocks to take Becca and her coat home. But she's—"

"What?" he prompted.

"A little addleheaded. She's been known to get side-tracked."

"You want me to go look for her?"

"No, not yet. She's been needing to talk to Becca's mother about some things. She's probably doing that."

The conversation lagged, until Jenna suddenly looked at him.

"I want to ask you something," she said.

"Go ahead." He expected that she'd get to the real reason she'd invited him here, but she didn't.

"I was wondering about your name..."

"My name?"

"Your first name—why you don't want anyone to use it."

He smiled slightly. "Because I'm a lot like Hernando."

"I don't understand."

"It's—" He shrugged. "I told you about how my mother wanted me to marry rich."

"Yes."

"Well, I wasn't just kidding around. It's the truth. Some people think winning the lottery or the magazine sweepstakes would be the answer to all their problems. Hazel thinks it's one of the two of us marrying money—not in a calculating way, but, like I said, the way it happened in the old movies. Luigi—he's the counterman at the Humoresque—he says she's always been that way. And she thinks if you can't be rich, you ought to *act* rich. She read someplace that in wealthy families a lot of times a son is given his mother's maiden name as his first name. That's why I'm 'Johnson.' I don't like it because it's a symbol to me—like Hernando's coat is to him." His eyes searched hers. "Do you understand?"

"I understand," she said. She understood completely. She just hadn't expected such candor. She didn't think he'd told many people that, and she felt as if he'd just given her a small but precious gift.

The minutes passed. They sat quietly. She could feel him looking at her. The door at the end of the hallway banged loudly.

"Mrs. Gallagher," he said, his voice low. "About the other night, at the Carvers' party—I was out of line."

She didn't say anything. She was sitting with her arms folded, and he couldn't see her face.

"Mrs. Gallagher, don't you ever say stupid things? You don't know why you say them, you just . . . do?"

"Yes," she said evenly. "I sometimes say stupid things." She looked around at him. "But I don't think you do, Detective Garth."

He could feel himself flush. He wasn't being entirely honest with her, and she knew it. "Mrs. Gallagher—"

"Your remark was cruel at best—I'm sure you know that. I'm sure you've had no problem understanding why I didn't want to spend an evening over dinner with you."

She abruptly got up and went to cover the children who were out from under their beach towels. Then there was a commotion in the hall—Debbie arriving out of breath and harried. As she came into the room, she tried to smile but didn't quite make it. She kept looking over her shoulder.

"What's wrong?" Jenna whispered to keep from waking the children.

"I...thought I saw someone," Debbie said, looking over her shoulder again.

"Who?"

"Oh..." Debbie said airily. She glanced at Garth. She had a slight frown, and she gave an offhand shrug. "Looked sort of like Hugh." She started to take her coat off but then apparently changed her mind. "Garth," she said, her agitation apparently growing. "Garth, could you take Jenna home this afternoon?"

Chapter Six

Debbie—" Jenna protested. Debbie was distracted at best, and Jenna was totally unprepared for this last-ditch attempt at matchmaking.

"Jenna, I'm sorry," Debbie said, moving away. "Something's come up. I have to take care of it today, and I don't know how long it'll take me. You don't mind, do you, Garth?"

"What?" he said, because he'd only heard his name in the middle of Debbie's run of conversation.

"Taking Jenna home," Debbie said.

"Sure," he said, glancing at Jenna. He'd do it, but from the look on her face, he was going to have one hell of a time getting her into the car.

"I'll take the bus," Jenna said—not unsurprisingly.

"Don't be silly," Debbie insisted. "It'll take you forever on the bus. Garth said he'd take you."

"Debbie, I don't want to impose any more on Detective Garth."

"It's no imposition, Mrs. Gallagher," he said lightly. She was feeling cornered again; he could see it in her face. But here was yet another opportunity—if he didn't screw it up.

Debbie looked at her watch. "What are you going to do, stand on the street in the cold and wait for the next bus?"

"I've done it before."

"When you had to," Debbie agreed. "This time you don't have to, does she, Garth?"

"No," he said. Some of the children were waking up and beginning to mill around. "Mrs. Gallagher, I would hate for you to do that on my account. It's the least I can do."

"See?" Debbie said, though clearly she didn't understand the obscure apology he was making.

"You don't have to *do* anything," Jenna said.

"I know that, Mrs. Gallagher. But I want to."

"Why?" She looked into his eyes, waiting to hear the answer.

"Because you were a cop's wife. Because you're my partner's friend. I don't want to leave you standing on the street in the cold waiting for a bus," he said evenly, and he didn't look away.

"It's out of your way."

"Yes," he agreed, because he felt as if this were some kind of trial suddenly. Would he tell the truth, the whole truth and nothing but? Or would she catch him in a lie—even a socially appropriate one—so she could dismiss him and his unwanted offer? "But today that isn't a problem."

"Detective Garth, I—"

But she was suddenly swamped by children. Mallory and at least two others were pulling on her skirt, and she turned her attention to that. He glanced at Debbie. She was frowning, and she kept watching the door.

"What's the matter?" he asked, walking over to her. She jumped.

"Oh, Garth! You scared me!"

"In broad daylight in the middle of a kindergarten class?" he asked, not quite teasing.

"I was thinking about something." She gave him a strained smile. "I forgot to tell Jenna I had this...errand this morning. Otherwise she could have driven herself instead of riding with me. I hate forgetting things the way I do—I don't know why I do it. Just me, I guess. Thanks for taking Jenna home."

Garth wasn't as certain as Debbie seemed to be that they'd gotten that settled, but he didn't say so. "Okay to get back to hammering now?" he asked. He'd been solicited to put cubbyholes together, too, and at least he knew he could finish that.

But he didn't get very far. Children, as they got their things gathered up and their coats on, kept coming to him, unabashedly hugging him before they lined up to go home.

Mallory was first.

"You are a very fine person, Garth," she said, hugging him hard.

"So are you, Miss Mallory," he responded.

"You are a fine person, Garth," the next two said.

Jenna was standing close by, watching.

"What is this?" he asked her when the children had trotted off to get cookies and juice, realizing now that he was participating in some kind of ritual.

"We always have hugs and positive reinforcement before they take their naps. I forgot today, so they're doing it now. Too many of them only hear that they're all right just the way they are from us—or from 'Mr. Rogers' on television. It's very important to them. They want to share it with you."

He gave up any further ideas of hammering, staying on his knees and waiting for the rest of the children to come and be hugged. Hernando was last.

"*I'm* a fine person," he said in typically Hernando fashion.

"The best, man," Garth agreed.

"I don't like cops."

"Yeah, I know," Garth said, giving him his hug. "What can I say?"

Hernando leaned back to stare at him for a moment. "Are you coming back here?"

"If I get invited."

"You ain't coming back, man. You're telling a *lie*."

"No. I'm telling you I haven't been invited yet."

Hernando studied him closely. "Okay," he decided. "Maybe I'll talk to Miss Jenna and Miss Debbie for you."

"You do that," Garth said.

Always "cool," Hernando slapped Garth's hand.

"Detective Garth," Jenna said, and he looked up at her. "I . . . can't leave until all the children are gone."

She was looking at him gravely. He thought that she was agreeing to let him take her home. He also thought that he could still blow it.

"Fine," he said. "I still have to finish the cubbyholes."

He went back to work. The less said on the matter, the better. The room grew quiet as Jenna and the last of the children went outside for whatever the going-home procedure might be. All in all, it had been a satisfactory day, he thought. Hammer or not, he certainly hadn't envisioned doing even minor carpentry, but his old high school shop training had apparently survived the years of police work, and the cubbyholes had been put together with minimal amount of aggravation. He'd had a conversation—of sorts—with Jenna. He'd liked the children. He would have liked to have had more time to work on whatever it was Jenna might know about Hugh, but maybe that would work out, too, if she'd decided to let him take her home.

The door at the end of the hallway slammed again, and he could hear someone coming—hurrying—down the long corridor.

"Forgot my purse," Debbie said, bursting into the room. It was lying on the desk, and she snatched it up in a hurried dash around the room. "Thanks for taking Jenna home," she called again as she went out the door, leaving him no time to reply. "You didn't have a date or anything, did you?" she asked, abruptly sticking her head back into the doorway.

"No. No date. I told Hazel I'd come to the Humoresque for dinner."

"Why don't you take Jenna?" Debbie said. "She'd love it."

He grinned. "Yeah, sure." He was trying to gain Jenna Gallagher's confidence, and a hole-in-the-wall café straight out of the pages of a Damon Runyon short story wasn't likely the place to do it.

"No, she would. She likes people. There are people there, aren't there?"

"I'm afraid so," Garth confessed.

"Look. Jenna isn't a snob. She'd like it. Really. I have to go," she concluded abruptly, disappearing from the doorway. He could hear her break into a run as she neared the outside door.

A bell rang somewhere, and the school emptied out in earnest, all the upper grades being let loose and all the appropriate commotion. He hammered the last few nails into the shelves and checked them for stability, remembering his own exhilaration at being let out of school for the day. As a boy, he'd considered school something just short of prison. But for Hazel's determination, he probably would have dropped out and ended up in a real one. He owed Hazel a lot for that, for making him stay in school.

He looked up, thinking Debbie had come back again.

"What did you forget this time?" he asked, but it was Jenna. They were both wearing black coats and the gold-and-black-school-colors scarf. "I thought you were Debbie," he said before she could reply.

"No, she's off on her errand. Are you finished?"

"Except for moving this section wherever you want it to go."

"Oh, next to the others, I think."

Jenna helped him slide the unit of cubbyholes across the floor and align it the others. *It was very kind of you to do this,* she almost said, but she didn't. She'd heard, loud and clear, that he didn't want to be thought of as "kind."

"Very nice," she said instead. "This should help cut down on some of the confusion."

He smiled. He'd spent the day here, and he was nothing if not battle scarred. "You think so, do you?"

"I hope so," she answered, smiling in return. "Every little bit helps."

"How often do you work here?" he asked idly, but he was more than aware of the fact that they were alone now, more than aware of how pretty she was and how nice she smelled.

"As often as they need me. The other regular teacher is pregnant, and she's having all the upsets that go with it. I'm hoping for something permanent. This gets my foot in the door anyway."

They stood there awkwardly. Garth couldn't keep from staring into her eyes. He wanted to know what she thought of him, and he supposed that he might see it there. The silence lengthened, and it occurred to him that he'd better tread lightly if he wanted the opportunity of taking her home.

"So," he said abruptly, "are you ready to go?"

She looked relieved.

"Yes. Sister Mary John would like to speak to you on the way out."

"I'm not in trouble, am I? I drank my milk, and I didn't swear—out loud."

"You should be in good standing then." She moved to the windows to open all the blinds. "When I was a little girl," she said over her shoulder, "we closed all the blinds at the

end of the day to help keep the heat in. Now they have to be
left open so anyone passing by can see if there are any sus-
picious lights or vandals or burglars."

"That's what the world's come to," he said, opening the
last few blinds for her. She went to the small closet at the
back of the room to get his coat.

"Are you sure you don't mind going all the way to Park
Slope?"

"I don't mind, Mrs. Gallagher."

She handed him his coat, and their fingers brushed. Hers
were warm, soft. He put the coat on on the way out, opening the door for her for no other reason than it would allow
him to get closer to her, albeit briefly.

Jenna walked alongside him to Sister Mary John's office, a bit disconcerted because the place was deserted now.
A school with all the children gone was a bit eerie, she
thought, though that wasn't entirely the reason for her dis-
quiet. The primary reason was Johnson Garth—kind, ac-
commodating Johnson Garth.

She glanced at him. She was a policeman's widow. She
was his partner's friend. Why shouldn't he offer to take her
home? There was nothing wrong with his offer. What was
wrong was her response to it. She wanted to be with him.
And she wanted to run for her life. And she was perfectly
aware that both responses were overreactions on her part.

Perhaps the duality of her feelings was because she was
lonely. And because she was still having some kind of wa-
tered-down version of her anxiety attacks. She didn't have
the weakness or the palpitations, but part of her certainly
wanted to run away. From him—or from herself—was the
question.

"About the dinner invitations," she said when they were
nearly at Sister Mary John's open door.

"Yes," he said without surprise.

"Detective Garth?" Sister Mary John called through the
doorway.

"They're still good—the invitations," Garth said with a wink just before he stepped inside the principal's office.

Jenna waited outside, exasperated because she was going to have to go into this after all. She should have known that subtleties wouldn't work with Garth. Not that it was entirely his fault. She *had* agreed to let him take her home.

She stood in the hallway, rubbing a small ache between her eyebrows that threatened to become a major pain.

"I thought you understood," she said when he came out again.

"I understand. I just wanted you to know the invitations stood anyway."

"Garth—"

"Friend of yours," he interrupted, nodding toward the end of the hallway.

But it wasn't a friend at all. It was Hugh.

"Hugh," Garth said when he reached them.

"What is he doing here?" Hugh said to Jenna, ignoring Garth, his eyes cold, his manner tense.

"I usually speak for myself, Hugh," Garth said. "What is it exactly you'd like to know?"

"I'm talking to Jenna," Hugh said, taking her by the arm.

Jenna pointedly removed it from his grasp. "And if I thought it was any business of yours whatsoever, Hugh, I'd tell you," she said.

Hugh hesitated, looking from Jenna to Garth and then back again. He suddenly smiled. "Jenna—Jenna, hey, I'm sorry. Patrick was my little brother. I was so used to looking after him—and with him gone, I guess it spills over to you sometimes."

"What are you doing here, Hugh?" Jenna asked. If he'd come because he'd somehow found out Garth was here, she wanted to know about it—and she didn't need him to remind her about Patrick.

"I was supposed to pick up Mom. She's here for some meeting about the Fall Bazaar or something. You haven't seen her, have you?" He continued to ignore Garth, but he was trying to handle her with that unsubtle charm of his that he could turn on and off at will. His assumption that he could cajole her into a better frame of mind grated on her nerves even more so than usual.

"No, I haven't," Jenna said, refusing to be assuaged. "If she's here, she'll be talking to Father Kevin."

"So how about helping me find her?" Hugh said, the smile still firmly in place.

This time Jenna smiled in return. "I think you know where Father Kevin's office is, Hugh. Patrick told me you were sent there enough when you were a student here."

Garth, who'd seen fit to stay out of the conversation thus far, spoke up. "I believe that's Mrs. Gallagher coming now."

Jenna looked around. Mamie Gallagher was coming down the corridor. She smiled broadly for a moment, but then, as she recognized Garth, the smile slid away.

"I was looking for you, dear," Mamie said to Jenna with the same studied indifference to Garth her son had displayed. "And how nice you look. Hunter green is your color, isn't it? So becoming. It's nice to see you taking an interest in that kind of thing again."

Mamie said the words, but her meaning was clearly the opposite. Mamie Gallagher still wore black, unlike her disrespectful daughter-in-law, who stood here in dark green—with another man.

Jenna smiled, a smile she had to dig deep for and strain hard to keep. "Mamie, you know Detective Garth."

"Mrs. Gallagher," Garth said, leaning forward to shake her hand before she had time to decide whether she wanted to or not. In the process, he shot Jenna an are-you-sure-you-know-what-you're-doing look.

Jenna did know what she was doing. She was working very hard at not being intimidated. Garth was here at her invitation, whether the Gallaghers approved or not, and she wasn't going to behave as if she'd been caught doing something wrong.

Because Mamie Gallagher had been schooled to be gracious, she smiled politely—for a second and a half. "Detective," she said, dismissing Garth without so much as a second glance. "You're coming to dinner tonight, Jenna." It wasn't quite a question. "We haven't seen you lately."

Jenna had no excuse for not coming, none except that she didn't want to have to explain her association with Garth. Garth was unexplainable—to herself, much less to Patrick's mother. "I—"

"You didn't forget about Hazel, did you, Jenna?" Garth interrupted.

She looked at him blankly.

"She's waiting at the Humoresque," Garth said. "You didn't forget, did you?"

She looked into his eyes. Hazel?

"Oh, Hazel!" she said abruptly. "I did forget," she said. She had forgotten that Hazel was his mother, certainly, and that she worked at the Humoresque; she wasn't playing entirely fast and loose with the truth.

"I think we'd better get going," he prompted, putting his hand on her shoulder. "Nice to see you again, Mrs. Gallagher," he said to Mamie. "Hugh."

"Nice going," Garth said as they crossed the parking lot to his car.

"Oh, sure—I can't believe I let you lie for me!" He now had her by the elbow, as if he thought she might not come along otherwise.

"I didn't lie," he said. "I only asked if you'd forgotten Hazel—which you had."

"It's the same thing—no, it's worse. It's…manipulation. I didn't have other plans."

"You didn't want to have dinner with the Gallaghers, did you?"

"No, but—"

"And you're all the old lady has left of her son, aren't you? You loved Patrick, and you don't want to hurt her feelings, right? So you can't very well tell her to take a hike, no matter how much you want to—"

She abruptly stopped walking and looked up at him. It was incredible to her that he understood the situation so perfectly.

"—can you?" he finished.

She sighed. "No."

"All right, then. Sometimes you gotta do what you gotta do, for your own sanity. This is the car."

He unlocked the door and opened it for her.

For my own sanity, she thought as she got in.

She looked back toward the school. Hugh and Mamie were coming out—to see if she was actually leaving with Johnson Garth, she supposed. She sighed again. "I live at—"

"I know where you live," he interrupted.

She didn't ask him how. She sat staring straight ahead, thinking about Mamie, thinking about what she should have said, but she gave a small wave as the car went past Mamie and Hugh on the way out of the parking lot. She was *not* going to behave as if she were doing something wrong!

"You're coming to dinner tonight, Jenna."

Thank you, no, she should have said. A big smile and a simple no, without explanation or excuse. It couldn't be any worse than letting Garth invent excuses for her. Why couldn't she just say that? Thank you, no!

Because she'd loved Patrick and because she was all his mother had left of him. And because sometimes you have to do what you have to do, for your own sanity.

"You still beating yourself up?" Garth asked when they'd gone a few blocks.

She glanced at him. "Yes," she said truthfully. She realized suddenly that they weren't going to Park Slope.

"Where are we going?" she asked abruptly and not without some alarm.

He looked over at her. "Take it easy, Mrs. Gallagher. I got you into a guilty conscience. I'm going to get you out of it."

She pursed her lips to ask how, then didn't ask after all. There was no point in it. For whatever unlikely reason, she believed him. She couldn't feel any worse; perhaps she'd feel better. Wherever he intended taking her, as it stood now, she'd go.

Chapter Seven

Jenna would remember their entrance into the Humoresque as a series of double takes—from the older woman in a green smock and a hair net waiting tables, from the old man in a T-shirt and a white apron working behind the counter, and from a nervous, ragged street person just inside the door, who stared at her, then immediately left.

The Humoresque was long and old and narrow. It had a big front window boasting its name, the lettering faded and barely still visible, and when Garth opened the door, it smelled of fried onions and fresh coffee and tired, down-and-out people. The floor was made of tiny hexagonal black-and-white tiles that made a whispery sound against the soles of her shoes when she walked, and everyone in the place looked up when she and Garth came in.

To her right was the grill behind a long counter with a row of wobbly wooden stools, and against the opposite wall, high-backed wooden booths with an assortment of patrons' initials carved into them. There were several small tables with bentwood chairs farther in back. Jenna looked up at the high ceiling. Probably the original embossed tin, she thought, and in spite of needing some repairs and paint, quite beautiful.

"Whatever you do, don't mention Walter O'Malley," Garth said as they made their way through the patrons to find somewhere to sit. The place was crowded with elderly couples, taxi drivers and little old men who slurped soup at the counter.

"All right," she said agreeably. "Who's Walter O'Malley?" She was feeling better already. Telling the truth in reverse like this was something she'd never done, but she had to agree that the guilt was fading. Somewhat.

"Who's Walter O'Malley?" Garth asked, his voice so incredulous that she shrugged and gave him an apologetic grin.

"On October 8, 1957," he explained hurriedly, "Walter O'Malley announced that he was moving the Brooklyn Dodgers to California—that's who Walter O'Malley is."

"I take it he hasn't been forgiven."

"Not in this world or the next. Ebbets Field—"

But he didn't get to tell her about Ebbets Field. The waitress in the green smock and the hair net swooped down on them.

"Well, what do you know?" she said loudly, giving Garth a hug. "My son the flatfoot," she continued in an exaggerated whisper. "And who is this?" she asked in a normal tone of voice, smiling at Jenna.

"This is Jenna Gallagher, Ma. I'm making an honest woman out of her."

Jenna gave him a hard look, but he only grinned.

"Good," Hazel Garth said, patting him on the cheek as if such announcements were commonplace from her irrepressible son.

"Jenna, this is the notorious Hazel of whom you've heard me speak."

Jenna extended her hand. "Mrs. Garth, it's nice to meet you. Actually, we just—"

"—came by for dinner," Garth finished for her.

"No, we didn't," she countered as nicely as she could.

"Yes, we did," he replied just as nicely.

Hazel was looking from one of them to the other. She shook Jenna's hand.

"Call me Hazel, Jenna. Everybody does. So how come you're out with a nice girl like this dressed like *that*?" she demanded of Garth. "You look like Roy Lee. How many times I got to tell you you got to dress for success, huh?"

"That makes about seventeen million, five hundred thousand and six, Ma," Garth said.

"Oh, you. You make the jokes. He ain't never serious, Jenna. So you want dinner? It's too early for dinner. Luigi's not ready for the dinner crowd. Who eats dinner this time of day?"

"Working people, Ma. People who've only had chicken and noodles and carrot sticks."

"You go find something else to do for a little while. Jenna! You seen the loft, Jenna?"

"Ah, no."

"You take Jenna up to see the loft." Hazel patted her on the arm. "It's a great place. There are people who'd give their eyeteeth for a place like that. You go show her," she said, giving Garth a little push. "Then you come back."

"Want to see a loft?" Garth asked, smiling into Jenna's eyes.

"Garth . . ."

"I'm telling you, it's a lot easier to just go. Trust me on this." He cut his eyes toward his mother.

Jenna smiled in spite of herself. "All right. Why don't I go see the loft?"

"Smart woman," Garth said, taking her by the arm. "Luigi!" he yelled down the counter. And apparently it was that kind of place, because hardly a head turned—even

Luigi's—for a raised voice. Clearly only entrances caused the clientele to take note. "Luigi!" he called again, motioning for the old man behind the counter.

This time the old man looked around, and he seemed delighted at Garth's summons, hurrying down the length of the counter and wiping his hands on his apron as he came.

"Luigi, posso presentare la mia amica, Signora Jenna Gallagher," Garth said to him.

"Signora, Giovanni?" Luigi said, eyebrows raised. *"Dove é il suo marito?"*—And where is her husband?—he continued in Italian, clearly bracing himself to have his sense of propriety offended.

"Lui é morto"—dead—Garth hastened to explain, glancing at Jenna to see if the conversation was disturbing her. No, he thought. She didn't understand Italian.

"Assassinato," he continued, because he knew Luigi had the gentlest of hearts, and it was suddenly important to him that the old man think kindly of Jenna. *"Lui era un poliziotto."* A policeman, murdered.

"Ah!" Luigi said in sympathy. *"Felice di conoscerla,"* he said to Jenna, clasping her hand warmly in his two big ones.

"Jenna, this is my friend Luigi Lufrano."

"Mr. Lufrano," Jenna said, smiling.

"Luigi, please, *Signora*. So. It's good to have so pretty a lady be your friend, Giovanni," he said to Garth. "You stay with us a while, Jenna. I fix you the best dinner you ever have."

"That would be nice," Jenna replied, because she liked him instantly. She glanced at Garth. If there was any complicity here, she couldn't tell it from Garth's face.

"You like . . . hamburger steak?" Luigi asked earnestly.

"Yes," she said.

"Good! I give you the best. Lots of onions and garlic." He squeezed her hand. "You go with Garth now while I get ready."

"This way," Garth said, leading her out through the back of the restaurant into a narrow hallway. "Through there." He pointed toward a door at the far end, one of dark wood with a textured, frosted panel of glass in the upper half. It reminded her of an office door out of a 1940s private-eye movie. In fact, the whole place reminded her of a 1940s movie set. No wonder Hazel Garth believed in Frank Capra miracles, working here every day.

"Luigi calls you John," she remarked, and he looked at her in surprise.

"You speak Italian?"

"No. I know Giovanni is John, but that about covers it."

"Interesting language," he said.

"You speak it very well," she said, wondering why he looked so relieved.

"Not really. I can hold my own with simple pleasantries. That's about it. And some simple *un*pleasantries," he added with a mischievous grin.

"That must come in handy," she observed. "Being able to swear in more than one language."

"Oh, it does, Mrs. Gallagher. Did you mean what you said to Luigi about staying here for dinner?" He fumbled in his jeans pocket for his keys.

She looked into his eyes. "I...think it would be nice," she said again.

"Good," he said, unlocking the door. It opened with a loud squeak. "I've got one question, though."

"What?" she said, waiting to see if he wanted her to lead or follow.

Follow.

"What's Luigi got that I haven't got?" he asked over his shoulder on his way up the stairs.

"Manners," she said dryly, and he laughed.

"Well, you've got me there. Hold on to the rail. And watch the steps. Some of the metal strips on the edges are coming up."

Her toe caught even as he said it, and he grabbed her arm to steady her.

"Easy," he said. His touch was warm and pleasant, but he let her go immediately. "I'd get these stairs fixed, but in this neighborhood you need all the booby traps you can get. So when's the last time you toured a loft apartment?"

"Never," she said, stepping well into the wooden steps as she climbed.

"Never? That's hard to believe. Housing is the only way New Yorkers know how to impress each other. You go to L.A., they want to show you their cars. You come to New York, all you hear about is apartments. I thought you would have seen everything by now—brownstones, penthouses, the works."

"No. Lofts I've missed."

"Well, you're going to love this. I figure this loft is right up there with, say, an '84 Porsche."

"I'm sure," Jenna said.

At the top of the stairs they came to another door with frosted glass.

"After you," Garth said, unlocking it. "The light switch is on the wall on your left."

She found it without difficulty and switched it on. The loft was huge and well lighted—the one switch seemed to turn on everything. As big as the area was, there were no dark corners. But there was a draft. One of the windows was slightly open, and the room was cold. She was glad to keep her coat on.

"So, how do you like it?" he asked, walking ahead of her, snatching up discarded clothes as he went and rolling them into a ball—which he tossed unceremoniously into a corner for lack of a better place.

"This isn't an apartment. This is a skating rink with furniture," she said, impressed by the vastness of the place. Some of the apartments she and Patrick had lived in when they were first married would have fit into this place twice.

"Not much furniture," he said, and he was right. There was a small grouping not far from the arched windows across the front of the loft—a sofa and a chair and a table with a telephone and a floor lamp. There was a double bed, made up but without a bedspread, at the far end of the room—a long way away. There was no kitchen table in the galley area, or anyplace else for that matter. She supposed he ate on a stool at the counter.

"But plenty of clocks," she said, noticing that there were four of them on the wall, identical except for the time. "Do you need this many clocks?"

"Yeah. I hate being bothered by bureaucratic nonsense like daylight saving time. You know how much aggravation that is? Setting and resetting clocks?"

"Yes," she said agreeably.

"Well, the first clock is Eastern Standard Time. The third one is Eastern Daylight Savings Time. This way I only have to reset my alarm clock."

"What are the other two?"

"Well, the second and the fourth one is what time I'll get to the station house, God willing, if I leave by whatever time is on the first one or the third one. See?"

She was grinning. She had no idea if he was serious.

"No," she said pointedly.

"See, it saves a lot of wear and tear on the Whip if I'm not late. The lieutenant *hates* ten o'clock scholars."

"I'm not surprised. Does the lieutenant know you go to all this trouble on his behalf?"

"Nah. I don't think he'd believe it, do you?"

"No," she said. "I don't believe it myself."

He gave her an incredulous look that made her laugh.

"This way for the view," he said, pointing to the arched windows.

As she walked in that direction, she noticed the photograph by the telephone. "This is you," she said, bending down to inspect it more closely. How handsome he was, she thought. And how happy. Somehow she'd never thought of him as being as young and carefree as this. She studied the other two people in the picture—the beautiful dark-haired girl Garth had his arm around and the skinny boy whose ears looked too big for his head.

"Who are the people with you?"

"Just . . . friends."

"You don't have any brothers or sisters?"

"No."

"The girl—she's so pretty. How old were you in this picture?"

"I was eighteen," he said, and something in his voice made her look up at him.

Something in his face made her stop asking questions. She straightened and walked to the windows to look down at the street below.

"You can see everything from here," she said, because she felt awkward suddenly and needed something to say.

"Sometimes more than I want to." He paused. "But sometimes it's nice. In the summer especially. Most of the businesses on the street are family owned, and everybody'll drag folding lawn chairs outside and sit on the sidewalk in front of their stores when business is slow. Parents, grandparents, the kids. It's . . . nice."

She looked back over the apartment. "Well, I'm impressed. I'm surprised Skip hasn't tried to talk you out of it."

"Skip hasn't seen it. I don't bring many people here."

He was standing close to her, and she looked into his eyes again. And once again, she believed him. She didn't think it was some kind of line he used on women. Perhaps that was why Hazel had insisted he show her the place. Jenna was someone new in Garth's life, and perhaps his bringing or not bringing her up here was, to Hazel, some kind of indicator, some kind of clue.

Signifying what? Jenna wondered, looking away from his eyes and back out the window to the street below. She had no idea what she was doing here—at least from his standpoint. Or was this still part of some police code of honor? She was a policeman's widow. She was his partner's friend. He'd been rude to her, and now he owed it to her to be a little more civil than was his custom?

She gave a soft sigh. She didn't think Garth *had* a code—at least not one that he wouldn't chuck at a moment's notice if he needed to.

What, then? What did he want? Maybe it was some kind of locker-room bet. Some plan to get even with Hugh. Or some plan to prove his sexual irresistibility to his skeptical peers. She'd been to enough department social gatherings to know the mind-set. *Five will get you ten old Garth can make it with the widow.*

She had to be careful. She had to stop feeling the things she was feeling. She liked him. And, while she couldn't help herself in that regard, it had to stop there, before someone got hurt. Her.

"What?" she said, because she realized that he had said something, her eyes searching his for some glimmer of intent.

"I said, he wouldn't like the onions."

She frowned, not knowing what he meant.

"You said you were surprised Skip hadn't tried to talk me out of this place. I said he wouldn't like the onions—the smell from the restaurant. It drifts up here. I have to leave a window open."

"Oh," she said absently.

He watched her closely. He'd lost her somewhere. Again. She'd remembered that she didn't want to like him, and the wall had gone up. He had to give her credit for determination. When she'd decided not to like someone, she stuck with it.

But, God, he wished she wouldn't look at him like that!
Those beautiful, sad, *knowing* eyes of hers. It was as if she
knew he wasn't being straight with her, but she was going to
let it play out anyway. Because she couldn't help it. Because neither of them could help it. The truth of the matter
was that he had to keep reminding himself what this was all
about. He wanted to know if Hugh had even remotely had
anything to do with Patrick's death. It was important, damn
it, and she was making him forget that. Standing here now,
he wanted to touch her. He wanted to put his arms around
her. He wanted to get as deep inside her as he could get. He
wanted to take away the sadness in her eyes and promise her
she'd be all right with him.

Like Mary?

The thought rose unbidden, and there was nothing he
could do about it.

"Are you ready to go?" he asked more sharply than he
had intended.

They went back downstairs—to a booth Hazel had cere-
moniously held for them with a small, worn RESERVED sign
she'd placed in the middle of the table. Jenna took her coat
off and put it with her purse in the corner.

"So, what'll it be?" Hazel asked as they slid in, order pad
out. "And if it ain't hamburger steak, it'll break Luigi's
heart."

Jenna smiled. "Hamburger steak will be fine—and this
goes on separate checks."

"You can have it well done or well done," Hazel advised
her. Hazel's eyebrows had gone up at the request for separate checks, but apparently she wasn't going to comment.

"I'd like it . . . well done," Jenna decided.

"Way to go. Two hamburger steaks, separate checks, with
the trimmings. You do want the trimmings?"

"With all our hearts," Garth said.

"Hush, you. You get what you get."

"Ever wonder why business is the way it is, Ma?"

"Listen, we got all the business we can handle. You want sweet talk, you let Jenna sweet talk you."

"I wish," he said, looking into Jenna's eyes. She smiled tolerantly, the way she would have smiled at some outrageousness of Hernando's.

Hazel left, taking their order—which surely would be no surprise—to Luigi. Luigi read it carefully, exchanged a few words with Hazel, then yelled "Giovanni!" in their direction.

"Excuse me," Garth said. "That's me."

"I know," she said dryly, and he grinned.

She watched him go. Apparently it was all right for Luigi to call him John, as long as it wasn't in English. The two men had a small conference, with Garth shaking his head no, then nodding.

He was grinning again when he came back. "Luigi wondered if you wanted french fries or hash browns."

"And what did I want?"

"Well, you'll try both," Garth said. "Because you don't know for sure."

"Ah," Jenna said. "Good thinking on my part. You two go back a long way, don't you?"

"He's the closest thing to a father I ever had. He even busted my butt good for me one time when I needed it. Man, he let me have it. And you know what? *He* cried. Big guy like that, crying because he had to put a good-for-nothing punk like me in his place."

"Giovanni!" Luigi yelled again.

"Luigi, what!" Garth yelled back, but Luigi had lapsed into a whirlwind of Italian. "Excuse me again," Garth said to Jenna.

Jenna sat smiling to herself, watching the drama at the grill. It was obvious that these two, regardless of the history of "butt busting," harbored a great affection for each other.

She suddenly looked up, realizing that someone was standing at the edge of the booth. It was the street person who'd been waiting just inside the door when she and Garth came in. He was nervous still, pulling at the grimy collar of his shirt. His eyes met hers briefly, then shifted away.

"Tony wants to talk to you," he said.

"Tony?" Jenna asked, looking in the direction he indicated. A man in a business suit was getting up from a table way in back. At a distance, he looked like any successful businessman in a well-tailored suit, and he was definitely out of place in the Humoresque. But as he came closer, the flashiness became more evident. The walk, the attitude, was all wrong for the world of legitimate business. He was wearing a pink silk shirt and too many rings—big diamond rings, two on each hand. He had his hair in the "wet look," combed straight back from his high forehead and into a queue. She could smell his cologne, expensive cologne— Drakker Noir, she thought—well ahead of him.

Jenna looked at him quizzically. She was certain they'd never met before. He smiled, but she didn't return it.

"I just wanted to say you are one beautiful lady," he said, his voice low and urgent, his dark eyes boring into hers. "Sometimes people don't take the time to appreciate beautiful things. Tony Zaccato takes the time. Life's too short—"

"Have we met?" Jenna said, growing uncomfortable under his scrutiny.

"Not exactly. You've got a nice body, beautiful lady." The smile became sly and knowing. "I noticed that when you took off your coat." His eyes slid down to her breasts and back again. "You be good to the cop there," he said, his head jerking sharply toward where Garth stood talking to Luigi. "You make him *real* happy, because he's not going to get—"

But Garth was coming, and he didn't finish. Jenna could feel the tension in him as he watched Garth approach. No, not quite tension. Expectation, perhaps, as if he'd deliberately wanted to provoke a reaction. When Garth was near, Tony Zaccato deliberately stepped closer to her. She thought for a moment he was going to put his hand on her shoulder.

"So," Garth said quietly, his gaze shifting from Jenna to the man. "Tony. It's been a long time."

"You know how it is, Garth," Tony Zaccato said. "It takes time to get over a great sorrow—for some of us, that is." He turned his attention to Jenna. "She's very beautiful. Even Mary would say so. Are you going to introduce me to her, Garth?"

"No," Garth said.

"No?" Tony said, both eyebrows raised. He gave a small smile. "You shouldn't be ashamed of such a beautiful woman, Garth."

"You're not going to start anything with me, Tony. You're back, and you've made sure I know it. That's the end of it."

"No, Garth. Not the end. But I don't want to start anything with you. I want to finish it, don't I?"

"Listen, you—"

Tony held up both hands. "Ah! Not here, Garth. Not in front of the beautiful lady. Another place. Another time."

He sidestepped Garth and walked toward the door, the street person hurrying to catch up with him before he got outside.

"Garth?" Jenna said, but he wasn't listening to her.

"Luigi!" he yelled. "You know he's here and you don't bother to tell me?"

"Hey!" Luigi said, throwing up both hands. "What, am I cooking with eyes in the back of my head now? Who sees Tony Zaccato? The man is a snake! He comes, he goes, like a snake!"

"Hazel!" Garth said.

"Yeah, I knew he came in and I didn't say anything!" Hazel yelled before he could start in on her. "And you want to know why? Because you'd act like you're acting now, that's why! Crazy! You can't do anything about Tony Zaccato! The less you see of him, the better for everybody. Now, sit down with Jenna—or do you want to chase him down the street so he can file charges of police harassment? Again!"

Garth swore under his breath; everyone in the place was looking on with great interest. He sat down, but he was still fuming. It was all he could do so sit still.

"Do you want to go?" Jenna asked, and he looked up at her as if he'd completely forgotten she was there.

He gave a short exhalation of breath. "No," he said. He shrugged. "The sonofa—Zaccato gets to me."

"Really?" Jenna asked quietly, and he half smiled.

He made a concentrated effort to get himself in hand. He'd expected to encounter Tony Zaccato sooner or later; he just hadn't expected it to be here, with Jenna. He had no idea what Tony had said to her. She didn't seem upset, but then he knew that Jenna Gallagher could keep a rein on her emotions if she had to. He took a deep breath. He was rattled, and not because Tony had turned up unexpectedly. It was because he'd been afraid for Jenna. When he'd looked up and seen Tony hanging over her, it had been all he could do not to behave like the street kid he was whose territory had been invaded. "Yeah," he said. "Really."

Hazel came by the booth carrying a pot of coffee and somebody's dinner. "Now look what you done," she whispered to Garth. "You got Luigi all stirred up. You know he can't cook when he's upset."

"Ma, tell him I'm sorry."

"*You* tell him you're sorry! You're the one who made him think he let Tony Zaccato sneak up on you."

Hazel went on with her plate, and Garth leaned against the back of the booth for a moment and closed his eyes.

When he opened them, Jenna was regarding him thoughtfully.

"What did Tony Zaccato say to you?" he asked, his voice quiet but filled with purpose.

"Nothing I understood. Some kind of macho pick-up line, I think."

"Did he know who you are?" he interrupted.

"Who I am? No. I asked him if we'd met—"

"He didn't mention Patrick or Hugh?" he asked, interrupting again.

"Why on earth would he do that?"

"Tony likes to name-drop. He might—if he knew who you were."

"He didn't. He only told me to—" She stopped. She hadn't wanted to tell him that part, but she fully realized that she was dealing with Garth, the cop, and not Garth, the man, and that the barrage of questions was his way of working, of getting information. He didn't give a suspect time to manufacture alternatives to the truth. And that was exactly the way she felt—like a suspect.

"He wanted you to what?" he persisted.

She hesitated, then decided to tell him. "To...be good to you."

Garth frowned. "Be good to me? He said that? Tell me exactly what he said."

"Garth, I don't remember exactly. I think he misunderstood. He thought I was your girlfriend. But that was the gist of it—he told me to be good to you."

They stared at each other; she couldn't begin to read his expression. Hazel came by again, this time carrying only the coffee decanter. She cleared her throat with great significance as she passed, and Garth looked around at Luigi. He sighed heavily.

"Excuse me," he said—for the third time since they'd come in the front door. He stood up, but he caught her by the hand and pulled her along with him. "I need the moral support."

That wasn't precisely the truth. What he needed was to touch her, and he couldn't think of any other way to do it. "I don't make apologies often. You can give me pointers."

That Garth would make the effort to soothe Luigi's ruffled feathers or that he would want her along while he did it was incredible to Jenna. But she went, letting him take her by the hand, his fingers warm, strong on hers. All day she'd had to keep changing her mind about him. The people at the Humoresque were his family, and he'd brought her here when there was no reason for it, or none that she could discern, regardless of his claim that he was making her an honest woman. Garth was a complicated man, and now he made a sincere apology, ignoring Luigi's gestures of dismissal until he had the old man in a better mood. The conversation ran in half-Italian, half-English until Luigi glanced around at Jenna.

"It's not a good thing to let Tony Zaccato see what you treasure," Luigi said, and Jenna wasn't certain if it were an explanation for her or a warning for Garth.

Luigi suddenly smiled. "Your pretty friend is hungry, Garth. You stand here a minute. I give you your dinner, and you can save your poor mama's feet."

They both waited, carrying their own plates back to the reserved booth as soon as Luigi pronounced the hamburger steaks done. The steak was excellent, Jenna thought, just the way she liked it, smothered in fried onions. Garth was very quiet.

"Tell me about Tony Zaccato," she said after a time.

Garth looked up at her. "You want more coffee?"

"No, I want to know about Tony Zaccato. Why did you think he might have mentioned Patrick or Hugh?"

She could feel him trying to decide—could he get out of answering her question or not?

"He's a two-bit hood," he said, apparently deciding the latter. "Drugs mostly, but he's not above a little prostitution and auto theft. I told you he likes to name-drop. If he knew who you were, I thought—" he shrugged "—he might have mentioned it." He looked into her eyes. "You never heard Patrick or Hugh mention him, did you?"

"No," she said. "Not that I remember. Can't you get anything on him?"

"Nothing that sticks."

They ate for a time in silence.

"Who is Mary?" Jenna asked.

Garth looked up at her as if he were startled by the question.

"Mary?"

"Tony Zaccato said, 'Even Mary would think so.' Who is Mary?"

He was growing restive again. He suddenly smiled, but his eyes shifted away. "So, how do you like Luigi's cooking?"

She didn't answer him. She was waiting for her own answers.

"Obviously you're worried about whatever this is with Tony Zaccato," she said.

"I'm not worried."

"You're a liar, Detective Garth," Jenna said mildly. "And as a participant or the bait or whatever I was just now, I think I'd be a little more at ease if I knew some of the details."

"I told you. Tony Zaccato is a two-bit hood."

"And what about Mary? Is she a hood, too?"

Garth looked into her eyes, and he realized he was going to tell her, that he wanted to tell her.

"Mary...is the girl in the picture, the one you saw upstairs. I was crazy about her when I was eighteen. After high school, I went into the Navy, and we lost track of each other. And then one day, about three years ago, she came walking into the Humoresque. I hadn't seen her in fifteen years.

Fifteen years, and it was still there. All of it. I wanted to marry her. She was Tony Zaccato's sister.''

''Was?'' Jenna asked quietly.

''She's dead. Tony thinks it's my fault.''

''Is it?''

He looked into her eyes. ''Yeah.''

They rode to Park Slope in silence. The streets were foggy. He had told her that he loved Mary Zaccato and Mary was dead because of it. He didn't know quite what he expected her reaction would be, but this wasn't it. He'd thought she'd be shocked, not uninterested. But she must be uninterested, because she hadn't said a word. He flipped on the radio to fill in the silence. Jazz. The radio station was playing jazz. He left it.

''You can let me out here,'' she said when they turned down her street. But it was dark, and a light rain was falling. He drove on and parked in a tight space.

''I'll come in with you,'' he said.

''You don't have to.''

''I want to see where you live.''

He opened the car door and got out, leaving her perplexed and uneasy. Again. He kept doing that to her—completely disarming her with the truth, when all the while she sensed that he would more likely be lying. And, though she couldn't explain it, she *believed* him. She believed the reason he'd given for wanting to be called Garth. She believed him about Mary Zaccato. She believed that he didn't take many people into his home and that he wanted to see where she lived.

She opened the car door to get out, and he was there to help her, offering her his hand. She took it, because she wanted to, and she pushed aside all her questions and misgivings to do it.

''I liked Luigi's cooking,'' she said as they walked along in the rain.

She could feel him smile. "Best short-order cook in Brooklyn," he said. "Which one?" he asked about the white or beige or brown row houses.

"The brown one there," she said, and he walked with her up the stoop.

Ten steps. Crazily he counted them. Ten. Somewhere in his flaming youth he'd learned that brownstones had a ten-step stoop.

The foyer was dark and smelled of the tenants' varied dinners—hot bread, coffee, seared meat with peppers and onions. Her apartment was the first one on the left. He waited while she unlocked the door and let him in. He was standing close enough to smell her perfume, or perhaps it wasn't perfume but simply her. He savored it, wanted more. He'd been with her all day, and he wanted more.

He followed her inside.

"Nice place," he said of the softly lit room.

She was about to take off her coat, and he reached to help her, then didn't help at all. He turned her around and, grasping her coat by the lapels, brought her to him.

Her mouth was both cold and warm. Cold lips from their brief walk from the car. Warm mouth because she parted her lips immediately.

She wants this, he thought incredulously.

He gave a soft moan as she returned the kiss and let him taste her, the way he'd wanted to for a long time now. A long time.

God, Jenna, he thought, perhaps said.

She leaned into him, and a warm, urgent pleasure suffused his body. His hands slid inside her coat, touching her soft breasts through the dark green sweater.

She had forgotten, she remembered—all at the same time. A man's touch. A man's smell. She'd been alone too long. She wanted to weep. She wanted—

"Garth, no," she said, trying to break away. "I don't—"

But he wasn't listening. His mouth came down on hers again. It was wonderful. She was afraid.

"Garth! I don't want this!"

He leaned back to look at her, his eyes searching hers. They were both breathless. She pressed her lips together to keep them from trembling.

"I don't want this," she said again, her voice barely a whisper.

He reached to touch her cheek—the way he might have if she had been Hernando or Mallory—and he gave a soft laugh.

"You're a liar, Mrs. Gallagher."

Chapter Eight

So. They were *both* liars, he thought as he walked back down the ten steps. It was raining harder now, but he didn't hurry. Walking in a cold rain was as good as a cold shower, he supposed. He hadn't wanted to leave her; it had taken everything he had in him to do as she asked—because he'd wanted her, because he knew she didn't mean it. He'd had the advantage. He could have persuaded her—into bed *and* out of any information she might have.

But he hadn't done it. She was afraid of him. He knew that, and he'd let the moment pass. But when had he gotten so altruistic? She was a very pleasant means to an end, and he kept letting himself forget that.

He suddenly smiled to himself, remembering the look on Jenna's face when they were about to leave the Humoresque—when Hazel had suspiciously asked her just how much she liked oatmeal, followed by a heavy-handed query into the status of her bank account.

Jenna. She'd let him take her into an absolute nuthouse, and she'd seemed to enjoy it, Hazel's unsubtle questions and Tony Zaccato aside.

He'd enjoyed it. He'd enjoyed the whole day.

Mrs. Gallagher, Mrs. Gallagher, what the hell are we getting into?

The headlights of an oncoming van lit the street. Garth could see the silhouettes of two men sitting in a car parked at the curb ahead of him. The car was expensive.

Two men. Now what would two men be doing sitting in a car here? Waiting for the rain to stop so they wouldn't get their Armani suits wet? Anyone but a former street kid might think so.

He hunted in his jacket pocket for the pack of stale cigarettes he carried. He didn't really smoke anymore, but cigarettes sometimes came in handy. When another car came down the street, he paused just short of the parked vehicle and lit one. And he read the license plate number.

The men in the car were watching, not waiting. He could feel their eyes on him as he passed, but he didn't hurry. He walked on, and he listened for the sound of a window rolling down or a door opening.

When he reached his car, he was careful not to look in their direction. He opened the car door and got inside, but he didn't leave. He got on the radio instead, and he waited for the report on the license plate number.

It didn't take long.

"Be advised that the vehicle in question is NYPD property."

"NYPD?" he asked to make sure he'd heard right.

"Ten-four."

A tail car. Not Tony Zaccato. NYPD.

He opened the door and got out, walking down the middle of the street toward the other car. When he was a few feet away, he held up both hands where the men in the car could see them. He could tell there was a hot discussion going on in the car, but after a moment the window on the driver's side slid down.

He immediately recognized the man behind the wheel.

"Rex," he said quietly. "And Putnam." He couldn't actually see the other man, but he had a good idea who it was. It was rare to see one without the other, even when they were off duty. They were both cronies of Hugh's.

"Garth," they both said.

"What are you two supposed to be doing?" Garth asked, because he knew they wouldn't tell him, and because anything they did say, he could check.

"Nothing," Putnam said testily. "Not a damn thing."

"Yeah? Well, as long as you're not doing anything, you can tell Hugh I left at—" he looked at his watch "—19:08. And tell him if he wants to know anything else, he can just ask me." He indicated the car. "This is a hell of a waste of taxpayers' money, guys."

He turned and walked away.

"I told you he'd get a make on us!" he heard Rex say as the window went up.

"Yeah, yeah, you told me," Putnam said. "You told me."

Jenna sat in the dimly lit living room, staring at nothing. She reached up and ran her fingers lightly over her lips. She could still feel the urgent pressure of his mouth on hers, still taste him. Garth and the peppermint candy Hazel had given her when they left the Humoresque.

I want him.

The thought presented itself, its import as significant as if it had been chiseled in stone. She didn't love him. Maybe she didn't even like him. But she wanted him.

What about Patrick? I loved Patrick.

Patrick was dead. She was alone. All the time. Patrick was dead.

She closed her eyes and took a wavering breath.

I don't want any more pain.

What else would she get from Johnson Garth? She could guess what his ideal woman would be like—overly willing, more than available, someone who would let him come and go without explanation and who would make absolutely no demands. But that aside, Garth was a cop. She didn't want to get involved with another cop! She didn't want to live on the fringes of a man's life; she didn't want to be afraid every time he left that she'd never see him again.

And she didn't want a purely sexual relationship between two strangers. She was certain of all these things, and yet...

She gave a heavy sigh. And yet she could still feel his kiss. Her body was alive with sexual desire, not just for a man, but for him. She was playing with fire, and she knew it.

The telephone rang, making her jump. She expected it to be Mamie, but it was someone from the Family Crisis Council.

"I hope you've had dinner, Jenna," the familiar voice said. "We need you to go to the hospital."

"Yes, all right," she answered, and she wrote down the particulars. For once she was glad to go. For once, going into a hospital would be better than staying here alone. She resolved that she would do whatever it took to get Johnson Garth off her mind. Maybe she'd even go out with the public defender she'd met in court who had asked. She would stay busy. That had always helped to take her mind off Patrick; it would help to take her mind off Garth. And she would stay away from Johnson Garth.

But she needn't have worried. She heard nothing from Garth. There were no more dinner invitations forthcoming, no telephone calls. She kept her resolve to stay busy, going to work in the Saint Xavier kindergarten the last three days of the week. But Garth was never far from her mind. One of the first things she saw when she arrived at Saint Xavier's was Hernando—sporting his new, pint-size, genuine leather bomber jacket. He proudly showed her all the zippered pockets and the World War II military patches. His father brought it to him, he said. Just like a surprise.

Jenna had no doubt about that, though the one most surprised was probably the heretofore notoriously uninvolved senior Mr. Cooley. She wondered how Garth had managed to persuade him to provide his son with a coat. With a well-placed foot to the man's behind? Garth would have done whatever it took, she decided. He had said he would get Hernando a new coat in a way that wouldn't make him feel worse about his poverty, and clearly he had.

Debbie didn't mention Garth at all. There were no questions about his having taken her home. Nothing. In fact, Debbie suddenly had little to say about anything.

"Do you feel all right?" Jenna finally asked her, and Debbie looked at her in surprise.

"I feel fine. Why?"

"Oh, you just seem...quiet. You're not pregnant, too, are you?"

"Good gracious, no!" Debbie chuckled. "Me, pregnant? What an idea!"

"Then what's wrong?" Jenna felt she had to ask.

"Nothing! I'm fine," she said blithely. And she became very busy somewhere else.

She's afraid I'm going to ask about Garth, Jenna decided. She knows something, and she doesn't want to tell me. Maybe that Garth had believed her when she'd told him she didn't want anything to do with him. He must have. Otherwise, given his earlier persistence, she would have heard something from him.

If anything, she told herself, she was relieved that he'd finally respected her wishes. Relieved—and disappointed that he'd apparently given up on her so easily.

But today was the day she'd know for certain. She had to be at the police station in the late afternoon. Family Crisis Council volunteers were meeting with a police representative, and Garth would likely be somewhere on the premises.

She left Saint Xavier's early, impulsively taking the writing exercises the children had done the first of the week with her. They had each drawn and colored a picture of Garth in the blank space at the top of the page, and on the blue lines below, they had laboriously copied the sentence: *Thank you, Detective Garth, for being our friend.* She found the exercises stuffed in the desk drawer, and she wondered why Debbie hadn't already given them to him. Or at least given them to Skip so he could pass them on. Pictures and a copied sentence were something the children did for all their guests, and she was certain that Garth would want his. She could leave them at the precinct for him; she didn't have to see him.

But she looked for him. From the moment she entered the front door until she went into the meeting. And then when she came out again. He wasn't there. She had the manila envelope with the pictures in it under her arm, and impulsively she went into the squad room.

"Where is Detective Garth's desk?" she asked a patrolman who was walking through.

He pointed it out, but she probably could have guessed. It was piled high with papers and folders, and if there was any rhyme or reason to the stacks, she couldn't tell it. She hunted down a pen from her purse and wrote his name on the manila envelope, hoping to put it in a place where he would see it—sooner or later.

"Is that for me?"

She jumped at the question.

"Garth—yes," she said, completely flustered because she hadn't seen him come in and because she had no business hanging around his desk, pictures or not, and because her knees went weak when she looked into his eyes.

"Yes," she said again, and she tried to walk away.

"Well, wait a minute," he said, catching her by the arm as he picked up the envelope. "What is it?"

"Some drawings. From the children at Saint Xavier's. They're...thank-you notes for spending the day with them."

He smiled and opened the envelope. "So what did they draw?"

"You."

He looked up at her and grinned. "Me? I can't wait to see this." He dumped the pages out and began to shuffle through them, chuckling from time to time, obviously pleased. "This is my favorite," he said, glancing up at her. "I look like Ma Kettle standing on a red boa constrictor."

She looked at the picture he showed her and smiled. He did look like Ma Kettle standing on a red boa constrictor.

"They're very... free-spirited," she said. "We try to let them do the pictures however they want."

He picked up another one. "Hernando did this one. That little sh—rascal knew I had a gun," he said incredulously.

"You had a gun?" Jenna said, not without some incredulity of her own.

"Under my pants leg—right where he drew it," he said, showing her the picture.

"You weren't supposed to come into the kindergarten with a gun, Garth."

"Old habits die hard," he said absently. He looked up from the pictures he had spread all over his already-messy desk. "Thanks for bringing these. Tell the kids I really like them."

She nodded and turned to go.

"Jenna?" he said, and she looked back at him. But looking into her eyes, he didn't know quite what he wanted to say. Well, he did know; he just couldn't say it here. "Nothing," he said.

"Jenna!" the lieutenant called from his office. "What is this? You come by and you don't take the time to say hello? Come in here. Come tell me how you're doing."

Jenna immediately walked toward the lieutenant's office, her relief at getting away from Garth written plainly on her face, but mixing with her dread of having to make a courtesy call on the lieutenant and listen to him reminisce about Patrick.

She's still in love with her husband, Garth thought.

He gathered up the pictures and put them back into the envelope, watching Jenna all the time she talked to The Whip, watching her when she left the lieutenant's office without a backward glance.

"My God," Skip said at his elbow. "There must be fifty case folders here. Did we get put on the scut detail or what?"

"Scut detail," Garth verified, sitting down at the desk and shoving some folders aside.

"Was it something we said? No, strike that. Was it something *you* said?"

"Probably. I'm not known for my tact."

"Do I get to know who's pissed off?"

"Alden!" Garth chided him. "Your language! What would Mummy and Daddy say?"

"Now, don't you do it again, Garth."

"Do what?" Garth said innocently.

"Stonewall me, that's what! You don't want to answer the question, so you give me a dig about my background. I know how you work, Garth, and since I'm the one who's got to help with all this, I want to know what's going on!"

"Take it easy, kid. You're going to give yourself ulcers."

"You're doing it again, Garth!"

"Okay! Okay! Hugh Gallagher's doing this. He doesn't want me seeing Jenna, and he's trying to help me understand that my happiness is going to be directly proportional to his. Unfortunately you get caught in the fallout."

"Hugh can't do all this," Skip said, gesturing to the piles of folders.

"He can call in a favor from someone who can."

"You think so?"

"I think so."

"This is crazy. You aren't seeing Jenna. She's going out with some lawyer, a P.D."

"Since when?" Garth wanted to know. "Who is it?"

"Since . . . tonight, I guess. She's going to the Peking Opera—or maybe it's tomorrow night . . ."

"Who is it?" Garth said again.

"I don't know. Debbie said Jenna was going out with some P.D. she met when she was in court with one of her Family Crisis Council cases—and that's all she said. Except that he has money."

"P.D.'s don't have money."

"This one does."

"What the hell does she want to go out with a lawyer for?" He realized that he could have used a bit of Hernando's "cool" at the moment, because his own had somehow escaped him. He didn't like the idea of Jenna going out with a shifty lawyer any more than he'd liked Tony Zaccato hanging all over her—money or no money.

"How should I know? Women can overlook a lot. Maybe if *you'd* asked her out, she wouldn't be hanging out with such trash. The Peking Opera, maybe even dinner at Lutèce—poor woman. What a downhill slide."

"Very funny, Skip. Very funny."

"Garth!" the lieutenant yelled out his door.

"You, too," Garth said to Skip as he wearily got up from his chair.

"My name's not Garth," Skip assured him.

"It's going to be crap if you don't get up off your can. That's his now-hear-this voice, and whatever's caused it, I'm not taking the heat alone."

"Gee, thanks," Skip said, reluctantly following.

"What are partners for?"

For more scut work.

"Don't take the time to sit down," the lieutenant said.

"One of our favorite gentlemen has inadvertently given us what we need to make an arrest."

"Who?" Garth said.

"Tony Zaccato."

Garth could feel the sudden rush of adrenaline. Zaccato. Another shot at Zaccato. "What have we got?" he asked, hoping against hope that this time it was something Tony's high-priced legal staff couldn't circumvent.

"Midtown got a really good collar from one of their buy-and-bust operations," the lieutenant said. "Tony's been trying to cut into this guy's territory of late, and the guy thinks Tony fingered him. It really pissed him off, so he's been singing like a songbird—names, dates, places. Seems he kept a lot of documentation for just such an eventuality."

"He'll testify? He's not scared of Tony?"

"Sure, he's scared of Tony. But like I said, he's pissed off. By the time he gets over it, he'll be in too deep."

"Do we know where Tony is?"

The lieutenant handed Garth a slip of paper. "This is the address Hugh got from one of his snitches. Maybe it's legit. Maybe not. I want you and Carver to go over and see."

"So how come Hugh's not going after him?" Garth asked, feeling Skip cringe beside him. It was not a proper question. Even Skip knew it.

"You got some problem with how I'm making the assignments, Garth?"

"No, sir. I understand." He looked into the lieutenant's eyes. He knew why he'd drawn the job, and it wasn't because no one else in the department knew Tony Zaccato as well as he did—though he had no doubt that that might have been Hugh's subtle suggestion at the time the lieutenant was making up his mind. And apparently the honeymoon for Skip was over as well. Garth looked again at the address. He wanted to get Tony Zaccato, but, God, he didn't want to try to do it using anything that came from Hugh Gallagher.

"Just how bad is this little task?" Skip asked on the way back through the squad room to the lockers.

Garth needed a few extra things, and he could feel the tension in the squad room when they passed through.

"Bad."

"You think it's the same thing as having all those case folders on your desk?"

"Something like that." Worse, he thought but didn't say it. A lot worse.

"Are you worried?"

"Yeah."

"Yeah?"

Garth gave a sharp sigh. "What do you want me to do, Skipper? Tell you it'll be a piece of cake?"

"That would be nice."

"It *won't* be a piece of cake. Nobody messes with Tony Zaccato, not even the official representatives of Truth, Justice and the American Way. And I'm not exactly at the top of Hugh Gallagher's Favorite Person list, now, am I? There's only one good thing about this, Skipper, and that's the chance, even a small one, of getting at Tony Zaccato."

"Are you going to carry all those guns?"

"Are you going to stand there and ask me all these damn questions? Yeah, I'm going to carry all these guns!"

"They're not regulation, Garth."

"You want me to be unofficially armed or both of us officially dead?"

Skip pressed his lips together and swallowed hard. "Do I need to carry something extra?"

"Nah. You're not used to it. You'd probably forget where it was and blow off something important. The only thing you have to do is what I tell you."

"You really think it's going to be bad," Skip said again on their way out of the station house.

"Skip, I really, *really* do."

He took a deep breath. "Okay, then. Just so I know."

It was bad. Very bad. Bad timing. Bad backup. Bad luck. Two patrolmen and a civilian wounded, and they didn't get Tony Zaccato. Garth had wanted Zaccato's arrest so bad he could taste it. Even if Zaccato had walked an hour later, he'd still wanted it. But once again the Tony Zaccatos of the world had triumphed. All he'd gotten was a spot on the six o'clock news.

"Can you explain what went wrong here, Detective? Detective? Detective!"

Yes, hell, he could. The other team played better ball. We just couldn't get it together out there, coach.

But he couldn't explain it to himself. He had more puzzle pieces than ever, and none of them fit. Tony never gave them a chance to say why they wanted to see him. And even though Garth had been ready for any eventuality, he had still been surprised by Tony's reaction, a reaction that came *before* he supposedly knew the you-know-what had hit the fan. Why hadn't Tony assumed that this little visit was like a thousand others, that they had just wanted him to come in and answer the same old routine questions they always asked, simply because it was part of the cat-and-mouse game. Big offenders like Tony expected it. A little cage-rattling. A little war of nerves. Tony had always cooperated. He was full of big-mouth threats, but he always came in willingly for those little sessions. In fact, Garth had always believed he enjoyed them.

But not this time. Why? *Why?* Because he'd known they were coming? No. Tony hadn't expected them; he wouldn't have been there if he had. Garth suspected that Tony had reacted the way he had because he knew that *if* they came for him, this time it would be the real thing, and that whoever had dropped the dime, whoever had pointed the finger, could make it stick. So who was Tony afraid of? Not some punk dealer in Midtown.

Who then?

Hugh Gallagher, Garth thought.

Maybe Hugh had wanted to get rid of two major aggravations at one time. In Garth's mind, it fit. *If* Hugh had some deal with Zaccato and wanted out of it, who would he want to bring Zaccato in? Somebody who would play it by the book? Or somebody who had a long-running feud with Zaccato, someone who was likely to provoke a major exchange of gunfire on sight. And they'd certainly had that. He had two bullet holes in his jacket sleeve.

It was well after midnight when Garth finished writing up the report. He was tired, hungry and depressed, and Skip was into Act III of "The Junior Detective, On His First Big Shoot-Out, Blunders."

"That little kid was in the way," Skip said for the hundredth time. Some cops internalized and said nothing. Skip Carver wasn't one of those. He was pumped up and talking.

"I know that," Garth finally said, knowing it was better for the kid to let off steam.

"I didn't freeze, Garth. I just couldn't take him out with the kid in the way."

"Skip, you're the one with every damned Annie Oakley shooting award the department gives. If you said you couldn't, you couldn't. Will you lighten up?"

"The whole damned thing was a mess!"

"I know that, too. Get out of here, will you? Debbie'll be worried. I'll see you tomorrow."

He sat at his desk for a while after Skip had gone, until he realized he had no alternative but to go home. But he didn't go home. He drove through Park Slope instead, telling himself that he was crazy—Jenna wouldn't still be up at this time of night.

But her lights were on.

He'd never find a parking space.

But there was one halfway down the block. Or at least three-quarters of one. With much juggling and not-so-gentle nudging of a Ford Escort and a Honda Civic, he parked. And sat in the car for a long time. Then he got out, walking up the dark street to the brown row house.

Her lights would surely go out before he got there.

They stayed on. And halfway up the ten steps of the stoop, he ran out of excuses. He also ran out of nerve. Maybe the lawyer was there. He just wanted to be with her for a little while; he didn't want to cause her any trouble.

He turned abruptly and went back down the steps.

Jenna saw him from the front window. She saw him come up on the stoop, and she saw him turn away again. She hurried out into the foyer, running the last few steps until she reached the front door. But she couldn't go any farther. She didn't have her keys, and she had to keep the door from closing.

"Garth!" she whispered, leaning out as far as she could. She could just barely see him, and he kept walking. "Garth!" she called out loud, and this time he heard her.

He came walking back, and she stood waiting, holding the door. The night was starry and cold. She didn't ask him what he wanted. Debbie had already called and told her about the day's events.

"Come inside," she said, shivering against the cold.

Tonight was lawyer night, all right, he thought. She was still dressed up. She looked so pretty. *Ah, God, Jenna, you look so pretty!*

"It's late," he answered. He was standing on the bottom step.

"Well, you're the man with the four clocks. You should know."

She could feel him smile in the darkness, and he climbed two steps.

Is the lawyer gone? he almost said, but he bit down on it. She wouldn't have asked him to come in otherwise. And surely he had some remnants of street kid "cool" left. But he was tired of tiptoeing around with this; she might as well know how he felt.

"I made a mistake," he said. "I was feeling sorry for myself, and I came here because I wanted you to feel sorry for me, too. I wanted you to feel sorry enough to let me into your bed. But I've changed my mind. I don't want the first time to be like that. I . . . think maybe we've got more going for us than mutual pity."

With that, he turned to go, not giving her time to say anything. Not that she could think of anything to say. He'd caught her completely off guard. Again.

"Garth?" she called when he'd reached the bottom step.

He looked up at her, and he was so handsome to her. She couldn't even *see* him and he was still handsome, rough, standing-with-his-hands-in-his-jacket-pockets Garth.

"I'm sorry about Zaccato," she said quietly, because she understood enough about the man to know how he must feel.

He shrugged, not asking her how she knew. "Story of my life, Mrs. Gallagher, you know?"

Jenna was awakened by the telephone shortly before seven. It was Debbie. In distress.

"Jenna, I need to talk to you," she began, her voice little more than a whisper.

"Now?" Jenna asked. She was awake, but just barely. "Why are you whispering?"

"I don't want to wake Skip. Jenna, I need some advice." There was a pause, and Jenna imagined Debbie checking to see if Skip were still sleeping or not. "I'm no good at being a cop's wife, Jenna. I thought I had the hang of it because I was a cop's kid, but I don't. Skip had a hell of a day yesterday—he thinks he's no good and Garth is going to dump him. I need you to tell me how to help him."

"Debbie, I don't know how to help him."

"Then just listen to me talk, okay? I don't have anybody who understands but you. Can you meet me at my dad's apartment this afternoon? I have to pick him up at the doctor's after work and take him home. He'll be tired, and he'll want to rest. We can talk there, and I won't have to worry about Skip coming in. Okay?"

Jenna didn't say anything. She had things she needed to think about, things that were disturbing enough to have kept her awake most of the night.

Garth.

She and Garth lied to each other about their true feelings. She and Garth considered each other pitiful. Was there more to their relationship than that? Yes, she thought. There was lust, at least, apparently in both directions.

"Okay?" Debbie said again, and Jenna gave a quiet sigh.

"Okay. I'll be there around six."

"Jenna, thanks. Thanks—I know you're busy today."

She *was* busy today. She had to go to court with a young rape victim who had sought Family Crisis Council support. The testimony for the defense was the worst kind—long and tedious and intimating that the victim was at fault. There was little Jenna could do for the young woman, nothing she could say that would lessen the ordeal of relentless media attention and having to relive the rape. All she could do was be there and hope that her presence somehow helped.

Jenna was emotionally exhausted by the time court adjourned for the day, and the last thing she wanted to do was play sounding board for Debbie and have to deal with even more distress.

But she went. Because she remembered what it was like to be a young cop's wife. Because she remembered the feeling of helplessness that came from being excluded when the man one loved couldn't share his failures and his pain. She remembered, too, how quiet Patrick had been before he'd been killed, and how little she'd been able to ascertain about what he was feeling. She had always thought it was because she'd had another miscarriage, her second, the month before, because he'd wanted lots of children and he certainly wasn't getting them with her.

Patrick's death had more than compounded the guilt she'd already felt. Had he been distracted, thinking about the disappointment, the unhappiness she'd caused not just in losing the babies, but in refusing to discuss future pregnancies? She hadn't wanted another pregnancy, not until she could distance herself from the ones that had already gone wrong. Twice she had lost a child, and she simply hadn't been prepared to face the prospect of losing yet another.

Had she said that to him? Yes. Yes, she had, but she still hadn't been able to break through the wall of silence he'd built around himself. It was only when he was dying that the wall had cracked, and then she couldn't get to him. He'd wanted her then, and she couldn't reach him.

Hugh. Hugh had kept her out of the room where Patrick was being treated, holding her back, keeping her away from him when he'd called and called her name.

"Oh!" she said, surprising herself that she'd spoken out loud. She hadn't thought of Patrick like that in a long while, and it was only because of Garth that she was doing it now. Garth with his pointed questions: *So why weren't you and Patrick getting along?* Garth with his surprising candor: *I want to see where you live. I wanted you to feel sorry enough to let me into your bed.*

Garth.

She didn't know anything when it came to him, except that she physically desired him. She wanted to lie with him in the dark and make love with him and fall asleep in his arms. She couldn't look at him without wanting it. She couldn't *think* about him without wanting it. It made things much worse knowing that he wanted it, too. And it was so hard *not* to think about him, now that she'd been to the Humoresque and to the loft. It was easy to imagine him in those places, being his irrepressible self, listening to The Drifters, bantering with Hazel and Luigi.

But she forced her mind back to the problem at hand, finding a parking space so she could go talk to Debbie. That wasn't so easy. She finally squeezed into a cramped space nearly two blocks away.

She walked briskly to the apartment house where Debbie's father lived. It was cold, but she needed the fresh air to clear her head. She liked Debbie's father, a stereotypical cop from the old school like Sidney, who monitored the precinct's telephones. Joe Eagan had been wounded in the line of duty and was paralyzed from the waist down. Still, he was self-sufficient and determined to be useful, going regularly to the police academy in a wheelchair to lecture from his vast storehouse of knowledge about being a New York cop. Debbie had met Skip when she accompanied her father on one of his lectures. New York's police brotherhood looked after its own, and he lived comfortably enough. The apartment house was in an older but nice neighborhood. Jenna had no qualms about the two-block walk.

In the building foyer, she located Joe Eagan's name and pressed the intercom button. Debbie answered almost immediately, releasing the lock so she could get inside. Jenna didn't see the man who came into the foyer behind her. He reached over her head to keep the inner door open, pushing his way in with her. She turned immediately, and immediately she recognized his intent. He lunged at her; he had on layers of old clothes, and he stank. She knew she should scream, make noise, but nothing came. She was terrified, and yet her mind registered such peculiar information—the faded blue-and-gray flannel shirt, the dirty navy-blue knit cap, the tattered raincoat with all the buttons missing. He kept shoving her backward toward the stairwell door. She looked around frantically for another person, but there was no one.

Surely it was money he wanted, credit cards.

"Here, take it," she said, thrusting her purse at him, but he slapped it out of her hands. The contents spilled out and skidded across the floor. He said nothing, grabbing her by the lapels of her coat, slapping her hard when she finally tried to scream. He slammed her against the door, knocking the breath out of her, and then dragged her through it into the stairwell.

"Please..." she managed with what little air she had left in her lungs.

He hit her again, hard enough to make her knees buckle. She had to grab on to him to keep from falling backward down the stairs. She held on tightly, so that he couldn't get in another blow, and she tried again to scream,

How unusual, she thought as she fought him. He was wearing thermal underwear. This close, she could read the inspection sticker just below the band on the neck. INSPECTED BY No. 2.

Chapter Nine

Roy Lee was out washing windshields again. Garth saw him from a block away.

"Don't make this next light," he said to Skip. "I want to talk to Roy Lee."

"You think he knows anything about Zaccato?"

"Yeah, he knows. They all do. But the question is, will he tell me?"

Skip drove slowly so as not to make the light, much to the ire of the cabbie behind them. When they got closer to the place Roy Lee had staked out for himself, Garth began to roll down the window. Roy Lee glanced in their direction.

"Roy Lee!" Garth yelled at him. But Roy Lee was already backing away. As Garth opened the car door, Roy Lee broke into a run, dodging through moving traffic toward the far side of the street.

"Roy Lee! Hey!"

But he didn't stop, and Garth couldn't get to him for the flow of traffic around them. He stood watching as Roy Lee disappeared into an alley.

"Now what the hell does that mean?" Garth said as he got back into the car. He had an understanding with Roy Lee. Sometimes he got information and sometimes he didn't, but because of the old days, there were no hard feelings.

"It means the answer to the question is no," Skip said dryly.

Sidney was looking for Garth when they got back to the station house.

"Line one, lad," Sidney said as he walked in. "Be a good lad and answer it now and save me the trouble of writing one of those piddling pink slips."

"Yeah, Sid," Garth said in passing. He went to his piled-up desk and uncovered the telephone, pushing the Line One button on the off chance that Sidney might, just this once, know what incoming call he was talking about.

"Detective Garth," he said.

"Yo! Garth!" a familiar voice said, and he smiled. "This is your old partner, Rosie Madden."

"The Rose!" Garth said. "What can I do for you?"

"This ain't no social call, honey. You see Hugh around anywhere close?"

Garth looked around him.

"No. Why?"

"I heard on the QT you've been trying to get into Hugh's sister-in-law's pants, you devil you, and Big Hugh ain't too happy about it. I got enough troubles, life being what it is. I don't want *my* desk covered up in case folders, too, and I want you to make sure he don't catch on to what I'm telling you."

Garth was shuffling papers as she talked, but Rosie certainly knew how to get his attention. "Jenna?" he said, responding to the only part of her spiel that interested him.

"Shh!" Rosie snapped at him. "Didn't you hear what I just told you? I don't want Hugh to know I'm calling—and how many of Hugh's sister-in-laws' pants have you been trying to get into? Yeah, Jenna!"

"What is it?" he asked, feeling the cold fist of anxiety in the pit of his stomach.

"Jenna's over here at Bellevue, Garth. Somebody roughed her up and—"

"I'll be right there," he interrupted.

"Wait a minute, will you! She doesn't know I'm calling you. She doesn't want anybody called, especially the Gallaghers. But like I said, I heard about you and her, and I thought you'd want to—"

"How bad is—"

"Will you quit interrupting and listen? She's not hurt too bad, but this is getting to her. It's about all she can do to hold it together. If she means anything to you, you sneak out and get your butt over here. She's still in Emergency. I got a partner with an itchy dialing finger, and he would have called Hugh already if he wasn't too dumb to think of it. I got to get off this phone before he figures out what I'm up to."

"What happened to her?"

"I'll tell you the details when you get here. I got to go!"

"Rosie, wait! She wasn't—"

"She wasn't raped, Garth," Rosie said, and he realized how tightly he'd been holding the telephone.

"I've done something maybe you won't like," Rosie Madden said.

Jenna looked at her sharply. She was sitting on the side of the stretcher in the cubicle they'd put her in, sitting because she couldn't bear lying down. She had the sheet over her lap, the top edge clutched tightly in both fists. Her hands were icy cold. She felt weak, dizzy; her heart was pounding, but she still couldn't lie down. The only thing she wanted was out of this place. Intellectually she knew that she needed to be X-rayed, examined, but it was all she could do to sit quietly and let them do it. It took everything she had to keep her anxiety hidden. If she let them see it, let anyone see it, she might have to stay. Every time she closed her eyes, she could see Patrick here. Every time she closed her eyes, she could see her assailant's face. So she sat rigid on the side of the stretcher and tried not to shake.

"What?" she asked Rosie Madden warily. There was a tremor in her voice she couldn't do anything about.

"I . . . called Garth."

"Why would you call Garth?" Jenna said, her voice rising, the control she was working so hard to maintain threatening to snap.

"Because," Rosie interrupted, equally loudly. "Because," she repeated in a softer tone, "I saw you and Garth sitting together on the stairs at Skip Carver's party. Because the word is you and Garth have a thing going. Because you need somebody here with you. Because Garth used to be my partner, and I care enough about him to make sure he knows what he ought to know."

Jenna swallowed hard and looked into Rosie's eyes. "Is he . . . coming?"

"Is he coming?" Rosie asked incredulously. "Now what kind of question is that? Is he coming? Of course he's coming. The man's crazy about you, honey. It was all I could do to keep him on the phone long enough to tell him what I wanted to tell him."

Jenna abruptly bowed her head, feeling the tears that had been so close to sliding down her face.

"Hey," Rosie said. "Now don't you go bawling. You don't bawl because a man cares about you and he's coming. You bawl because he don't and he ain't, see?"

Jenna understood the logic perfectly, but it didn't help. She tried to smile—Rosie Madden was trying to be kind to her—but she couldn't. She didn't want Garth here, and she wanted him here more than anything else in the world. Was she never going to feel anything but completely contradictory where he was concerned?

It didn't take him long to get there. She heard him before she saw him. The long time seemed to be until he actually reached her cubicle. She knew when he was finally standing right outside. She knew when he pulled back the curtain, and slowly she turned her face to let him see.

At first he thought she wasn't hurt; seeing her in profile, she looked fine. But then she looked at him and gave him a funny, lopsided smile that faded almost before it had begun.

Oh, God, baby.

He didn't say anything. He reached for her instead, holding her tight, careful of her bruised and swollen cheek and eye. He could feel her trembling, and she clung to him with all the desperation he'd seen in her face.

"Get your clothes on," he said, leaning back to look into her eyes. "I'm taking you out of here."

She stared back at him, not knowing whether to believe him. She was going?

"Hurry up," he said, "before the doc changes his mind."

"The X rays—" she began, her voice husky with unshed tears.

"They're okay. I told him you'd be better off at home. You're not going to tell me you want to stay in this joint, are you?"

She shook her head, overcome by the sense of relief. "No," she managed. "No—Garth—thank you."

"Hey, Mrs. Gallagher. What are friends for?" He gave her a mischievous smile that belied the concern she saw in his eyes. "Now get your clothes on." He stepped outside, fully aware that that particular phrase was one he'd certainly never expected to ever say to her and mean.

But he did mean it—this time. He needed to get her out of here before Hugh turned up. Rosie had been right in her assessment of Jenna's emotional state. And in his estimation, a confrontation with Hugh or Mamie Gallagher would just about push her over the edge.

Jenna took off the hospital gown and gathered up the clothes she'd been wearing when she came in. She tried to hurry, but in her haste, she fumbled with buttons and zippers.

"You decent?" Garth asked once.

"No," she said, putting her hands to her face in exasperation. But that hurt, and she took a long, deep breath.

"Now?" he called a moment later.

"Yes, all right," she answered. She was more or less together.

Garth slid back the curtain. "Where's your coat?"

She gave him a bewildered look. "I don't know."

"You know where her coat is?" Garth asked a nurse who stood nearby.

"She wasn't wearing a coat when she came in."

"Were you wearing your coat, Jenna?" Garth asked her.

She shook her head. "I don't know—yes. I don't care about the coat. I just want to get out of here."

"No coat when I got here," Rosie put in.

"Here," Garth said, stripping off his jacket. "You can wear mine."

"I don't want to take yours," Jenna said, but she let him put her into it anyway.

"It's not what you want in this world," he said philosophically, "it's what you need."

"Get," Jenna corrected as he turned her around to lift her hair out from under the collar. "It's what you get." She felt like one of the kindergartners. She felt like a woman who was being gently cared for by the man she very much needed right now.

"Whatever," Garth said. "It's cold as a witch's—"

"Whatever," the nurse and Rosie supplied, and he grinned.

"Could we go find the doctor? I'd rather not wait here," Jenna said to Garth.

"Let's go," he said, taking her by the arm. "When we find the doc, try to look a little perkier, okay? He wants to give you the lowdown on the X rays and stuff like that."

"All right," she said, taking a deep breath and working on "perky."

"Can you make it?"

"I can make it," she assured him.

Her knees were wobbly, but she managed to listen to the doctor's report on her condition and his instructions about rest and the names of the over-the-counter medicines she could take for the pain. But all the while she could feel the panic rising, the illogical fear that somehow something would keep her here and she wouldn't get out after all. She was finding it hard to concentrate. She felt that the lights were too bright, the noises too loud. But she stood firm. She'd been through enough anxiety attacks to know that that was what she was experiencing now, and that they were only that—a rush of adrenaline and her body's response to it. She'd had counseling for them; she understood them; she just didn't want to have to explain them. So she tried to look "perky" instead.

"I'm sorry you were hurt, Mrs. Gallagher," the doctor finally said. "But you were very lucky. I know it's been a bad . . . year for you."

It didn't surprise her that he recognized her name; she'd made a lot of public appearances in the past few months. But she made no comment. He, however, apparently felt the need to explain. "I was working the day the officer—your husband—was brought in. . . ."

The sentence hung in the air, and Jenna swallowed hard, giving Garth a plaintive look. "Let's go," he said, cutting the physician short.

"She can wait here while you get the car."

"It's close," Garth said, and he hustled her out.

"You okay?" he asked as soon as they were outside.

"Yes," she said, not really knowing.

"I lied about how close the car is."

"I know," she answered. He put his arm around her as they walked.

"It's down there. I thought the hike to the car was the lesser of two evils."

She nodded. "Why?" she suddenly asked, because she knew her reasons but she didn't know his.

"Skip . . . told me you have a hard time in hospitals."

"Not always," she answered, wondering what else Skip had told him.

"Panic attacks, right?"

"Yes," she said.

"And you keep going back into hospitals anyway."

"I'm . . . supposed to. The first thing anybody does after an attack is to try to avoid the place where they had the anxiety—because they think it will happen again."

"Can't it?"

"Sometimes. But if you keep doing that, pretty soon you aren't going anywhere."

"So what do they do for panic attacks—give you pills for them or what?"

"Sometimes. Why are we talking about this?"

"To take your mind off your other troubles."

"This is taking my mind off my troubles?"

"Okay—because I want to know. Do you take something?"

"No, I wait."

"For what?"

"For the attack to be over. I know I'm not dying, so I just . . . wait."

"And then you go on about your business."

"Something like that. Did you say something to the doctor to get him to let me go?" it suddenly occurred to her to ask.

"I told him the truth. Mrs. Gallagher, don't look so incredulous. The truth comes in very handy now and again. I think we'd better hurry—unless you want to talk to Hugh."

She had thought they *were* hurrying, but she picked up the pace as he hustled her toward the parking lot. The wind was sharp and cold, scattering bits of trash and leaves across the pavement.

"No, I don't want to talk to Hugh. And it doesn't matter if you told the truth or not. I was leaving anyway."

"Well, let's don't let the doctor find that out. Let's let him think he was persuaded."

They walked on, and she stumbled once.

"Maybe I should have let the car warm up for you," he said, hurrying her on.

"For me? I'm the one with the coat."

He suddenly grinned. "You know what I like about you, Mrs. Gallagher? You had a hell of a day, and you've *still* got enough spark to be a smart-ass."

She didn't say anything to that.

"You'll feel better when you get home," he said.

She stopped walking. Home. She didn't want to go home. Somebody was surely going to tell Mamie her daughter-in-law had been beaten up in an apartment house stairwell. She closed her eyes. She didn't want to have to deal with Mamie. Mamie was high-strung, emotional, still mourning Patrick. She'd weep; she'd use the incident to try to talk Jenna into coming to live in the Gallagher house, where Mamie thought she belonged. With her. So they could wear black and talk about Patrick.

"What?" Garth was saying.

"I don't want to go home, Garth. I don't want to go home!" She couldn't keep her voice from rising, and she was doing it again—running away because she didn't want to have to deal with the Gallaghers. Sneaking out before Hugh got here. Panicking, because she'd have to see Mamie if she went home. She was ashamed of it, and she couldn't help it. "I don't want to go home," she said again, trying to sound more reasonable this time.

"Okay. No problem."

"I just...don't want to have to talk to anybody," she said, feeling that she had to make some kind of explanation or Garth would think she was crazy.

"Okay," he said again.

"If you could—"

"Take it easy, Mrs. Gallagher. I'll take care of it. The car's over there."

She believed him. He'd take care of it.

He opened the car door, and she got inside. She huddled on the cold seat, and, relieved of the responsibility of deciding what to do next, she suddenly gave herself up to physical and emotional exhaustion. She hurt. Her body. Her soul. No one had ever deliberately hurt her before. Nobody.

She tried not to shiver as Garth got in on the other side. She could feel him looking at her, but he didn't say anything. She was thankful for that. She didn't want to talk; she didn't want to explain. She drew inward, because she didn't want to think about anything anymore. She just wanted to sit here, thinking nothing, feeling nothing.

No. There was feeling. She hurt. Her face hurt. Her eye. She reached up to tentatively touch the place that throbbed so, but Garth caught her hand.

"Leave it alone," he said. "If you think it hurts now, just go poking around." He pulled her closer to him, and he slid his fingers between hers. She didn't try to move away.

"How...bad is it?" she made herself ask.

"You look like hell."

Of course, she thought. I look just the way it feels. She closed her eyes.

"Jenna?" Garth said, and she opened them.

Not Mrs. Gallagher. *Jenna.*

But he wasn't holding her hand anymore. He was outside the car, holding the door open. She looked up at him. "Come on," he said kindly.

She slid across the seat to get out, wincing when he took her arm.

"Sorry," he said.

She didn't answer.

She looked around. A deserted parking lot. She looked up. The moon was full. Frosty and full in the night sky. It was so cold out here.

"I'm not going to take you in through the Humoresque," he said. "It's still open, and Hazel and Luigi will go nuts if they see you. Come on."

She went.

"Come on," he said again when they reached a fire escape. "Can you make it?"

"I can make it," she answered.

It was a long way up.

"Okay," he said when they reached the first landing. "You need to rest?"

"No," she said. "Do you?"

He chuckled softly. "Smart-ass," she thought he said.

But she did need to rest. She needed to rest so badly. Just to sit down. Here—anywhere—for a few minutes—forever.

"Come on, baby," Garth said, his face close to hers. "You can do it."

"I know." She could do it—because he wanted her to.

She climbed, and she stood on the last landing while he wrestled with the door locks. She looked up at the moon again. Beautiful—unlike herself. She lifted her battered face to the moonlight.

Garth had the door unlocked, and when he said it was all right, she followed him inside. He went around closing windows; it was nearly as cold in the loft as it was outside. Why was it he left the windows open? Oh, yes. Onions. Luigi's fried onions.

She stood where he left her, shivering.

"Come sit down," he said, and she went to sit in the chair next to the table with the telephone. She looked at the picture again, the picture of Garth and Mary Zaccato.

"It'll take a while to get warm in here."

"She was very beautiful," Jenna said.

There was a pause before he answered. "Yes. She was."

"And you ioved her very much."

"Mrs. Gallagher..."

"Don't call me Mrs. Gallagher."

"All right," he said, his tone of voice indicating that he'd humor her.

"And you loved her very much," she repeated.

This time he answered. "Yes. I loved her very much."

Jenna nodded. It was important to her, knowing precisely how he'd felt about Mary. She felt better, knowing. She had loved Patrick. And he had loved Mary Zaccato. She looked down at his jacket. It had holes in it, holes she didn't remember from the day he'd spent at St. Xavier's.

"Jenna?" Garth said, and she looked up at him. "Will you take some advice from an old hand at having the living daylights kicked out of him?"

She tried to smile. "Why not? I don't have any... prior experience."

"I know you're tired, but I'm going to run the tub. I want you to take a hot bath. And then you can take some aspirin and go to bed. You won't be nearly so sore in the morning if you do that, okay?"

She looked into his eyes. He was going to take care of it. Of her. Of everything.

"Okay?" he asked again, and she nodded.

"Good. Maybe it'll be a little warmer out here when you get done."

She did as he suggested, but it took her a while to get past her reflection in the bathroom mirror. Garth had been right about both things. She looked like hell, and if she thought her eye hurt left alone, she should just try poking around. She didn't seem to have many other bruises—a few on her arms, scraped knuckles on one hand.

Garth had a huge clawfoot tub—necessary for a man used to having the living daylights kicked out of him, she supposed. She slipped gingerly into the hot water, and she lay with her eyes closed, savoring the warmth until the water grew cool.

But it wasn't warmer when she came out. The loft was too cavernous to have recovered from an all-day airing out. Garth had given her one of his flannel shirts to put on, and a pair of sweatpants, and wool socks, but she was still shivering.

"Nice outfit," he said when she came out, but she couldn't smile. She was too dammed up with feeling. She wanted to smile, but she wanted to cry more, and as a result, she could do neither.

He took the clothes she'd been wearing out of her hands and put them aside. He gave her two aspirin, and he gave her his bed, making her sit on the side of it while she drank what she thought was going to be coffee.

It was hot chocolate. She had thought she had no appetite for anything, but it was wonderful.

"Courtesy of the Humoresque," Garth said. "Luigi wanted to send you a dish of ice cream, but I told him you were too cold. When he was a young man—when he first came to the United States—he had to have his tonsils out. They gave him ice cream in the hospital. Impressed the hell out of him, even if he couldn't eat it. He thinks ice cream fixes everything.''

She did manage to smile at the anecdote about Luigi, and she drained the whole cup of chocolate, sitting there on the side of the bed. Then she crawled between the crisp, cold sheets. It was so good to lie down. Garth had been right about the hot bath. She lay quietly, trying to get warm while he covered her in blankets and a quilted brown comforter. He had music playing softly.

"The Drifters," she murmured, her eyes growing heavy as the bath and the aspirin and the hot chocolate did their work.

"Yeah," he said.

"I like The Drifters."

"Good. They kind of go with the territory."

"Garth?"

"Yeah?"

"Thank you."

"It's okay, Mrs. Gallagher—Jenna."

She felt so tired, but sleep didn't come.

"Garth?" she said after a time.

"Yeah?" His voice was still close by, but she didn't open her eyes to see exactly where he was.

"Hernando's coat. How did you get his father to buy it for him?"

"You don't want to know," he said.

She gave a half smile. "That's what I thought. He's so...proud of it. Garth?"

The telephone suddenly rang, and he went to answer it.

"Yeah, Debbie," he said, and she turned her head to look at him. He gave her a questioning look, and she shook her head no. She didn't want to talk to anyone—except him.

"No, she's all right," Garth continued. "No. I'm sure, Debbie. I wouldn't tell you she's all right if she wasn't. Yes, she's out of the tub now, but she's just about asleep. Yeah, I talked to Skip. No, Debbie, it's not your fault. No, Jenna doesn't think that. I'm sure—I'm positive. Okay. Good night." He hung up the phone.

"Second time she's called," he said. "She thinks it's all her fault. She let you in, and then she got busy on the telephone and she didn't realize how long it was taking you to get upstairs. And then she couldn't find out what had happened to you. She's pretty frantic."

"I'll call her tomorrow," Jenna said. She suddenly put her hands to her face. She was going to cry again. Suddenly she was going to cry.

"Don't," Garth said quietly. "Not now. I want you to talk to me instead. I want you to tell me everything that happened. Everything you remember, no matter how minor or how silly it seems to you. And I want you to do it now."

"Garth, I can't. I've already told Rosie."

He came and sat on the side of the bed. "Yes, you can, and I want you to tell *me*. You tell me, and then you can sleep. But there's one other thing first. I need to ask you a question."

She tried to wipe her eyes with her fingertips, and she looked at him. "What?"

"Your name."

"My *name*?"

"I promised the doc every two hours I'd make sure you knew what planet you were on."

She sighed. If he'd promised, he'd promised. "Jenna Gallagher."

"And today is . . ."

"Friday," she supplied.

"The date?"

She told him that, too.

"Very good. Joe Eagan called while you were in the tub."

"Is that the truth, or are you still testing?"

"Both. You get to tell me who Joe Eagan is."

She looked into his eyes. He was so serious about this. "Joe Eagan is Debbie Carver's father. He's a retired cop— retired because of wounds received in the line of duty. He's in a wheelchair. He lectures regularly at the police academy about things like keeping a little notebook—an 'auxiliary brain,' he calls it, because a street cop never knows when an unimportant detail might become an important one—how am I doing?"

"Well, *I'm* impressed," he said. "How did you know about the auxiliary brain?"

"Patrick told me. He kept one. A lot of you do, don't you?"

He looked away; there was a long pause.

"Yeah, I guess we do," he said finally. "The test is over. Now, tell me what happened to you."

Garth paced around the loft. The moon was shining in the arched windows, leaving patches of moonlight on the floor. And damn, this place was still cold! He glanced from time to time at the clocks and at Jenna sleeping quietly in his bed. He'd have to wake her soon for another name and day of the week run-through to make sure she was all right. But at the moment, he had other things on his mind.

Patrick Gallagher kept a notebook. Had anybody looked in it? *He* certainly hadn't. That unofficial spiral pocket notebook Joe Eagan advocated hadn't been part of the murder investigation, and he hadn't thought to ask for it.

He still remembered Joe Eagan's lecture from when he had been at the academy. "If you got a great memory, don't keep a little book," he'd told them. "I had a partner like that. Remembered everything he ever heard—names, addresses, everything. Of course he got hit by a bus over on Second Avenue one night, and everything he could remember didn't do anybody a damn bit of good."

Where was the notebook now? Garth wondered. If it was significant, Hugh would have done something with it—*if* he had known it existed. But maybe he hadn't thought of it, either. Some rookies took Joe Eagan's advice to heart; some didn't. Which brought him to the problem at hand. If the book still existed, Jenna must have it. How was he going to get it?

Ah, Jenna.

He closed his eyes. He'd been scared for her. He was *still* scared for her. The mugging hadn't been a robbery. Attempted rape? He didn't think so. What, then? All he had were questions.

He went to the telephone, quietly dialed the station house and asked for Skip.

"Skip!" he said when his partner answered. "What's the word?"

"Quiet," Skip said. "Hugh's not around. Some of us have to pull a twelve and some of us don't. I imagine he's heard about Jenna, though. Everybody here has. The brotherhood is pretty riled about this happening to her. She made the evening news, complete with clips of Patrick's funeral. How is she?"

"Asleep."

But she wasn't asleep. Even as he said it, she made a soft whimpering sound.

"Skip, I want Roy Lee picked up," he said hurriedly. "Take care of getting that out, will you?"

"You got it. And you take good care of Jenna."

He hung up the phone and walked toward the bed to see if Jenna was all right. She was quieter now, her breathing deep and even again. He stood staring down at her. She was so beautiful to him—even with a black eye. Her hair was loose and spread out over the pillow. She had a black eye, no makeup; she was wearing a man's flannel shirt, and she was still beautiful to him. He tried not to think about how much this had scared him. If something had happened to her...

Like Mary.

He realized that he was scared for her and for himself. He was scared of what he was feeling, scared of this need he had to be with her, to bring her into his life and keep her there. He didn't want any encumbrances; he *knew* that, and yet...

He was about to move away from the bed when she suddenly sat up.

"Jenna?" he said, but she didn't hear him. "Jenna," he said again.

"Don't!" she cried out. He reached out to touch her, because she was on her knees. "Don't!"

"Jenna!" he said sharply, taking her by the shoulders. She began to fight him, flailing out with both arms.

"Don't! Don't!" she cried.

He caught her to him, holding her tightly. "It's all right. You're all right," he whispered urgently. "Jenna!"

She suddenly went limp in his arms. "Oh, Garth! Oh, Garth! He wouldn't take the money—I tried to give him my purse. He wouldn't take it!"

"It's okay," he soothed. "It's just a dream, baby. It's okay."

"Don't go anywhere, Garth. Please!" She clung to him desperately.

"No, I won't. Here. Cover up. It's cold." He tried to pull the covers up around her, but she wouldn't let go of him so he could. She was trembling. Careful of her bruised face, he stroked her hair, rocking her gently, as if she were a child.

But she wasn't a child, and in a very little time, they both knew it. She suddenly stiffened in his arms, pushing herself back so she could see his face. She regarded him gravely, and he was lost again in her eyes, those sad, knowing eyes of hers that saw everything and still forgave.

The Drifters sang.

Her hands rested lightly on his shoulders. And slowly, so slowly, she lifted her mouth to his. He tried to stay passive under the tentative sweetness of her lips.

She tasted him.

Again.

And then again. He let her, his breathing growing heavier, his hands moving over her back in spite of everything he could do.

Don't do this, he told himself. He understood, and he wanted to tell her that he did. He wasn't the one she needed. She'd been hurt, and she needed her husband to comfort her. She needed Patrick; she didn't need him. He didn't want to take advantage of a moment of weakness. Hers. Or his. In the cold light of day, she'd be sorry, and he didn't want to see that in her eyes.

But he was all she had, and her kisses were warm and soft. Her body was warm and soft. He shivered with desire and buried his face in her sweet-smelling neck.

Ah, God, he wanted her.

"Jenna," he whispered, some part of him still needing to protest.

But she slid her hands into his hair, and she parted her lips under his, so that he wouldn't be passive anymore. His arms tightened around her.

"I don't want to hurt you, baby."

"You won't," she promised him. "You won't." She knew that he didn't necessarily mean now. She knew that he was giving her the chance to stay Mrs. Gallagher.

But she didn't want the chance. She wanted him. He'd been watching over her while she slept, and he was so cold. She wanted to warm him. She wanted to be close to him. She wanted to belong to him, and she purposefully moved his hand to her breast. She could feel the trembling in his body and in her own, and she wanted to shut out everything but him. The physical pain she felt was nothing compared to the pain in her heart. She wanted his comfort and, yes, his kindness. She would ask for nothing else.

"Jenna," he said, holding her away from him.

She gently placed her fingertips against his lips. "Don't say anything. You don't have to say anything. I don't want any promises in the dark."

He took her hand and slid his fingers between hers the way he had in the car. "Yeah?"

"Yeah," she answered.

He pulled her closer and placed both her arms around his neck. "Well, I do," he said quietly, staring into her eyes. "I want you to promise me everything. I want you to sweet-talk me and make me feel good. What do you think of that?"

She thought she would die from the pleasure of it.

Making love with him was not the way she had thought it would be. He talked to her, touched her, looked at her, made her laugh, made her cry. He filled her with urgency, an urgency that the effort to discard clothes and emotional baggage didn't diminish. Her body sang the familiar refrain that had come into play almost from the beginning:

I want him.

She felt no jealousy that he was prepared for the possibility of lovemaking, that he kept what he needed near the bed for just such an eventuality as this, regardless of the fact that supposedly he rarely brought anyone here and regardless of the fact that he most certainly hadn't intended them for her.

She didn't care.

She didn't care about the women he'd had here or the potential liaisons he'd bought condoms for. She didn't care that he didn't meet the Gallagher standards of what an acceptable police officer should be. She didn't care that he'd come from a world she couldn't begin to understand. It was only Garth himself that mattered. She'd sweet-talk him. She'd make him feel good.

He sat up and piled pillows behind his back to lean against, bringing her leg over his so that she sat astride his thighs. They were face-to-face; she could look into his eyes.

Hide me, Garth. Just for a little while.

"Are you all right?" he asked her.

"Yes," she whispered, her voice so tremulous she hardly recognized it.

"Where can I touch you? I don't want to hurt you." His fingers moved lightly over her shoulders to her breasts.

"I'll tell you if you hurt me—oh, Garth—"

"What? What? Did I hurt you?"

"No," she murmured, her mouth finding his. She kissed him deeply, reveling in the moan of desire she elicited from him.

She pressed her body against his. Her breasts flattened against his chest. She wrapped her arms around him and held him tightly. "You're so cold."

He laughed softly against her ear. "No, baby. I'm *not*."

Even so, he took his time. He wanted to make it last. He had no illusions about her need of him. He knew that this would likely be his only time with her, and that when the morning came, they would both remember who they were.

What if I love you? he thought. But he didn't say it. He tried to make her feel it instead. It was such an ache within him, that he might be in love with her and that she might be thinking of Patrick.

When he entered her, she could still look into his eyes.

Don't be sad, Garth, she thought. Why was he so sad? Because she wasn't Mary?

And then she said it, cupping his face in her hands, kissing his eyes, his mouth. "Don't be sad, Garth. Please."

"I'm not," he whispered, thrusting into her, trying not to hurt her and yet trying to take all the pleasure she could give. It was so good with her. So good. "You—make me happy. You—"

She clung to him, letting the rise of his passion fuel her own. Incredible, she kept thinking. Incredible, her need of this man. She loved being with him like this. She loved the smell of him and the taste and the feel of him. And she found that she was jealous of his other women after all. And Mary.

"Garth," she murmured. "No, don't stop—oh, Garth—"

But it was he who did the "sweet-talking." He told her how good she felt around him. He told her how long—how *long*—he'd wanted to do this, how he'd thought about making love with her ever since the night they'd met. He told her she was beautiful, so beautiful—shiner or no. He told her—showed her—how much he wanted her.

And even when their passion had peaked, even when she thought she would die from the pleasure he had given her and she began the slow spiral downward into reality, she believed him.

Chapter Ten

They lay together, bundled under blankets and the brown quilted comforter. Her body was warm against his, and her hand rested lightly on his chest. He didn't think she was asleep.

He covered her hand with his. Who was he kidding anyway? He was crazy in love with this woman.

What do you think of that, Jenna? I love you.

But he didn't tell her.

"The lawyer you went out with," he said instead. "The Peking Opera one," he added in case she had any doubts about which one he meant.

"What about him?" she asked sleepily.

"Whoever he is, I hate his guts. I just wanted you to know that."

There was a long pause.

"I wasn't too crazy about him myself," she said finally, and they both burst out laughing. He hugged her to him.

She made him so happy. Just being with her made him happy.

Until he remembered—Mary, and Hugh Gallagher, and how he'd come to have Jenna in his bed in the first place.

I love you, Jenna, and by the way, could I have Patrick's notebook? You see, I want to break his mother's heart and ruin his family.

But he didn't want to think about that. Not now. Not now. He abruptly rolled her over on top of him, and his mouth found hers. She gave a soft cry of surprise, but he didn't stop.

"That dress you wore to the opera," he whispered against her ear. "One day I want you to wear it for *me.*" His hands moved over her, as if he could memorize the feel, the softness of her body before she was gone. "Jenna."

"Yes," she said, returning his kiss. For now, for this night at least, he was her lover. And she wanted him.

She must have slept, because she seemed to have awakened, but what had awakened her she couldn't say. Some disturbing dream not quite remembered—the man in the stairwell again?

She gave an involuntary shiver and moved closer to Garth.

"You okay?" he asked, pressing a small kiss on her forehead. He brought the covers more snugly around her.

"Yes," she said. "I . . . can't stop thinking about the man—oh!" she said softly as the memory returned, strong and disturbing and not at all muted by the pleasure she'd shared with Garth.

"You're safe here. Try to sleep."

But she couldn't go back to sleep. Not because she was afraid of the night, but because she dreaded the morning. She wouldn't be able to hide then. She would have to deal with everything—with the memories, with the fear, with Patrick's family, with the possibility that Garth would re-sent her intrusion. She would leave early, she decided. Before he even wanted her to. She couldn't bear the thought of being here when he wanted to be rid of her. He was a private man, and she'd imposed upon him without mercy.

Still, she thought, lying here with his breath coming soft and warm against her neck and his hand cupping her breast, her imposition wasn't without compensation. The problem was that she wanted to be more to him than a double-edged sword.

She finally slept, only to be wakened for another of Garth's orientation quizzes. She knew who she was—she knew only too well who she was, and what planet she was on, and whatever else it took to prove that her mental faculties were intact. It wasn't her mind she was concerned about. It was her heart. In spite of herself, she'd given it to him—and he didn't even know it. She understood the kind of man he was, that he would be driven to isolate himself from personal involvement. And she had never wanted just a sexual relationship between strangers.

Neither had she wanted to become involved with another policeman. It was too lonely, too filled with worry. And commitment, if Garth were capable of it, would be on the run, falling somewhere well behind his mistress, The Job. Yet what was the alternative? Quietly returning to her widowhood, the way Mamie wanted? Going back home to live along the Susquehanna River?

She gave a sad smile. Hazel had wanted Garth to marry "up." Jenna's mother had wanted the same—only where she came from, marrying up would be to a nice white-collar worker from IBM instead of someone from the shoe factory—neither of whom would be anything at all like Garth. No one was like Garth. No one. She suddenly tightened her arms around him.

"What?" he asked.

"Nothing. Nothing..."

She left his bed at dawn, dressing quietly in the bathroom because the best she could do for him would be not to bother him anymore. She still looked like hell, or perhaps worse. Her eye was still swollen, and her cheeks tingled from the chafing of his beard. The pleasant memory of his lovemaking immediately surfaced, making her give a soft, ragged sigh.

When he finally woke, she was standing in front of the arched windows, waiting, her arms folded over her breasts.

"What are you doing?" he asked, trying to rub the sleep from his eyes.

She turned to look at him. "I'm going to go home now, Garth," she said quietly.

"Now? What time is it?"

"It's early, but—"

"What's wrong?" he asked, cutting in the way he always did when he wanted answers.

"Nothing."

"Don't do that! Tell me what's wrong."

"Nothing is wrong. I . . . need to get home."

He stared at her across the room. When he was right, he was right. He'd known her regrets would get the best of her this morning. Regardless of the night they'd spent, in the cold light of day, she was done with him. And he, *he* had said too much, revealed too much about what he was feeling. He knew enough to keep things to himself, and he hadn't done it. And that lapse made him angry.

"You mean you need to get away from me, don't you? It's all right, Mrs. Gallagher. You can tell me. I can take it." He got up from the bed, looking for his shorts.

"That's not what I meant."

"You mind if I shower first? Or can't you wait that long?"

"You don't have to take me. I've called a cab."

"I see," he said. "So what's the hurry?" he asked as he crossed the room. "Are you afraid somebody will see you leaving?"

She had only meant to relieve him of the responsibility he'd had to take for her, a responsibility he'd really had little choice about, but instead she'd insulted him somehow. Because they'd rushed their intimacy, she thought. Because they really didn't know each other. "You know better than that," she said.

"Do I? You know Hugh has you watched when you're with me, don't you? You know that?"

"No, I don't know that!" she said sharply. "Hugh wouldn't—"

"Yes, Mrs. Gallagher, he would. So tell me. How was I? Was I worth that aggravation? Was I worth the guilt you're feeling now for your little lapse in propriety? Am I as good in bed as Patrick was or not?"

She walked toward him with every intention of hitting him, and it surprised her that he didn't realize it. Even when she swung at him, he hadn't anticipated her intent.

He caught her hand, pulling her around and pinning her arms, his eyes filled with incredulity that he'd misjudged her.

"What is the matter with you!" he cried.

"Why don't you tell me if I'm as good as Mary Zaccato, Garth! Did you tell her the same things you told me? And while you're at it, you can tell me what's the matter with *you*! Why are we having this conversation!"

"Because I don't want you to go, that's why!" he yelled at her. He held her away so he could see her face. "Because I don't want you to go," he said, bringing her to him, wrapping his arms around her and holding her tightly.

"Garth—" she said, leaning into him. She put her arms around his waist and laid her uninjured cheek against his bare chest. "Garth—"

"What, damn it!"

She gave him a hard hug. "I'm trying not to bother you anymore, you big dummy."

"When I'm bothered, lady, I'll tell you."

She leaned back to look at him. "Maybe I don't want you to tell me. Maybe I'd rather—" She stopped because someone was knocking on the outer door at the fire escape.

"I'll get it," she said, because he wasn't dressed.

"No," he said, picking up his jeans and getting into them. He didn't bother to button and zip, and he quickly crossed to the chair where he'd hung his gun holster. He took the gun out.

"Garth?" Jenna said, but he held up his hand to keep her quiet. He walked barefoot to the door as the knocking continued. He stood well to the side against the brick wall.

"Who is it?" he yelled to whoever was outside.

"Open the door, Garth! I want to talk to Jenna!"

They both recognized the voice immediately. Hugh.

Garth cursed softly and unlocked the door. "About what?" he asked Hugh as he opened it.

"Now, that's not any business of yours, is it, Garth?" Hugh said, pushing his way into the loft without an invitation. Jenna watched as his sweeping glance took in everything—her, the rumpled bed, Garth's half-dressed state. Hugh, on the other hand, was wearing an expensive suit and a tailored winter coat, but neither his unexpected arrival nor his wardrobe rattled Garth in the least. He slammed the door shut behind him and casually walked to put his gun back into the holster.

"Making your rounds kind of early, aren't you, Hugh?"

"I want to make sure Jenna's all right."

"You want to catch somebody with his pants down."

"Well, I didn't miss by much, did I?"

"I'm fine," Jenna interjected before this got out of hand.

"That's just great, Jenna," Hugh said. "But none of the family would know that, would they? It didn't occur to you that we'd be worried? A phone call would have been nice.

You know mother hasn't been well since Patrick died, and—"

"She wasn't thinking about making telephone calls," Garth cut in.

"You stay out of this!" Hugh said, turning on him. "This is a family matter."

"Is Mamie all right?" Jenna asked, but no one heard her.

"She wasn't thinking about making telephone calls," Garth said again. "I could have done it for her, but I thought it might make things worse for your mother to get a telephone call from me. And I was sure it wouldn't take you long to find out where she was. I really expected you sooner, Hugh."

"Look, do you mind? I'd like to talk to Jenna alone!"

"That's up to her," Garth said.

"It's all right, Garth," Jenna said. She might as well get it over with. "Hugh, say whatever it is you want to say—and, Garth, this is your home. You don't have to leave."

"No problem," he said, looking into her eyes. "We don't want to get Hugh any more bent out of shape than he already is. I'll be in here. Yell if you need me." He walked into the bathroom and closed the door. In a moment, Jenna could hear the shower running.

"I can't believe this," Hugh said, running his hand over his cropped hair. "I cannot *believe* this! Jenna, what are you doing here with him? Don't you know what people are going to say!"

"I know what your friends will say, but, for me, that isn't a consideration. Garth helped me when I needed help."

"Yes, I can see how he *helped* you. I understand your problem, Jenna—a woman as attractive as you is bound to get lonely. But don't you have any respect at all for my brother? Patrick was a good man. He was worth ten of Garth."

"Don't talk to me about Patrick, Hugh! Patrick is dead. I loved him, but he's dead."

"Jenna, use some sense, will you? I read the report on your so-called mugging. The man who attacked you didn't want your money. It was deliberate—he probably would have raped you if he'd had the time. I think—a lot of us think—it was because of him," he said, jerking his thumb toward the bathroom door. The water abruptly shut off. "He's got a foot on both sides of the law, Jenna, and his old friends make bad enemies. If he steps on their toes, if they even think he's stepped on their toes, they're not above setting up some kind of retribution. I want you to stay away from him. I don't want to see you hurt."

"Hugh, I appreciate your concern, but I have to make my own judgments. I know you and Garth don't get along, and I'm sorry about that. But it doesn't have anything to do with me—"

"It's got everything to do with you! Do you think he'd come sniffing around if it didn't? You're not even his type, Jenna. Don't you see?"

Her temper rose at Hugh's choice of words, but she didn't get the chance to say anything. The bathroom door opened, and Garth came out wearing one towel around his waist and drying his hair with another.

"Sorry," he said to Hugh. "I was getting pruney."

"I've said all I came to say," Hugh said, heading for the door.

"I think you're right, Hugh," Garth said when he reached it. "I think Jenna's mugging was a message—but I don't think the message was necessarily for me."

"What is that supposed to mean?"

"It means, Hugh, that fifty case folders on my desk or a hundred and fifty case folders on my desk—or playing clay pigeon for Tony Zaccato—I'll find out."

"What was that supposed to mean?" Jenna asked as soon as Hugh had gone.

"What?" Garth said, his tone of voice neutral enough to make her angry.

"Don't give me that, Garth! I want to know what that 'fifty case folders' and the 'clay pigeon' thing means."

"I don't want to tell you."

"I'd suggest you do," she said evenly.

He looked at her from under the towel and grinned. "You have got a lot of sonofabitch in you, Mrs. Gallagher. You know that?"

"Yes. It comes from having to deal with condescending police officers. And—"

"Sure you weren't raised on the wrong side of the tracks, too?"

"Don't change the subject! I want to know what that means."

He sighed and dropped his towel—the one that mattered—and walked blithely toward the sleeping area, hunting through various drawers for his underwear. The sight of his bare backside caused an immediate internal flutter in her. He knew she liked his body—she'd certainly done everything she could last night to convince him of that—but she was determined not to let him get away with this flagrant ploy to distract her from the topic of conversation.

"Garth . . ."

"Jenna, it means that Hugh has seen to it that I keep busy." He put his shorts on.

"Why?" she asked pointedly.

He didn't answer.

"Let me guess. Another message?"

"Something like that."

"Because of me?"

He didn't answer that, either.

"All right—that brings us to the mugging, which all of a sudden isn't one at all. Were you going to tell me about that?"

"Nope," he said easily. He put on a T-shirt.

"Why not!" she cried, trying not to think how seductive it was to stand and watch a man put his clothes *on*.

"Because I know what I think it *isn't*. I don't know what I think it *is*. So there's no point in it."

"Who's the message for then, if it's not for you? Hugh?"

"Maybe. Maybe not."

She rolled her eyes upward in exasperation. "Maybe the message is for me, Garth. Maybe *I'm* the one who stepped on somebody's toes with these committees I'm on. Or maybe it's because of somebody I've gone to court with."

"Maybe," he said noncommittally.

"Maybe it's not a message at all. Maybe I was just in the wrong place at the wrong time."

"Maybe," he said again.

"But Hugh—and some of the others—think it's your fault. And you think it's Hugh's fault. And Debbie thinks it's *her* fault, right? And don't say 'Maybe'!"

"Don't forget Joe Eagan," he put in.

"Joe Eagan?"

"Yeah. He thinks it might be *his* fault. He's made a lot of enemies in his time, and you were on your way to his place."

"Good Lord," she said in aggravation. "And just who would know that?"

"Debbie said some man called Saint Xavier's looking for you when you were in court. Something about a change in a meeting. He wouldn't leave a message. *Had* to talk to you. Debbie told him she was meeting you at Joe's apartment yesterday afternoon so he could call you there."

Jenna stared at him.

"What else haven't you bothered to tell me?"

"You weren't feeling up to hearing this last night," he said instead of answering.

"Today I'm feeling better! What else?"

"I've got a couple of things I want to check out."

"Like what?"

"Oh," he said airily, "like the sticker on your assailant's underwear."

"That's very funny, Garth." A car horn blew several times in the parking lot below. She went to the window to see if her cab had arrived. "Very funny. I'm not stupid. And I'm not weak, regardless of the way I behaved last night. If you explained things very carefully, I could probably follow it."

"I told you I didn't want you to go," he said as she picked up her purse.

"Nevertheless, I'm going. Thank you for your... hospitality."

"Take my coat," he said when she reached the door.

"I don't need it."

"Take the damn coat!" he yelled, grabbing it and shoving it at her. "Have you got money?"

She stood staring at him, then finally accepted his jacket. "Yes. I have money."

"We won't be seeing each other," he said, trying to look into her eyes. She wouldn't let him.

"No," she agreed.

"Until we know more about your assault," he qualified. "In case I am the reason."

She opened the door to go down the fire escape. He was trying to be kind to her. He was a kind man, regardless of what he said.

"Jenna?"

She looked back over her shoulder at him.

"I want you to be careful. Don't go anyplace alone. Don't take any chances."

"I won't."

"Jenna," he said again. He wanted to say something about last night, something so she'd know how special it had been to him. But he didn't. He knew the price of revealing too much. "The notebook you said Patrick kept," he said instead. "Do you still have it?"

"I think so. Why?"

"I'd like to look at it. I'll…pick it up when I pick up my jacket."

He stood in the arched window staring at nothing for a long time after she'd gone. The sun was just coming up. He had a lot to do and no inclination to do it. He could see what she had done. She'd tried to take away every trace of her having been here. Nothing was out of place. She'd put the sweatpants and flannel shirt he'd loaned her into the dirty laundry. The bathroom was straight. She'd even washed the cup that had held the hot chocolate.

And yet she was still everywhere he looked. He hadn't wanted her to go, damn it all, and he hadn't known how to keep her. The only thing he'd known to do was to *say* that he wanted her here, and that certainly hadn't worked.

He went to the station house—early, because he didn't want Hazel and Luigi to give him the third degree about Jenna and because he had to think. He wanted to get Skip so they could go looking for Roy Lee. If anybody on the street knew what getting to Jenna was all about, Roy Lee would.

He was surprised to find Skip already at work on the pile of folders. The kid looked like hell, as if he hadn't slept at all.

"What's the matter with you?" Garth asked, and none too kindly. The last thing he needed was a partner who was ailing.

"Oh, nothing much," Skip said, waving a folder in the air. "Debbie's having an affair."

Garth laughed, when he thought that he felt nothing at all like laughing. "Sure," he said. On the way here, he'd formulated a plan, and he needed Skip to carry it off. "Skipper, I want you to—"

"I tell you my marriage is over, and all you can say is *sure*?" Skip demanded, causing a few heads in the squad room to turn.

Garth leaned back to look at him. The kid was serious.

"Look, Skip, you can't stay in bed *all* the time. Sometimes you have to get up. And when you do, words fly. It's nothing to—"

"How the hell do you know? You don't know a damn thing about it!"

"Well, you got me there," Garth said, trying to humor him. "You want to tell me what's going on, or do you want to keep acting like a complete idiot?"

"Oh, so I'm acting like an idiot. Sure, blame me."

Garth's temper snapped. He was worried about Jenna. He did *not* have time for this. "Knock it off and tell me what's going on!"

"Read my lips, Garth! Debbie is having an affair!"

"Damn it, Skip—" Garth began, but he needed to exercise more control here, before he hit the kid on the head with something. "Skip," he said, trying hard, "what makes you think that?"

"What makes me think that? She's been acting crazy! That's what makes me think that!"

Crazy for Debbie or crazy for everybody else? he almost asked. "Like what?" he said, revising his first impulse.

"She keeps disappearing—going places with some kind of vague explanation of where it is and when she'll be back. She's all nervous. She's scared of the telephone."

"Did you *ask* her what's wrong with her?"

"Ask her? No, I didn't *ask* her."

That did it for Garth; he cuffed Skip sharply on the ear. "What is the matter with you! Don't I have enough to worry about? You get me all involved in this thing with you and Debbie, and you don't know any more about the situation than I do!"

"Don't you hit me, Garth," Skip said, bristling and pointing his finger into Garth's face. "I don't like it!"

"Don't hit you? You don't *like* it? I'm going to throw you out the damn window, kid!" Garth jerked him up by his lapels.

"Teacher's watching," a patrolman said in passing.

"What the hell is going on out here!" the lieutenant yelled, bursting out of his office. Garth let go of Skip's lapels. The Whip would stay out of most squabbles unless it came to breaking up the furniture, and he and the lieutenant both knew he was only a hair away from that.

"What the hell is the matter with you two? Didn't I tell you I don't want to be bothered with personality clashes! We got television people coming in here today—all I need is for them to see two of my detectives kicking the holy crap out of each other!"

"It's nothing, sir," Skip said, straightening his jacket. "A hands-on learning experience. That's all."

The lieutenant made a noise of disgust and went back into his office.

"Here!" Garth said, shoving the telephone receiver into Skip's hand. "I want you to call your old man."

Skip gave him an incredulous look. "I don't call my father, Garth, and you know that."

"Today you do. Today you call him and you tell him what happened to your friend Jenna Gallagher. And you tell him you and your partner want the case. You remind him of who Jenna is and the tragedy she's suffered, and you tell him it's really important to you. Then you tell him to mention that to his squash-playing friends at One Police Plaza or Gracie Mansion or wherever the hell they are so they can pass the word down ASAP."

"I'm not going to do it, Garth."

"Yes, Skip, you are."

"I don't ask my father for favors!"

"The favor isn't for you. It's for me. I want Jenna's case, and I won't get it any other way. I'm your partner, and sometimes you have to put yourself out for your partner. You're going to do this for me, do you understand?"

"What do I get out of it?" Skip asked.

"I don't kick your butt all around the squad room?" Garth suggested.

"No—you talk to Debbie for me."

"Talk to Debbie? I don't want to talk to Debbie! I'm not a marriage counselor."

"She likes you. She respects your opinion. You talk to her. That's the deal."

Chapter Eleven

The day, for Jenna, was an incredible study in extremes. She was exhausted emotionally and physically, but she had no time to recoup her strength. She had to deal with a visit from Mamie and with the news that Mamie had seen fit to call Jenna's mother and tell her that she'd been beaten senseless in an apartment house stairwell. She had to talk again with Rosie Madden—this time about the matter of her missing coat. She didn't *know* what had happened to it— perhaps she'd been beaten as senseless as Mamie had led her mother to believe. She got a special-delivery letter from a lawyer in the city who represented the college friend of Patrick's from whom they'd sublet the apartment four years ago when he'd taken a job abroad. He was back. He was very sorry about Patrick, but he wanted his apartment. She had a message on her answering machine from a rather harassed-sounding Sister Mary John.

She had all these phone calls to make—to her mother, and to the lawyer, and to Sister—if the phone stopped ringing long enough so she could. Television people were hounding her for an interview about the mugging, the overly sympathetic tones of voice suggesting that they all believed "mugging" was a euphemism for "rape." And while she was at it, perhaps she'd talk about her life since Patrick had died and her ideas for making New York a safer city. In her desperation, she referred them all to Detective Rosie Madden of the NYPD.

She didn't have an apartment anymore. She didn't have a winter coat. All she had was her battered self and a misplaced devotion to Johnson Garth. She couldn't stop thinking about him. She didn't want to deal with any of this; she wanted to hide some more. With him. She wanted to go to the Humoresque, where black eyes wouldn't be so out of place, and eat one of Luigi's hamburger steaks. She wanted to sit in Garth's lap and have him tell her everything would be all right.

But she was a responsible, mature person. She called her mother, trying her best to reassure her that she was fine—not an easy task, because she could see her reflection in the mirror in the foyer as she talked. It was hard to sound convincing when one was looking directly at one's black eye.

"Jenna, honey, don't you want to come home now?" her mother pleaded. "Mamie was so upset."

"No, Mama."

"But, Jenna, it's not safe—you shouldn't be living by yourself!"

"I'll come for a visit as soon as I can. We'll talk then."

"When?" her mother asked, trying to pin her down.

"Soon, Mama," she repeated, because she couldn't say "as soon as the black eye's gone."

She called Sister Mary John next. Incredibly it was an offer to work at Saint Xavier's full-time. She wanted—needed—the job, but Sister Mary John wanted her to start tomorrow. She tried to explain about her black eye. Sister wasn't impressed. She'd start tomorrow.

The lawyer Jenna ignored. Her current coping limit seemed to be two major demands per day.

She set about looking for the notebook Patrick had carried instead, finding it in a desk drawer where she'd put it just after he'd died. She hadn't looked at it then or since. But she sat down to look at it now. How strange it was seeing his handwriting again. Patrick. She smiled to herself. He had terrible penmanship, but she could read his entries. None of it made much sense, however. There were names, addresses, notes to himself: *Don't forget Jenna's birthday!*

Her eyes fell on Joey Malaga's name, the boy who had shot him. Patrick must have written it down the first time they'd met so he'd know it the next time he saw him—so the boy would know that his name, that he himself, had mattered, to at least one cop. She silently shook her head and continued to turn the pages. There was nothing significant to her until several pages later. At the top of the page was a vaguely familiar address. In the middle, Patrick had drawn a triangle. At two of the corners he had a question mark. At the other corner, he'd written a name. *Mary Zaccato.*

"Are you going to sulk for the rest of the day?" Garth asked when they stopped long enough to buy something to eat—a luxury Garth allowed only because they were going to eat on the move. He wanted to find wherever Roy Lee was holed up before it got dark.

"I'm not sulking," Skip said. "I'm worried about my wife. When are you going to talk to her?"

"Skip, I can't do it today. I want to find Roy Lee. I'll...do it tomorrow. I'll come by and—"

"You can't come by, Garth!"

"Well, how the hell am I going to talk to her?" he snapped. His head ached from lack of food, and as far as he knew, Skip's old man hadn't come through with the favor.

So he'd taken it upon himself to start the hunt for the whys behind Jenna's being hurt anyway.

"You can't talk to her with me there, Garth. You'll have to meet her someplace."

"Oh, sure. I just ask Debbie to meet me and she's going to do it, particularly when I tell her I want to talk about the affair you think she's having."

Skip gave him a stricken look.

"Yeah, well, see? It's not going to be easy, kid."

"You could say you wanted to talk about Jenna," Skip said as they got back into the car.

"No, I couldn't."

"Yes, you could. You're crazy about her. Everybody knows it."

Everybody knows it, he thought. *Except Jenna.* For once he didn't waste his time trying to deny it. Okay. So he was crazy about her.

"I'll...stop by the school tomorrow. I'll talk to Debbie there. Pull into that alley."

"Now where are we going?"

"We're looking for Roy Lee, remember? You look for a rat where he lives. Hold that," he said, handing Skip his Polish sausage. "And don't eat the damn thing while I'm gone."

Garth walked the length of the alley, stepping over sleeping men, staring into old faces, into young faces with old eyes. He didn't see Roy Lee. He moved on toward a pile of cardboard boxes, knowing Roy Lee used to sleep in one of the bigger ones.

"Roy Lee!" he yelled because he didn't want to stick his head into some wino's sanctorum if he could help it. "Roy Lee!"

"Roy Lee ain't here, man," a voice said crabbily.

"Where is he?"

"How the hell do I know? He ain't here. That's all you need to know, sucker."

"Which box is his?" Garth asked the voice coming from a refrigerator box to his right. The voice didn't answer, and Garth kicked the side of the box hard.

"Hey, man, are you crazy?"

"Which one is his!" Garth yelled.

"That one!"

"Which one!"

"Kenmore!"

Garth knelt down to shine his mag light into the box with the Kenmore logo, making certain first that no one was behind him. The pavement was wet with God only knew what, and the box stank of unwashed human, as if it had just been vacated. There was nothing inside but a rolled-up coat. He pulled it out. It was a woman's coat—black. He held it up so he could see, running his hands into the pockets. He found a piece of paper. A memo from Saint Xavier's.

"Let's go!" he said to Skip.

"What is that?" Skip asked, dodging as Garth threw the coat into the back.

"Jenna's coat."

"Don't tell me we've got a crazy who falls in love with women's coats?"

"No, we've got a crazy who sleeps on the street and needs all the insulation he can get." He didn't tell Skip what he was thinking. That for once Roy Lee *had* spent the money he'd given him on something besides booze, and that he'd taken Jenna's coat because he'd been living on the street too long to let a chance like that pass him by. An INSPECTED BY No. 2 label and the missing coat in a Kenmore refrigerator box in an alley full of winos wouldn't stand up in court, but it was enough for him. Roy Lee had worked Jenna over, but the question was *why?* Roy Lee had no animosity toward anyone. Unless it was bought and paid for. "Where's my sausage?" he asked abruptly.

"Oh—I, ah, gave it away."

"You gave it *away*?" Garth said incredulously.

"Well, this old guy was staring in through the window. He was hungry...."

"What the devil do you think *I* am?"

"I told you the guy was hungry!"

"Yeah? Why didn't you give him *yours*? Jeez! A man could starve to death with you for a partner!"

They kept looking, checking the bars, all the places Roy Lee hung out, Garth taking one side of the street and Skip taking the other. He wasn't there. He wasn't anywhere, and no one would admit to having seen him. Just before sundown, it began to rain.

"Now what?" Skip said tiredly.

"We call it quits."

"Why is it I don't believe you?"

"No, I mean it. We've looked everywhere I know to look. Go home to Debbie."

"Good idea—if she's there. What are you going to do?"

"I may look some more."

"If you're still looking, so am I."

"Or I may go see Jenna."

Skip grinned in the dark interior of the car. "Yes, sir. Old Garth has bitten the dust on this one, hasn't he?"

It was late when the telephone rang. Jenna had been crying for a long time, and she wanted desperately to let it keep ringing. But it would cause more problems than she already had if once again she couldn't be accounted for. The last thing she needed was to have Hugh or Mamie come over because she hadn't answered the phone.

She wiped her eyes and picked up the receiver. "Hello?"

For a moment all she could hear was traffic and some kind of steady background noise—the rain, she supposed. She didn't hang up. She knew it wasn't a crank call or a wrong number. She knew Garth was there, and she waited.

"I want to see you," he finally said, and her knees went weak.

She marveled at her loss of resolve. She didn't spar with him; she didn't pretend to be coy. There was no token "It's late" or "You said we wouldn't." He was the source of her unhappiness, and he was the only one who could comfort her. She didn't have to be persuaded. She had only one thing to say, and she said it.

"Hurry."

He closed his eyes at the need he heard in her voice. "Baby," he whispered into the receiver. He could feel it—a loneliness and a longing that matched his own. He didn't say goodbye; he didn't say anything. He stepped out into the rain. And he hurried.

She washed her face in cold water and waited for him, answering the door ahead of his knock, not knowing what she would do until she saw him face-to-face.

He looked so tired—and so good. He was a beautiful man to her. She stared into his eyes; she tried to find her anger and couldn't. She didn't care that he was rain soaked; she stepped into his arms, her body warm and soft against his.

How pretty you are, he thought. Her hair was hanging free to her shoulders. She was barefoot, and she was wearing what looked like a man's white cotton nightshirt. He buried his face in her neck and hair. She smelled so good! Sweet, sweet woman smell.

"You make me crazy," he whispered against her ear. "You make me crazy."

"Good," she answered simply. Her arms slid around his neck, and her mouth found his.

So good, he thought. Her kisses, the feel of her body pressing against his, drove him immediately to the brink. It was as if they'd never made love before. He reached down to find the edge of her nightshirt, sliding his hand up under it.

Soft, soft skin. Warm, dewy places that were already ready for him. He was so hungry for her. Nobody did it for him the way she did.

Nobody.

He leaned back and lifted her up off the floor; she locked her legs around his hips. He carried her through the apartment, looking for the bedroom door.

He found it easily because she'd left the light on. Her bed was full of pillows, pillows and pink-and-purple flowered sheets. He had the vague concern that this was the bed she'd shared with Patrick, but then he realized that it was narrow. This was *her* bed, a replacement, not the one she'd had with Patrick, and if she brought a man into this one—if she brought *him* into it—it was because she wanted him there.

He set her down among the pillows and the flowers, trying to get out of his jacket, his clothes, and still touch her. He didn't want to break contact, not for a second. She helped him. On her knees at the edge of the bed, she undid buttons, unsnapped snaps. He kept one hand on her, stroking her unbruised cheek, her soft breasts through the opening in her nightshirt.

He held her close for a moment before he sat down with her, hugging her to him. Once again Jenna could sense that he didn't want to hurt her—physically, at least. She was still on her knees on the edge of the bed, and he kissed her forehead, stroked her hair. She didn't want him to feel her desperation, but she couldn't keep from clinging to him.

She should have told him immediately about Mary's name being in the notebook, but she didn't. Even knowing that its being there had ended everything between them, she didn't. She would tell him about the notebook—but not now. Not now. She wanted this one last time. She would tell him goodbye in a way she hadn't been able to say goodbye to Patrick.

He was aroused, and so was she. She could feel him, hot and hard against her belly.

He could feel her trembling, and he leaned back to look into her eyes. "What is it?"

She shook her head, giving him a small smile to fool him, and she kissed him tenderly, deeply, to fool him more.

"Love me, Garth," she murmured, the words flowing from her mouth into his. She moved backward to make room for him, holding up the covers in invitation. He slid into bed beside her, and she held her arms out to him.

He lifted her up and took her astride his thighs, so that he could see her face, touch her breasts. She surprised him. God, she surprised him. When they'd first met, he'd thought her buttoned-up and shy. She *was* shy, and that made this all the sweeter. He caught the edge of her night-shirt and pulled it off over her head, giving it a sling and not caring where it went. He put his arms around her and pressed his face against her breasts. She smelled so good, felt so good. He could get lost here. He wanted to get lost here.

She gave a soft moan when he took a tightly budded nipple into his mouth. When he gently suckled her, her head arched back.

Her hands slid into his hair.

"Garth," she whispered. "Garth—"

And, God, he loved that, too, hearing her say his name.

She brought his mouth to hers, and for a moment, he did his best to stay passive. He liked for her to kiss him; he liked the taste of her warm mouth. He liked the feel of her warm hands stroking his chest, her warm, *bold* hands that now moved downward. He closed his eyes. She kissed his eyelids. And all the while her hands—her clever hands—stroked and encircled and caressed.

"Yes," he hissed in her ear. "Like that—oh, baby— Jenna!"

He was awash in pleasure. His hips thrust upward. "Wait—" he whispered urgently as her ministrations continued.

But she didn't want to wait, and she told him so. He wrapped his arms around her and thrust himself into her. He tried to hold back as the exquisite pleasure she'd begun intensified. It was torture not to move. She was so hot and tight; he trembled with the effort to make the pleasure last while everything in him screamed for release.

In a moment, he made the first tentative thrust. It was so good! He needed this—no, he needed *her*. "Jenna."

She gave herself up to pure sensation, to his loving intrusion into her body. She wanted him inside her. He filled that great emptiness she'd had since Patrick died. He filled it, but he was not a substitute for Patrick. He was himself. The emptiness she would have after he'd gone, no one else would be able to fill. She wanted to cry again, but suddenly there was nothing but the sweet oblivion of his body joining with hers. He made her feel so good! The pleasure swirled around her, took her away from everything but him, until at last it peaked and shattered, and she tumbled earthward, her face covered in her own tears.

"Don't cry," he said after a long time of listening to her try to hide it.

"Can't help it," she answered, trying to sound reasonable and in control. But her voice was husky and strange-sounding even to herself.

"What's the matter?" he insisted, trying to make her look at him.

She sighed. "Just . . . one of those things, I guess."

She lay quietly in his arms, and her silence made him afraid. She wasn't telling him the truth.

"You know I . . . care about you," he offered.

"Don't!" she said sharply. She turned on her side to look at him, wiping quickly at her eyes with her fingertips as if by doing so she could minimize the emotion she was feeling. "I told you before. I don't want any promises in the dark."

"What do you want?"

"This is enough," she said, but she avoided his eyes.

"Great sex, you mean? Making the earth move?"

She forced herself to look at him. "We don't know each other well enough for anything else." It was both the truth and a lie. Chronologically, she hadn't known him long, but he had been giving her small pieces of himself ever since they'd met. She knew him well enough to admire the person she thought he was and to care about him; she knew him well enough to care a great deal.

"What if I want more?" he asked.

"Do you?" she countered.

He didn't answer.

"I think we'd better end this conversation while we still feel kindly toward each other," she said. She moved to get up, but he wouldn't let her.

"I'll tell you what I don't want. This is a small bed. I don't want three of us in it."

"Or four?" she asked.

"Mary is dead."

"I have something for you," she said, moving to get up again. This time he let her. She picked her nightshirt up from the floor where he'd slung it and put it on.

"What is it?" he asked, but she was already going into the living room.

He heard her opening a drawer someplace, and in a moment she came back again. She handed him a small book with a black plastic cover.

His lips were pursed to ask what it was when he realized that she'd given him Patrick's notebook. He looked up at her, but she was already going back into the other room. He stared after her for a moment, then down at the book.

Jenna stood in the dark by the bow window, looking out at the rainy street. Every now and then a car went by. She could see the raindrops in the headlights. She took a deep breath to gather up her courage, and she walked back to the bedroom.

Garth was sitting on the edge of the bed—fully dressed.

"I have to go," he said when he glanced up and saw her. He stood. "You read this?" he asked, sticking the note-book into his shirt pocket.

"Yes. I read it. But I don't know what it means."

He didn't offer to enlighten her.

"Mary—and Patrick. That's what this has all been about, hasn't it?" she said, moving out of his way as he bent to pick up the change and keys that had fallen out of his pockets in his haste to make love to her.

"I don't know what you mean."

"I mean, Garth, there was some connection between the two of them. And you've been using me to try to find out what it is."

He came and stood closer, and he reached out to touch her, but he didn't at the last moment, letting his hand fall to his side. "Not exactly," he said, and she gave a short laugh.

"Not exactly? For a cop, you are the worst liar in the world, Garth."

"Jenna—"

"Take the notebook. Take it, and your jacket, and your half-truths and go. Or is there something else I can do for you? I've already told you I never heard Patrick or Hugh mention Tony Zaccato. I'll tell you now that I never heard either of them mention Mary, either."

"Jenna, it's not what you think—"

"It doesn't matter what I think. I certainly can't pass any judgments. I'm the person who figured out this afternoon that there was some kind of rhyme and reason to your sud-den interest in the widow Gallagher and your unsubtle questions. I figured it out, and I went to bed with you just now anyway. You see, I always thought you were doing a number on me, but I wanted you, so I let you do it. That doesn't say much for my integrity or my good sense, does it?

But tell me. At Skip's party, if I'd said no, Patrick and I weren't getting along before he was killed, what would your next question have been? Would you have asked me right then and there if he was having an affair with Mary Zaccato? The truth is, *I don't know*."

"I didn't think he was involved with Mary!"

"The thing I can't understand is, what does it matter? They're both dead. What does it matter?"

"I can't explain it to you. You have to trust me."

She smiled; a tear ran down her cheek anyway. "Now, that's the strange thing, Garth. I do trust you. Or I did. Even thinking you had to be up to something, I believed everything you told me. I guess you're a good liar after all." She gave a tremulous sigh. "Ah, well. Live and learn."

"Jenna, don't—"

"Don't? You needn't worry about this, Garth. I'm all right. If I can get over Patrick's dying, I can certainly get over you."

"Jenna, I can't explain this to you," he said again. "It's too complicated. I don't know all the answers myself."

"Then we'll just have to let it go, won't we?"

"We have to talk about this—"

"No! Please, please! Just go, and we'll call it even."

He stood staring at her; it was all he could do not to try to take her in his arms. But he saw in her eyes that he had been relegated to another place, to that place where she put pesky television cameramen, and demanding Gallagher in-laws, and anybody else who wanted to take a piece of her for their own gain.

"Okay," he said finally. There was nothing he could say to her. Nothing.

Chapter Twelve

He hadn't slept. He'd looked for Roy Lee all night. And all morning he had vacillated between being hurt and being angry. He didn't know what to do, and indecisiveness was an entirely new emotion to him. Should he call her? Try to see her, talk to her?

Damn it all, Jenna!

She was a strong person; he knew that. Last night he'd looked into her eyes and listened to what she said, and he'd had no doubt whatsoever that she meant every word of it.

"Just go, and we'll call it even."

Well, he couldn't just go. She had tried to make it sound so simple. He'd used her, she'd used him, and that was supposed to be the end of it. It wasn't the end of anything. The idea that he couldn't see her, that she'd been so loving and then so cold, was a relentless ache in him he couldn't do anything about. He kept remembering the way she'd made love to him. Why had she done *that* if everything was over?

He couldn't think about anything else, but how the hell was he going to explain anything to her? He didn't know himself. All he had was bits and pieces and one of those gut feelings a cop got and could never explain to anybody—except another cop. All he'd known was that Hugh Gallagher hadn't wanted him investigating Patrick's death. But, my God, how had Patrick known Mary? It was incredible to him that this mess might somehow have cost him *both* women he'd loved.

But what to do about it? He'd never been a man who could just wait. He had to *do* something, talk to her. God, he wanted to talk to her.

And I can't, damn it! I can't!

He worked at his desk when he should have been out looking for Roy Lee again, fiddling with the endless paperwork that always needed doing. But he didn't register any of it. His mind filled with idea after idea for making Jenna understand—none of them worth a damn. His temper grew shorter and shorter, and even the news that Skip's father had come through and he and Skip would take over Jenna's case from Rosie Madden did nothing to improve it. Once again he marveled at the inner workings of the police department. After all his years of being a cop, it was still incredible to him that somebody's squash partner could influence a detective's assignment. Not that he didn't welcome it this time. He intended to take care of Jenna, whether she wanted him to or not, and if he couldn't be with her, the least he could do was find out for certain who had hurt her and why.

"Just how involved are you with Jenna Gallagher?" the lieutenant asked before he made the assignment change.

He looked the lieutenant in the eyes and told him the current truth. "I'm not."

"That's not what Hugh says."

"Hugh is full of—"

"Be that as it may," the lieutenant interrupted. "I'm not having you harass Patrick Gallagher's widow—for what reason, I don't even want to think about. What I want is for you to tell me what the hell's going on. Now, you may think I don't see your heavy hand in all this, and if you do, you're not as good a cop as I thought. Before I do or don't do what I'm being leaned on to do, I want you to fill me in on why you're using your partner's contacts to get this case."

He didn't say anything.

"Hugh suggests that of late his sister-in-law has been the victim of your unwelcome attentions. He suggests that you won't take no for an answer. He further suggests that your having this case will compound and aggravate the misery you have already caused her by your uncouth behavior."

"Have you had any complaints from Mrs. Gallagher?"

"No. And that's why we're having this little tête-à-tête instead of me busting your butt. The only thing I've had is a letter from a Sister Mary John at Saint Xavier's telling me how kind and helpful a Detective Garth was to the children there. Jenna Gallagher also signed it. As you are the only Garth we've got, I put it in your file—it's kind of lonely in there, considering some of the past complaints that have come in, but I like to be fair. Now," he continued, his voice unnaturally controlled and quiet, "this is where you tell me why you're rattling cages to get this case. And, I might add, this is your last chance to do it."

Garth gave a short exhalation of breath. He'd learned a long time ago that sometimes you had to give to get—and this was one of those times.

"I don't think Jenna—Mrs. Gallagher—was mugged. I think it was more."

The lieutenant's eyes narrowed. "Like what?"

"Maybe the company she was keeping—me. The day I was at the school I took her to the Humoresque for dinner. Tony Zaccato saw us there. He even made a point of talking to her."

"You're going to all this trouble because of that old grudge you've got with Zaccato?" the lieutenant said, shaking his head.

"Yes."

"The Job is no place for personal grudges!"

"No," he agreed, but they both knew that that was neither here nor there.

"You got any hard evidence?"

"No. A gut feeling. That's all. I think I know who did it. He's from my old neighborhood, and he owes me. If I can put enough heat on him, I think he'll drop a dime on Zaccato."

The lieutenant looked at him over the top of his glasses. "Okay. You got until something else more important comes up—and *I* decide what that is. Now get out of here. Garth!" he said sharply when Garth reached for the door. "I hope you and Carver get the sonofabitch, but, personally, I think he's vacationing in sunny Colombia."

"He's here," Garth said. "He wouldn't give the nod to get to Jenna and not be around to see what I'm going to do about it."

"Is this as good as it gets?" Skip asked. "Or can I look forward to some small improvement in your current disposition? Anything, anything at all, Garth, no matter how minute, no matter how seemingly insignificant, would be ever so appreciated."

Garth glanced at him but didn't feel the remark was worth a comment—tossing him out the window, but not a comment.

"You're supposed to talk to Debbie today," Skip persisted. "Remember? The mood you're in, I'll end up divorced."

The fact of the matter was that he hadn't remembered. He had other things on his mind. No, he had *one* other thing: Jenna.

"So what's wrong with you?" Skip asked.

"Nothing," Garth said.

"Oh, yeah, everybody in the whole station house can see that it's nothing. Didn't you see Jenna last night?"

"I saw her—and I don't want to talk about it."

Unfortunately the only way he could manage that was to leave—in which case, he might as well go talk to Debbie. And he didn't tell Skip he was going; the kid was strung out enough already.

He arrived at Saint Xavier's shortly after the end of the school day. As before, Sister Mary John flagged him down when he passed her door. He liked Sister Mary John—even before he knew she'd written a complimentary letter—and, for some reason, she seemed not in the least surprised to see him. The reason for that became apparent when he came out of Sister Mary John's office and walked into Jenna. The stricken look she gave him made his heart sink. He had kept trying to tell himself that maybe things with Jenna weren't as bad as he thought, but they were. He had only to look into her eyes to know that.

"I didn't know you would be here," he said immediately, because she looked so upset. She was tired, and her face was still bruised, and he had never wanted to put his arms around anybody so bad in his life. But he knew from experience that she wasn't above taking a swing at him if she thought she needed to. It was one thing he'd admired about her—her feistiness. One of many, many things, all of which came to mind when he looked at her.

"What are you doing here, Garth?" She had a stack of papers in her arms, newly mimeographed papers; he could smell the familiar, pungent smell of the mimeograph fluid. She held them tightly in front of her, as if they were some kind of barrier that would keep him at bay.

He decided to tell the truth. "I'm here to save Skip and Debbie's marriage. Well, it's the truth!" he said when she frowned.

"That's what worries me," she assured him. "I didn't know there was anything wrong with Skip and Debbie's marriage."

"He thinks there is. He's been driving me crazy. He thinks she's having an affair."

"Is he crazy or are you?" she said incredulously.

"Yes," he said, and he thought for a moment she was going to smile.

But she was an old hand at not letting him amuse her, and she squelched it immediately. She started walking down the hall, and he went along with her.

"I want **us** to talk," he said, his voice echoing in the deserted hall.

"There is nothing to talk about."

"Jenna!" he said in exasperation, but she stopped walking and turned to him.

"I understand how you must have felt. You loved Mary. You wanted to know the truth. I would have felt the same way. I do feel the same way. It's just that I would have done it differently." With that she walked off, and he would have followed if Hernando hadn't appeared.

"Garth! You came back, man!"

"Yeah, Hernando. I came back," he said, watching Jenna until she went into the classroom. He looked down at Hernando. Hernando was frowning now, his head cocked to one side.

"You going to give me five?" Garth asked, holding out his hand, but he got no response.

"Did you hurt Miss Jenna?" Hernando asked, watching Garth closely, apparently for some sign that he might lie.

"No. I didn't hurt Miss Jenna," Garth said, because he knew that Hernando meant her black eye.

"You looking for the sucker that did?"

"I'm looking."

"You ain't going to find him."

"I don't know, sometimes I get lucky. Hey, that is some coat. Turn around here and let me see."

"The *real* kind of leather," Hernando said proudly.

"The real kind? Yeah, it looks like the real kind. And a Screaming Eagles patch. You are one tough dude."

"I know it," Hernando assured him. "Did you get your pictures we drawed? Did you get *my* picture?"

"Yeah, I got them. I've got them on the wall in my apartment."

"*All* of them?"

"All," Garth said.

"Mallory can't draw, man," Hernando pointed out.

"I put her picture up anyway."

"You crazy, man—you don't supposed to put up *ugly* pictures in your apartment."

"It's the thought that counts, Hernando," Garth said, wondering if someone had told him that about his own pictures. "Beauty is in the eyes of the beholder. Give me five."

"You crazy, man," Hernando said again, but he slapped Garth's hand and ran down the hallway toward the outside doors.

Garth walked on toward the classroom Jenna had gone into, catching bits of conversation as he neared the open door.

"—I'll make the visit," Jenna said.

Debbie responded, but he couldn't hear the words.

"No, Garth's here. He wants to talk to you," Jenna said.

"Has something happened to Skip?" Debbie said, alarm clearly evident in her voice.

"No," Jenna said quickly. "I'll make the visit. You stay and—"

Their voices dropped again, and he couldn't understand any more. When he reached the doorway, Jenna came out of it, wearing a coat—a new or borrowed coat, he supposed. She looked into his eyes, but she didn't say anything. He stepped aside to let her pass.

"Jenna!" Debbie said, running out into the hallway and all but bumping into him.

"Easy!" Garth said, catching her briefly by the elbows to keep her steady. "Debbie, I need to talk to—" He stopped because she wasn't listening to him. She was staring distractedly after Jenna. "Debbie," he said again.

She looked at him.

"I need to talk to you."

"I can't talk now, Garth. I have to—" She was wringing her hands, and she didn't tell him what was so pressing.

"Debbie, Skip sent me to talk to you."

"Skip?" she asked, her eyes darting from him to the far end of the hallway. And she kept trying to edge away from him. Her hands were shaking, and he thought she was about to cry.

"Honey, what is the matter with you?" he asked, deciding that Skip had cause for concern after all. "Are you all right?"

"No," she said, her face crumpling. "I'm not all right, Garth."

"Debbie—"

"You have to go get Jenna. Don't let her go there—I should have *said* something, but I'm afraid they'll hurt Skip. Garth, stop Jenna—she might see them!"

"Who? Honey, I don't know what you're talking about—"

"They'd know her. Everybody knows her. Garth, do something!" Debbie was pushing her way back into the classroom. She ran to the desk and picked up a small index card. "Here! Take this!" she cried, shoving it into his hands.

Becca Sullivan he read on the card, and then the address. The address was the same as the one in Patrick's notebook.

Chapter Thirteen

He could see Jenna ahead of him, walking briskly down the sidewalk, piquing the interest of the unoccupied males who loitered on the steps and in the doorways along the way. He had no idea what he'd say when he caught up with her but, nevertheless, he would do what Debbie asked and deter her visit to Becca Sullivan. He was reasonably content to find out *why* he was doing it later. Even if he didn't know what the hell Debbie was so upset about, he didn't consider the action entirely inappropriate. He had specifically told Jenna not to go anywhere alone, yet she'd parked her car three blocks away—in this neighborhood—and elected to walk rather than circle for a closer parking space. He himself didn't waste the time looking; he simply double-parked, leaving the vehicle with its dubious talisman on the dashboard for protection—a NYPD Official Business plate.

The day was cloudy and cold, and a panhandler waylaid him at the end of the first block. By the time he disengaged his arm from the man's persistent grasp, Jenna was well into the third block. He ran to catch up, but she went into the building before he got to her. As he entered the ground floor, it occurred to him that Jenna wasn't likely to let him dissuade her from doing whatever it was she was doing—in which case, he'd just have to go along. She wasn't apt to like that, either, but he considered his company the lesser of the two offenses.

He took the stairs two at a time, catching up with her on the second landing. She turned sharply around at his boisterous approach, clearly frightened for a moment, and he damned the impulsiveness that had let him forget her recent experience with Roy Lee.

"Garth, what are you doing here?" she said. She looked relieved, regardless of the exasperation he heard in her voice.

"I'm going with you."

She gave a small sigh. "I thought you were busy saving marriages."

"Well, Mrs. Gallagher, as far as I can tell, it's become a matter of shifting priorities. I told you not to go anywhere by yourself. You didn't listen to me. So here I am. What are we doing here—aside from the fact that this is the same address that was in Patrick's notebook?"

She stared at him, her lips pressed into a tight line. He tried not to look at them, tried not to think how much he wanted to hold her and kiss her until her mouth became soft and responsive.

"You did make the connection?" he said, looking into her eyes.

"Patrick's notebook has nothing to do with this—and, yes, I made the connection. I'm here to see Becca Sullivan's mother. Becca hasn't been coming to school, and Sister Mary John wants to know why."

"Couldn't she telephone?"

"She tried. The number has been disconnected—why am I explaining this to you?"

He ignored the question.

"You know, of course, that there was a reason for Patrick to have written this address down. And Debbie's all to pieces over this little jaunt of yours."

"Debbie's *always* all to pieces of late."

"Right—hence my other quest. But you take precedence."

She looked into his eyes, then looked away. "I didn't come here because of some whim I had about Patrick, Garth. Sister is anxious to know about Becca. Debbie was supposed to come, but then you arrived to save her marriage or whatever it is you think you're doing—"

"Right," he said again. "So here you are, in spite of what I told you. How many times do you have to be roughed up to get the message?"

"Do you mean literally or figuratively?"

"Touché, Mrs. Gallagher. Pardon me while I bleed."

They stared into each other's eyes.

"Nobody followed me, Garth."

"I did."

"Please!" she said, holding up both hands. "Can we stop this? I have to see about Becca."

"Lead the way," he answered.

"You don't have to go with me!"

"I know that. But I'm going. Now we can stand here and argue, or we can get on with it." He held out his hand for her to go first.

She went, climbing the stairs quickly.

"Your face is looking better," he called after her, but she didn't respond.

"New coat?" he asked on the third landing.

She gave him a hard look.

"It's very nice. Not as nice as the other one, but nice."

"Thank you," she said, but she certainly didn't mean it.

"You're welcome," he said, knowing it would annoy her even more. But he'd rather have her angry than the way she was last night. "So which one of the Terrible Twenty was Becca? I can't place her."

"She wasn't there. She had to go home early—her coat was flushed."

He suddenly remembered meeting Debbie and Becca at the outside door. Becca had been carrying her coat in a plastic bag, and Debbie had stayed gone all day. She'd been here in this building, and she'd been very worried about Jenna's coming back.

"Garth," Jenna said when they reached the fifth floor. "I don't want you to—"

"Jenna, don't start up with me. We've covered this. Let's find the apartment. You look on that side."

She hesitated, but he walked off without her, reading apartment numbers. She followed, and she sensed that the people on the other sides of the doors they passed were watching through their peepholes to see where she and Garth would stop.

"There is no reason for you to be here!" she suddenly burst out.

"Yeah, well, that's a matter of opinion—it's down that way."

He took her arm, walking her in the direction he'd pointed, but after a few steps Jenna balked, digging in her heels so that he would stop.

"Garth," she said, turning to face him. She held on to both his arms, her eyes searching his for understanding. "You're going to have to leave me alone. Do you understand? I can't . . ." She abruptly looked down, and he could feel her struggling for emotional control. She looked up at him. "I can't make it if you don't."

"I'd do anything for you," he said. "Anything. But not this, not now." He reached up to lightly touch her cheek, and she turned away. He tried to keep her close, but she pulled free of him. She couldn't explain it to him; he didn't understand at all. She cared about him; she couldn't be near him and have him touch her in that gentle way he always seemed to use with her.

"Hey!" someone—a man—yelled. He was standing at the end of the hallway, and from behind the nearest door a child suddenly began to cry.

"What do you think you're doing?" the man demanded.

Jenna thought he meant the argument she and Garth were having, but he didn't mean that at all. Their argument was the least of this man's concerns. "Get out of the hall! Now!" he yelled. "How many times do we have to tell you people!"

The child behind the door cried louder. She expected Garth to do something—and he did. He was going to leave and take her with him.

"Come on," he said, taking her firmly by the arm. "Now."

"I have to see Becca's mother," Jenna insisted. The Sullivan apartment was just in front of her, and she stepped up to the door, intending to knock. The child's crying was coming from in there, and the door opened abruptly before she could knock on it.

"Mrs. Gallagher, come in here!" Becca's mother whispered urgently. "Get out of the hall!"

She went in—with Garth right behind her. Becca sat on the couch sobbing, clinging to her mother frantically when the woman took her into her arms.

"What's going on?" Garth said, but Becca's crying only escalated.

"You were a big help," Jenna whispered to him.

"You get the civilians out of the way first, and then you find out what's going on. *Then* you help. Mrs. Sullivan, what's happening?"

Becca's mother looked up at him. "Who are you?"

"Detective Garth, NYPD."

"Oh, God! Why did you bring him here?" she cried, looking at Jenna and rocking Becca back and forth.

"Mrs. Sullivan," Jenna said, "I didn't bring him. I just ran into him on the stairs. Detective Garth was concerned about my being out alone. I was mugged a few days ago." She stopped, glancing at Garth. The woman was too distraught to listen.

"Mrs. Sullivan," Jenna said, beginning again. She waited until the woman looked up. "Sister Mary John has been worried because Becca hasn't been in school for a while. I just came to see if she was all right. We weren't able to telephone you."

"How could she go to school with *that* going on!" she said, flinging one hand toward the door. "What are you going to do?" she asked Garth. "I haven't said anything. None of us has said anything!"

"Mrs. Sullivan," he said quietly. "I'm going to ask you again. What's going on?"

"If you don't know, *I'm* not going to be the one to tell you."

Garth stared at her, then moved to the door.

"What are you doing!" she cried.

"Be quiet!" he said sharply. He cracked open the door enough to see down the narrow hall. The "hall monitor" was still there, and some nondescript people were coming up the stairs. These people, however, seemed not to be trespassing. He watched them—three men and a woman—disappear into the next apartment, stay a few minutes and then leave one at a time. And they left happy.

He looked back at Mrs. Sullivan. Jenna was holding Becca now. "What are they selling?" he asked. "I'll find out," he said when she remained silent. "Sooner or later. The guy in the hall—he's seen me come in here. He's going to think you told me anyway."

Her eyes shifted to Becca before she answered. "You remember Alice's Restaurant?" she said obscurely, reaching out to touch Becca's hair. She gave a wavering sigh. "Crack mostly."

He nodded, understanding that her concern now was for her child. "Are you willing to relocate for a while—maybe let us use your apartment?"

She looked hesitant, worried, and he didn't blame her. She was in a dangerous situation, and they both knew it.

"Jenna, can you get them shelter with the Family Crisis people?" he asked.

"Either there or through Saint Xavier's," she said, letting Becca go back to her mother. She stood up and came to stand beside him. "What are you going to do?"

He gave a heavy sigh. "Clear out the civilians. Mrs. Sullivan, how long will this go on? How long are you supposed to stay out of the hall?"

"It goes on as long as it takes them to get rid of whatever they've got," she said. "Sometimes into the middle of the night."

"We aren't going to wait that long. Is there another way out?"

"Just the fire escape."

"Get your clothes together. Go on," he said when she didn't move. "Pack whatever you and your little girl will need for a few nights. We all have to do our part, Mrs. Sullivan," he added. "Inconvenience isn't such a big price, is it?"

"We're talking about more than inconvenience here, and you know it!" she answered.

"Yes. I know it. But I don't know of any other way to deal with it. They're not going to just disappear. How long has it been going on already? A year? Two? I'll do my best to help you, but I need your cooperation."

"That's what you think now," she said doubtfully. "You'll help us?"

"I give you my word."

"Excuse me if that doesn't exactly thrill me, cop."

"Look! What choice do you have?"

She stared at him. "Yeah, right," she said. She got up from the couch, taking Becca with her into the next room.

"Garth—" Jenna began.

"Yeah, yeah, I know. You *hate* going up and down fire escapes."

For a moment, he thought she was going to smile. "I'm not crazy about it," she admitted, her brief flash of amusement taken away by the seriousness of the situation. "What are you going to do?"

"Whatever it takes," he said.

When she was about to object to his vagueness, he held up his hand.

"These people shouldn't have to be living like this. Nobody should have to live like this."

He went back to watch through the crack in the door. Whoever was involved in this operation was certainly confident about it. The man in the hall hadn't been the least bit concerned about who he and Jenna might be, certainly not that they might have been working narcotics. It only mattered that he didn't recognize them as customers.

"Do you think Patrick knew about whatever is going on here?"

"I don't know, Jenna," he said, but he did know. He believed that Patrick had written down the address of this apartment building for a reason, just as he believed that Debbie had been caught here in the same way he and Jenna had. It must be that that had her so rattled.

But if Patrick had known what was going on here, why hadn't he done something about it? Or Debbie, either, for that matter? Mrs. Sullivan and the rest of the tenants had apparently been living like prisoners in their own homes, staying out of the way of the drug transactions because the man in the hall ordered it.

But Garth's concern was that Mary's name had been written down on the same page as the address. And if Patrick knew about Mary, then it logically followed that he must have known about her brother Tony and that Tony must be in this somewhere.

"Mrs. Sullivan," he said when she came back into the room. "Why haven't you called the police?"

She gave a short laugh and shook her head. "Why haven't I called the police? These people—these animals who have to sell their drugs here—they *are* the police."

Becca, at least, enjoyed the jaunt down a rickety fire escape in a high wind. Some part of Jenna's mind presented the fact that she'd never even been on a fire escape before she met Garth, and she was now embarking on her third trip. This fire escape, however, didn't go all the way to the ground, and it took some determined maneuvering on Garth's part to get the last segment of ladder down. He managed, swearing under his breath in a way Jenna found all too endearing. He carried Becca down, and Jenna stood on the sidewalk, guarding Becca's hastily packed Barbie overnight case and holding her hand while he went back up to help her mother and get the other suitcase.

The street was more or less deserted. A few men in a nearby doorway watched with jaded interest. Everything around her was cold and bleak, but not as bleak as she felt. She tried not to think about Patrick and Mary Zaccato, or why he might have come here.

"Using the fire escape is something you do only in an emergency, Becca," she said as the teacher in her reasserted itself. "Fire escapes aren't to play on or anything like that."

"Where is it, Miss Jenna?" Becca asked, sniffing heavily, her nose red and running from the cold.

"The emergency? Not down here where we are."

Becca looked up at her. She had the hiccups from crying so long. "Is my mommy scared?"

"Not so much now," Jenna promised her, hoping it was the truth. But what did she know about it? Where she had come from, people didn't have to live in a self-imposed prison in their homes in order to survive.

"I was scared. And I cried and cried," Becca said, her voice quavering.

"I know. But Detective Garth is going to help, and we're going to find another place for you and your mother to stay for a while."

"Not here?"

"No, not here."

"Okay," Becca said.

Jenna watched as Garth came the rest of the way down the fire escape ladder. *The Job,* she thought. He'd become even more intense and purposeful than he usually was; he reminded her of the night they'd met at Skip's party. He was completely in his element, and she and the Sullivans were impediments to his ultimate goal. He wanted to do what he got paid to do, and he wanted the civilians out of the way so he could do it.

She fell in step with Mrs. Sullivan and walked down the street ahead of him, still holding Becca's hand. In a moment, he was at her side, but he didn't say anything. She glanced at him. His face was grim.

She understood his quandary. Becca's mother had said the men involved were police. It was likely the truth. But was it a legitimate undercover operation? Or were they dirty? The problem would come for Garth if the latter were the case. She knew that the best compliment a cop could get from his peers—from his superiors, too, for that matter—was that he was a "stand-up kind of guy," a guy who would do anything—look the other way, perjure himself in court, anything—to preserve the honor of the brotherhood. What kind of choice was that for a man like Garth who put personal, individual honor first?

She understood the situation perfectly; she had been a policeman's wife. But because she'd been a policeman's wife, she knew that it would likely never occur to Garth that she, someone outside The Job, could be capable of such empathy. And that was yet another thing that made their being together so impossible. She didn't want to live on the outside of a man's life again; she wanted to be part of it. She wanted to matter enough to share the good times *and* the bad.

She glanced at him again, and this time he caught her at it.

Ah, Garth, she thought. It wasn't the choice that troubled him. She thought he'd already made it. It was the consequences of his choice that would bring him pain.

He helped get Mrs. Sullivan and Becca and their suitcases into her car, but when she was about to open the door and get in herself, he stopped her.

"What?" she asked, because he *still* wasn't saying anything. He was looking into her eyes, and he reached up to take a strand of hair the wind had blown across her face and tucked it behind her ear.

"I love you," he said simply and without prelude. "You understand? I didn't want to, but there you are. I can't help it. I love you a lot, and regardless of what you think of me, I want you to know that."

She wanted to say something, but she couldn't. Her heart soared, only to have the reality of their situation bring it down again. First Garth had seen her as a means to an end, and now he claimed to love her. And he'd actually said so—and not in the throes of passion, but on a windy New York street in broad daylight when he didn't have to say anything at all. Her mind couldn't get anywhere past that or past the fact that once again, fool that she was, she believed him.

His eyes, his beautiful eyes, searched hers, and then he suddenly smiled.

"Bowled you over with that one, didn't I, Mrs. Gallagher?" He opened the car door for her, but he didn't wait for her to get in. He turned and walked away, leaving her with her bewilderment.

Chapter Fourteen

Jenna waited. To hear something from Garth. To see something on the evening news or in the papers. There was nothing. Becca and her mother were safely tucked away in a shelter for women and children, and they, too, waited.

She tried to find out something from Debbie when they were together at Saint Xavier's, but that was entirely futile. Debbie didn't want to talk about going to Becca's apartment building, and, if anything, she was more addled than ever. She claimed no knowledge about whatever Skip was working on at the moment, and she knew even less about Garth. Her only concern seemed to be her supposed betrayal of Jenna's friendship—which she couldn't explain without dissolving into tears. Jenna tried pressing her, but it only upset them both. There was no sense in mentioning Garth's assertion that the Carver marriage was in difficulty. Debbie was so distracted it was likely she didn't even *know* she was having marital problems. Finally, Jenna just let it alone. The bottom line, anyway, was that she wanted to see Garth.

How like a cop, she kept thinking, to announce his love and then disappear. She spent every free minute of her time trying to decide what he had really meant. It couldn't have been a simple declaration of affection. Nothing was simple where he was concerned. But what ulterior motive he might have, she couldn't decide. And she didn't know which worried her more, that he might have an ulterior motive, or that he might not.

She missed him. She *missed* him. It was all too apparent to her that she needed him in her life, just as it was apparent to her how crazy she was for wanting him there. Everything was turned upside down; she had to pacify her mother and her mother-in-law, she had to find a new place to live, and she understood nothing about Patrick and Mary Zaccato. And all she could think about was Garth.

And she began to have nightmares about the man in the stairwell. She woke up repeatedly, thinking she heard noises, dreaming he was there in the apartment. Suddenly it all seemed to catch up with her. She didn't want to go out alone. She didn't want to go out at all. Once, she even dialed Garth's number, hanging up after the first ring.

Three days later, Rosie Madden telephoned her at Saint Xavier's, asking her to come to the station house to look at some pictures. She went, without seeing Garth anywhere in the place, and after nearly an hour of looking at what had begun to seem the same basic faces, she recognized two men. The man who had been with Tony Zaccato at the Humoresque, and the man who had assaulted her—Roy Lee Anderson.

"Well, this is a surprise," Rosie said, looking at the second mug shot Jenna indicated. "You're sure?"

"Yes, I'm sure. Why is it a surprise?"

Rosie looked up at her. "This dude is from Garth's old neighborhood. They kind of looked out for each other when they were kids. I always thought they still did. Well. Thanks for coming in. I'll let you know if we need you again.''

Thus dismissed, Jenna had no alternative but to leave— or to swallow her pride and ask the question she'd been trying not to ask ever since she'd arrived.

''Rosie, have you seen Garth?'' she said, letting the question out before she had the time to agonize about it anymore.

''This afternoon, you mean? Nah, I haven't seen him this—'' She broke off and looked at Jenna closely. ''Oh, you mean have I *seen* him? Yeah, yeah, I've seen him here and there. He and Skip have been running around here doing their Frick and Frack, Two Stooges impersonations. No, that's not what you mean, either, is it? The question is, why haven't *you* seen him, right? Well, Jenna, I don't know. All I know is there is something going down around here. Garth's been in there with the lieutenant with the blinds shut—nobody knows nothing, and nobody can find out nothing. But unless I miss my guess, our Garth is knee-deep in the middle of some heavy you-know-what. Now you know how a cop is when he's working—especially if he loves it like Garth does. He don't know he's on the planet. It's just him and The Job. You know what I mean?''

Jenna gave a small smile. ''I know what you mean.'' She turned to go.

''Hey,'' Rosie called after her. ''I'm going to hand you some advice, okay?''

''What is it?''

''When he does show up, be glad he did, okay? Don't give him a lot of grief about why he wasn't there sooner. Believe me, we all hate that. You were married to a cop. You know how it is.''

''Yes,'' she said quietly. ''I know how it is. I was just . . . worried about him.''

Rosie grinned. ''Jenna, if you don't worry about a man, he's not worth having, I always say.''

Again, Jenna turned to go.

"Hey," Rosie said. "I think he could use a friend about now. You wouldn't happen to know where he could get one, would you?"

"Maybe," Jenna answered.

"Good. I'll tell him. You know, that sucker is one lucky dude—having two fine women like us caring about what happens to him."

Jenna didn't know about that, but she left in a better mood than when she came, and she couldn't say precisely why, except that it was a relief to talk to someone who understood. Rosie Madden knew she cared about Garth; she didn't have to pretend otherwise for fear of offending or for fear of being thought a fool.

She headed for home, intending to have a hot bath and a quiet meal. She still had nights when she didn't sleep well, and she was so tired suddenly.

But her mind kept presenting her with worrisome information, things she'd rather not consider—like that the man she had identified as the one who had beaten her was a friend of Garth's. Coincidence or not? She didn't know, but she was almost certain that Garth did. Perhaps Hugh had been right. Perhaps her association with Garth had been the reason the man had hurt her.

She had her bath and her dinner, but, as tired as she was, she didn't want to go to sleep early and then lie awake half the night. She put on a sweat suit, and, just to keep occupied, she began to pack up the books and the bric-a-brac she had in the apartment, putting as much as she could into what few boxes she had. Another chore to add to the list. Finding boxes. Finding an apartment. Finding Garth.

She tried not to think about him as she methodically put away the pieces of her life with Patrick—books he'd given her, a photograph of the two of them the day he'd graduated from the police academy, a David Winter cottage he'd bought her for her birthday, an old celluloid Kewpie doll with pink and blue feathers he'd won at Coney Island when he was a little boy.

She worked on, not stopping for anything as long as she had space in the boxes, until someone knocked at the door. It was too late for visitors, and she reluctantly went to see who it might be, checking through the peephole and not failing to note how hope flared that it might be Garth.

But it was a woman, one she didn't recognize, standing on the other side of the door. There was a man with her, and perhaps one other person.

"Who is it?" Jenna called.

"Mrs. Gallagher," the woman called back. "I'm Jay Jay Coleman. I'd like very much to get your—"

The woman turned her head toward the man with her, and Jenna couldn't understand the rest of the sentence. She opened the door, leaving the chain on. The minute the door was cracked, a bright light hit her full in the face.

"Mrs. Gallagher!" Jay Jay Coleman said. "What do you think of the investigation and the arrests?"

"What?" Jenna said, shading her eyes. Someone stuck a microphone through the crack in the door.

"The investigation! Did you know about the alleged drug dealings?"

"I don't know what you're talking about," Jenna said, trying to close the door. The man in the hall was holding it.

"Our information is that you're personally involved with one of the detectives on the case. Did you know about the lengthy investigation? Don't you think it's ironic that the cop who was instrumental in solving your husband's murder case is also responsible for—"

Jenna managed to get the door shut.

"Please, Mrs. Gallagher!" Jay Jay Coleman yelled through the door. "We'd like to have your comment!"

The telephone was ringing, and Jenna dashed to answer it, looking back over her shoulder at the door. They were still out there, still calling out questions for her to answer.

My God, what's happening?

She picked up the telephone. "Hello?" she said, her voice wary.

"Jenna, it's Garth."

"Garth, what—"

"I'm coming over. I'll tell you when I get there."

"No! Don't come. There's a television crew outside the door."

"I'll be there in a few minutes."

"Garth!"

But he hung up. She looked at the front window. Someone was hanging over the banister on the steps outside, trying to see into the apartment. She crossed quickly and pulled down the shades, knocking one of the plants on the windowsill onto the floor. She left it lying there with half the dirt spilled out.

She kept pacing around the apartment, trying to make some sense of Jay Jay Coleman's questions. The only reason the woman could be here is that it had something to do with Patrick.

She abruptly sat down, only to get up again and pace. She could tell the moment Garth arrived. There was another barrage of questions outside the door, all of which he apparently ignored.

"Can you give us your name, sir!" Jay Jay was calling as Jenna opened the door. She let him in quickly, standing well back out of Camcorder range.

"I wanted to get here ahead of them," Garth said, slamming the door closed behind him. "At least they don't know who I am."

"What have they found out about Patrick?" Jenna said. "Garth, you tell me what it is!"

"It's not Patrick, Jenna. It's Hugh."

"Hugh?"

"Hugh was arrested a little while ago—let's get away from the door. I wouldn't put it past one of them to have an ear at the keyhole."

She followed him into the living room.

"Garth, tell me!"

"I'm going to turn on the music," he said, walking to the stereo on the nearly empty bookshelves. "I want to make sure they can't hear." He punched the radio on, adjusting the volume so that the room filled with quiet jazz.

He turned to look at her. "What's all this?" he asked about the boxes and the packed books.

"I have to move. What about Hugh?"

"Jenna, why are you moving?"

He was stepping on the ends of her questions again, the way he did when he wanted to know something, and her temper flared. She had such a contradiction of feelings where he was concerned. She was glad to see him, and upset about his arrival, and annoyed with his questions all at the same time. But she still wanted to be with him. She remembered her mother giving her a piece of sage advice once about how to gauge your affection: If a man makes you mad enough to kill him, but you never think of leaving—it's love.

"I have to move," she said evenly. "The apartment belongs to an old school friend of Patrick's. We were renting it while he was out of the country. He's back now, and he wants it. Now will you tell me what is going on!"

"I'll tell you what I know," he said.

"Well, that would be a refreshing change."

"Now, don't start up with me," he warned her. "I've had a hell of a day. I came here to tell you about Hugh in person because I didn't want you to hear about it on the six o'clock news or read it in the newspapers. It was really *very* nice of me."

She stared at him, then threw up her hands, half in capitulation, half in token apology. He looked so tired, she suddenly realized.

"So tell me," she said, not yet willing to be pacified.

"Becca's mother was right. The drug operation in the apartment house was being run by cops. It wasn't part of a sting. It was being done on the sly for a big cut of the profits."

"And Hugh's in it?"

"Hugh—and others."

"How?"

"I don't know for sure, but IAD—Internal Affairs—does. From what I've heard, it may have started as a joke."

"A joke?" she said incredulously.

"Jenna, you know how cops are. They raided the place, and somehow this guy came looking to make a buy. He was either too dumb or too strung out to realize he was shopping in the middle of a bust. As a lark, they sold him an ounce or two. They asked for a ridiculous price, and they got it. And all of a sudden there was all that stuff just lying there waiting to be sold. They stayed open. They even cut a deal with the original supplier to keep it running—only his percentage was suddenly a lot less. But a quarter of a pie is better than no pie at all."

"How do they know Hugh's in it?"

"They picked up the guy we saw in the hall first. He was from another precinct. They gave him a choice of taking the heat alone or wearing a wire to get what they needed to nail the rest of them. He went for the wire."

"Does Mamie know about any of this?"

"Hugh was at her house when they picked him up."

"Did they have to do that?" she said sharply. Poor Mamie. Her police officer sons were her reason for being, and Hugh was all she had left.

"Jenna, when the word comes down to pick him up, that's what you do."

"You arrested him?"

"No, not me. I had very little to do with that part of it—because of the fight Hugh and I had that time. IAD didn't want a defense lawyer to be able to suggest that I might have planted evidence to get back at Hugh or anything like that.''

"So you just had your little talks with the lieutenant with the blinds closed."

He frowned. "What is it with you?" he said. "What are you mad at me for? I'm not the one running drugs and terrorizing five-year-olds!"

She looked into his eyes. What was it with her? He'd just given her very bad news about her late husband's brother, but all she could think about was that he'd said he loved her, and she was desperately afraid that she loved him back. *That's* what it was with her.

She stepped away from him, because she was perilously close to throwing herself on him. Once again she wanted his comfort, his closeness. Nothing seemed as bad if he were near. How could she tell what she really felt about him, if she could never get past that? And how incredibly unfair it was to have one's only source of comfort also be one's source of pain.

"Tell me the rest," she said.

"They're going to indict him. I don't think he'll get off."

"I'd better call Mamie," she said, crossing to the telephone. She quickly dialed the number. A woman whose voice she didn't recognize answered the phone almost immediately, and there seemed to be a lot of commotion in the background.

"I'd like to speak to Mrs. Gallagher," Jenna said, not certain she had the right number.

"Who is this?"

"Jenna Gallagher."

Jenna could hear a hand being put over the receiver and then muffled conversation. A voice in the background began to rise.

"Hello?" Jenna said.

"I'm sorry," the woman said in a rush. "Mamie asked me to tell you that she can't talk to you at the moment—"

"That's not what I said!" Mamie cried in the background. "You tell her what I said!"

"Mamie..." the woman on the telephone said. And then she spoke to Jenna. "I'm sorry. Mrs. Gallagher is very upset. It would be better if you didn't call again."

She hung up, and Jenna stood holding the telephone receiver. She looked at Garth. "She wouldn't talk to me."

He didn't say anything.

"What's going on, Garth?" she asked, hanging up the phone.

"She...thinks you have something to do with Hugh's being arrested."

"Why would she think that!"

He shrugged. "Hugh has her ear. I don't."

"You're not answering me!"

"Hugh and I are enemies. You and I have been seeing each other," he offered.

"And?" she said, because she sensed there was more to it than that. Much more.

He looked into her eyes. He was going to have to tell her, so he might as well do it. "I think—" He broke off. He didn't *think* anything. He knew it; the lieutenant had told him. Mamie Gallagher had called the lieutenant personally to ask him, with all the influence she had, to get rid of Detective Garth, to make him admit what he'd done to her son—to both her sons. But Garth wouldn't tell Jenna that part of it. "Hugh told her that you and I were together...before Patrick was killed. He told her that that was the reason for his fight with me. He said he'd kept it to himself all this time out of respect for his brother."

"Garth, he wouldn't do that!" She didn't want to believe it, couldn't believe it. Still, she asked the question. "Why would he say that?"

"He knows I have Patrick's notebook. There's only one way I could have gotten it."

"There's nothing in the notebook, Garth. Nothing but the address of that apartment house."

And Mary Zaccato's name. The unspoken phrase lay heavy between them.

"Hugh doesn't know that," Garth said.

He wanted to look away from her, but he couldn't. He could see the worry and the pain in her eyes, both of which he'd helped put there. He wanted to tell her that Hugh had always been a man to cover his bases, and that he was certain Hugh was doing it now. If Mamie Gallagher thought the worst of Jenna, she wasn't likely to listen to anything Jenna might have to say about what was in that notebook. Maybe Hugh thought he could bluff his way through all the rest of it—with his mother at least. He could tell her he was undercover, that things went wrong and now his superiors were letting him take the blame for it. It wouldn't work on a street-wise woman like Hazel, who knew human nature inside and out, but it might work on someone like Mamie Gallagher, who needed desperately to keep intact whatever prestige her husband and sons had given her. The only thing that could throw a wrench into a plan like that was whatever Patrick knew and had written in his notebook.

But Garth didn't say anything. Hugh was Patrick's brother, and Jenna had loved Patrick.

"What else?" she asked.

"That's it."

"What about Patrick?"

"He wasn't in it."

"How do you know?"

"I don't *know*. I just don't think he was."

She closed her eyes for a moment and took a deep, steadying breath. Her mind was whirling. Hugh. And Mamie. My God, how was she ever going to convince Mamie that she hadn't known Garth until a few weeks ago?

"We have to talk," Garth said.

She walked away toward the spilled dirt and the over-turned plant. She began to scoop up the dirt with her hands, dumping it back into the pot.

"Jenna," Garth said, following her. He stood to one side as she worked at cleaning up the mess, and she worked at it as if it were a matter of life and death.

"We have to talk," he insisted.

She didn't look up at him.

"You don't think so?" he asked. "Will you stop doing that! Sometimes keeping yourself busy isn't the way to go."

She looked up at him. "I don't know what you mean."

"I mean sometimes you can't hide from your troubles, Jenna. You have to deal with the problem head-on, be-cause it isn't going to go away. Sometimes keeping yourself busy—the way you did after Patrick died, the way you're doing now—doesn't work. Look. Do you think I'm going to tell you I love you and not want to hear what you have to say about it?"

"I don't have anything to say. I've told you how I felt about you."

"You told me you ignored your personal principles be-cause you wanted to go to bed with me. Period. I want to know how you feel about us."

She got up from the floor, wiping her hands on her sweatpants. She picked up the pot and put it back on the windowsill. "There's a lot more we need to talk about be-fore we get to that, Garth."

"Like what?"

"Like the truth about why you came looking for me at Skip's party."

He didn't try to deny his duplicity in what had seemed a chance meeting. "It doesn't matter now," he said instead.

"It does to me. At Skip's party, you suggested that Pat-rick and I weren't getting along before he was killed." She looked into his eyes. "Sometimes I think you did that be-cause you wanted to find out if Patrick and Mary were involved with each other. Sometimes I think you did it because you suspect me of having something to do with his murder."

"If you think that," he said, "then we're a hell of a lot farther apart than I thought."

"That's the problem, Garth, don't you see? We *are* far apart. We were... lovers too soon. We were intimate before we really knew each other. I think now that maybe I can't trust my own judgment where you're concerned."

"I never lied to you."

"Didn't you?"

"No, goddamn it!"

"Is omission a lie?"

"I don't know what you mean."

"I mean that the woman out there with the television crew suggested it was ironic that you were the cop who was instrumental in solving Patrick's murder. I didn't know that, Garth. No one ever told me it was you—or if they did, I was too upset about Patrick to remember it. And you certainly never mentioned it."

"Jenna, I did the legwork on Patrick's murder investigation. Somebody dropped a dime on Joey Malaga. I went out and found him—"

She could keep from wincing at the sound of Joey Malaga's name. She could see him in her mind's eye, angry, unrepentant, a boy murderer.

"—but it wasn't because I knew it might upset you that I didn't say anything about that. I didn't tell you because the whole thing with Malaga was too easy. It was so easy it worried me. I never thought it was you who might have had something to do with Patrick's death. I thought it was—"

"Who, Garth?" she asked when he didn't continue. "Tell me."

"Hugh. I thought it was Hugh."

She turned from him. "My God, Garth, they were brothers!"

"I told you before, I can't explain it to you. I don't have anything concrete. It was a thousand little things that don't add up to much separately. Hugh was scared of something. He didn't want me asking questions on the street. During the investigation, he wouldn't let me talk to you about Patrick. At Skip's party, he still didn't want me anywhere near you. I said what I did that night because I wanted to know if Patrick was worried or distracted enough not to be paying attention to what he was doing. I was looking for a reason not to think what I was thinking. I was looking for an alternative."

She stood staring at him. He didn't go on because he didn't think she was listening anymore. He could feel it, her distancing herself from her feelings and him. He wanted to touch her, hold her, *make* her understand that, no matter how it had started, he loved her now.

"We weren't getting along," she said after a moment, her voice very quiet.

"What?" he asked, because he didn't understand. She was standing so rigidly in the middle of the room, her arms folded over her breasts as if her only source of comfort was herself.

"Patrick and I. We weren't getting along. He was very... unhappy. We couldn't have children—it was my fault. I kept having miscarriages. I didn't want to try anymore. It hurt too much, losing the babies. But he—"

"Don't," he said, reaching out to touch her shoulder. She didn't move away, but he didn't take it as an invitation. "Don't go beating yourself up again, Jenna. You can keep doing that, but the guilt's still there when you're done. I know."

He came closer. She could feel how close he was; his breath ruffled her hair.

He could smell her scent, the soft, tantalizing essence that was her and no other. He felt the faint stirring of desire, and she suddenly leaned against him. He put his arms around her. She gave a resigned sigh and rested her head against his shoulder. She felt so good to him, but he didn't press his advantage, if indeed he had one. They were on the very edge of not making it, and he didn't want to do the wrong thing.

She said something he couldn't hear.

"What?"

She lifted her head and looked at him. "I said, tell me how you know."

"Mary," he answered simply and with a candor that surprised him. He'd been all through his relationship with Mary Zaccato for IAD the last few days—because her name was in the notebook and because IAD field representatives liked to impress upon the rest of the department just how much so-called personal information they knew. The ordeal had left him touchy, defensive, the old wounds raw. He hadn't intended to speak of Mary to anyone again. Ever.

But he looked into Jenna's eyes, and he had to make her understand. "I loved her. I cared about her. But she was my chance to rattle Tony Zaccato's cage. I should have gotten her away from him, gotten her out of this town, but I waited too long. She was caught in a raid of one of Tony's operations. He was her brother. He was the only family she had, but she'd had enough of it. She wanted out." He paused. "She didn't make it. She was killed."

"Did you know about the raid beforehand?"

"No. I was off duty, waiting for her to meet me at the Humoresque."

"Did Hugh know about it?"

He'd forgotten how quick she was. He wondered if Patrick had known what he had in this woman, if he'd ever bounced ideas and problems off her, ever made use of her intuition and her logic.

"It's all tied together, isn't it? Hugh and Mary and Patrick."

"I don't know."

She walked a few steps away, then turned to look at him. "I think you do know, Garth."

"Jenna..."

"I'm not stupid, Garth!"

"Baby, I know that—"

The telephone rang, and she went to answer it.

"For you," she said, holding out the receiver to him.

He hesitated, then reached for it. No one knew he was here but Skip; it would have to be important for him to call.

"Garth," he said tersely. But it wasn't Skip. It was Sidney.

"Your Roy Lee Anderson's been run aground, lad," he said. "He's at St. Vincent's, and if you want to talk to him in this world, you'd best be getting over there."

Jenna watched Garth closely. He suddenly frowned as he listened to whatever the desk sergeant was telling him. She could see him changing; how easily he made the switch from Garth, the man, to Garth, the cop.

"I have to go," he said to her as he hung up the phone.

"Yes," she answered without surprise.

"I have to go to St. Vincent's Hospital to see Roy Lee Anderson."

She was surprised he told her, but she didn't ask him for details or whether he knew that Roy Lee Anderson was the man who had attacked her. She turned away, expecting to hear the front door closing behind him.

"Jenna," he said, his voice close, startling her because, in her mind, he'd already gone. "Jenna..."

She looked back at him. The jazz still played quietly in the background, the kind that made a woman want to sit in the dark and feel sorry for herself.

He reached for her hand, his fingers closing over hers, and he brought her to him. His arms slid around her, and, for a moment, he held her tight.

She gave him a brief hug in return, savoring the feel of his body against hers. *I love you, Garth.*

"Be careful, will you?" she said, because she knew he wanted to go and because she could do that much for him— help him take his leave. And because she hadn't said it enough to Patrick.

"I'm always that," he answered.

"The hell you are," she said, and she could feel him smile. She closed her eyes tightly so that she wouldn't cry.

"I love you, baby." The words were soft and warm against her ear. "You hear me?"

"I hear you, Garth."

He leaned back to look at her, his eyes searching hers. She thought he was going to say something else, but he didn't. He was in too much of a hurry to be gone.

Chapter Fifteen

It suddenly occurred to Garth that he hated hospitals as much as Jenna did. He'd certainly never been in one except when something bad had happened. He could see Skip at the end of the corridor, motioning for him to hurry up. He walked quickly, nearly colliding with one of the housekeeping staff who was pushing her cleaning cart out of a side room.

"Sorry," he said to the woman, and he kept going.

"Where is he?" he asked Skip, falling into step with him as they moved rapidly down the corridor.

"Down this way. Intensive Care. He's in isolation."

"Is he going to make it?"

"The doctor said if he'd been worth killing, he wouldn't have made it this far. But since he's not, it's fifty-fifty either way—sorry," Skip added as if he suddenly remembered that Roy Lee Anderson and Garth used to be friends.

"For what?" Garth said. "I know what Roy Lee is. Are they going to let me see him?"

"Yeah. He's been asking for you. And there isn't exactly a line ahead of you."

No, Garth thought. No line. As far as he knew, he was the closest thing to a family Roy Lee had.

"Did he say who did it?"

"No. He didn't say much of anything except to get you here—that way," Skip said, pointing around a corner. "You'll have to put on a gown and a mask before you go in."

"Why?"

"Third-degree burns," Skip answered, and Garth didn't ask how Roy Lee got them.

He could see through the glass partition ahead of him, but he couldn't tell if the patient in the first bed was Roy Lee or not. He rapped lightly on the glass so that the closest nurse would look up.

She seemed to be expecting him. He didn't have to wait to get in. He didn't get any hassle about upsetting schedules or trying to visit in the wrong quarter-hour. All he had to do was get the gown and mask on and come inside.

"Mr. Anderson is right there," the nurse said, pointing out a bed in a small glassed-in cubicle.

He looked at her doubtfully. At first glance, he had thought the patient in the bed was an old man.

"That's him," the nurse assured him, and he walked forward, letting himself into the small, closed-off room.

The door shut behind him, cutting off the whirring and beeps of the medical machinery outside. Of course there was machinery in here as well, but none of it seemed to be doing anything, except the green screen that flickered with the path of a heartbeat. And the closer he came to the bed, the more inclined he was to think the nurse had made a mistake about who was in here. This couldn't be Roy Lee; this man had no hair.

But he could see the name tag on the side of a bag of IV fluids that hung on a pole at the corner of the bed. ANDERSON, ROY L. The name was the only thing that was familiar, certainly not the man in the bed. Whoever Roy Lee had offended had more than meant to pay him back.

He moved closer, trying to decide if Roy Lee was conscious or not and trying not to bump into any of the medical paraphernalia that stood ready for whatever the rest of the night might bring.

"Roy Lee," he said after a moment, and Roy Lee's eyes flickered open. His eyelashes were gone.

He turned his head slightly. "You took your time, man," he said, his voice hoarse and grating. "Where the hell have you—been?"

"I've been busy."

"With her? Jenna—Gallagher?" Garth didn't answer him, and he smiled. "You're pissed, aren't you, man? Because I did the job on her."

"Yeah, Roy Lee. I'm pissed."

"How did you know it was me?"

"You didn't take the sticker off your new thermal underwear," Garth said. "And I found her coat."

"Big shot cop."

"That's me, Roy Lee. Why don't you tell me why you did it?"

"She could have got worse than me, man," Roy Lee said, his raspy voice now hardly more than a whisper.

"What is that supposed to mean?"

"It means I did you a favor."

"You hurt her, you bastard."

"No! No, I didn't hurt her—not the way Tony wanted her hurt, man. I hurt her just enough for you to get the message."

"What message?"

"How the hell do I know?"

"What message!" Garth said again.

"Tony Zaccato always wins, man. *That's* the message. You got to be careful now. He's mad, Garth. He's *real* mad—you can look at me and tell that." Roy Lee tried to laugh, but it deteriorated into a string of coughs.

"I know all about Tony, Roy Lee."

"Not just Tony, man. Hugh. Hugh Gallagher. You got to watch Hugh, too."

"Hugh's in jail."

This time Roy Lee did manage to laugh; at least the sound he made Garth took for a laugh.

"Now I—see what it is. Now I see."

"See what, Roy Lee?"

"I—thought I got this for cutting out the dude that was supposed to work her over. I thought Tony found out it was me that beat his man to it. She's pretty, Garth. Real pretty— I seen her on TV one time. I tried not to hurt her face much."

"Roy Lee, I don't know what you're talking about."

"I'm talking about *this*, man. This! They did me good. I thought it was because Tony found out I got to Jenna before he could. But it wasn't—"

"It wasn't Tony?"

"Yeah, it was Tony, man! Can't you *listen*? It was Tony— but it was for the *wrong thing*. He kept saying how I told you, how I *told* you. I didn't know what he meant." He tried to smile. "He was a little too cranky for explanations, you know? But he must think I dropped a dime on his little business with Hugh. He didn't even know I took care of Jenna for you."

"For me?"

"So she don't get hurt the way Tony wanted. It was better that it was me that did the job first, see? I hurt her just a little bit. Not bad. I owed you, Garth. I wouldn't hurt her bad, see?''

Garth looked away for a moment. The worst part was that he *did* see. He understood perfectly the convoluted logic that would let Roy Lee hurt Jenna himself, only a little bit, because he owed Garth for a pair of thermal underwear, rather than coming to him so that he could try to keep it from happening in the first place. Tony Zaccato had ordered Jenna hurt; to Roy Lee's mind, it wasn't negotiable. And what kind of track record did Garth have against Tony Zaccato? None. Nothing.

''Why was Tony sending me a message, Roy Lee?''

''You know why—''

''Tell me again.''

But Roy Lee drifted off, telling him nothing.

''Garth,'' he said abruptly after a moment.

''What?''

''You got to teach her, Garth.''

''Teach who, Roy Lee?''

''Your woman—Jenna. She don't know—nothing, man. She don't know how to take care of herself, how to fight. If she's yours, you got to teach her, Garth—take her and *show* her what to do, so when Tony...''

Roy Lee drifted off again.

''Is it night or day?'' he said abruptly.

''Night, Roy Lee.''

''Jeez, I hate the night. You remember how I always hated the dark? Ever since I was a little kid.''

''Yeah. I remember.''

''Mary and me, we were scared of the dark, but not you. You weren't scared of nothing. Don't go yet, Garth, okay? Stay here till the sun comes up. Please, Garth—''

''Take it easy, Roy Lee—''

"Please, Garth! I don't want to be by myself if it's dark—" He was trying to sit up, and Garth would have restrained him if he could have found a place to put his hand. But Roy Lee had no place where he could touch him. All over, he was either bandage or raw skin. The pattern on the green screen darted around crazily.

"Lie down, Roy Lee," Garth said. "They'll throw me out of here if you don't."

Roy Lee suddenly relaxed. "You know what, Garth?"

"What, Roy Lee?"

"I think I'll get to see Mary."

The sun was coming up, and Skip was sleeping in the waiting room. Garth was half-surprised to see him still here, and watching him snoring softly with his head thrown back, oblivious to everything, Garth suddenly felt worn-out, used up, old. He'd felt that way before he'd ever become a cop, and The Job certainly hadn't made it any better. At this particular moment he couldn't have said why he was so hell-bent to have Jenna. She was loving, giving. What would she want with a burned-out cop like him? He had nothing to offer her, and she probably had the good sense to realize it.

He kicked Skip on the bottom of his shoe to wake him up, handing him one of the cups of coffee he'd brought with him.

"Thanks," Skip said, sitting up and taking a sip. "Where did you get this? This isn't the machine stuff. This is good."

"From the nurses' lounge."

"Do they know it or do I have to hide the cup every time I see one of them?"

"Yeah, they know it," Garth said, sitting down heavily. "Two cups of real coffee, free of charge. If there's anybody nurses feel sorry for, it's two dumb cops—and vice versa."

"I'll remember that. So how's Roy Lee?"

"He died," Garth said without emotion.

"I'm—sorry, Garth."

"Don't be. He's been dead for years. This was just the official leave-taking. He's a damn sight better off—" He felt a sudden lump rise in his throat, and he abruptly got up and walked to the window. The sun was just topping the buildings across the street. He took a deep breath. He wanted to see Jenna. He wanted to go to her and put his head in her lap until he felt better. She'd be kind to him, even if she'd never once said she loved him.

I need you, Jenna.

He closed his eyes against the great emptiness he felt.

Don't give up on us, baby. Not yet.

He realized that Skip was talking to him. "What?"

"I said Debbie told me what happened."

He looked around. "What happened where?"

"At the apartment house the day she took the kid with the wet coat home."

Skip had his attention. He walked back and sat down. "And?"

"She recognized a couple of the men hanging around in the hall as cops. She didn't say anything to them because she didn't want to inadvertently blow somebody's cover. They didn't seem to recognize her, so she just kept quiet. But then she realized what they were doing there—the drug deals going on. The walls in the Sullivan apartment were thin, she said. She could hear voices in the next apartment. Loud voices. A fight about somebody not getting his fair cut. She thought she recognized one of the voices—Hugh's. She kept hoping it was some kind of legitimate operation, but then Hugh came to the school just after she'd gotten back from that place. She thought he'd followed her—to see if she knew anything, I guess. And then Jenna was beaten up. She thought it was meant for her—she and Jenna both wore black coats, and they both had one of those gold-and-black school scarves, and it was done in her father's apartment building. She was afraid to say anything—she knows enough about the way things work to know that Hugh could probably have gotten out of it if it were just her word alone. She was afraid Hugh and his friends might do something to *me* if she came forward or if she told me about it. That's why she's been acting so crazy. She's been scared to death, and she was ashamed because she didn't do anything and Jenna got hurt.''

"It wasn't her fault about Jenna," Garth said. He told him about Roy Lee's "favor." "Hugh must have been giving Tony trouble about his share. That's why Zaccato wanted to kill two birds with one stone—to make sure Hugh understood his family wasn't safe, to make sure I knew he hadn't forgotten me, all of it—by getting to Jenna.''

"What are you going to do?" Skip asked, apparently because he'd been Garth's partner long enough now to know that the question was appropriate.

"I'm going to go home and shower. And then I'm going looking for Zaccato. I'm going on the street. Anybody I can scare, I'm going to scare. Anybody I can't scare, I'll bribe. But I'm going to find him. I want him bad, Skip.''

"Yes, well, count me in on that.''

"I'd rather work alone.''

"Well, that's tough. You've got a partner, and there's not a damn thing you can do about it.''

But they split up to cover more territory, and they stayed out until midafternoon, when Skip summoned Garth with a loud whistle across a windy waterfront parking lot.

"Come on!" Skip yelled at him. "They want us in!''

"Did they say why?" Garth asked as he jumped into the car Skip didn't bother to completely stop. He was half expecting Skip to tell him that Hugh had slipped the noose after all.

"No."

"Did you *ask*?"

"Yes, I asked.

"Well, what did they say?"

"They said to come in! And don't you start about what a lousy partner I am just because they wouldn't tell me anything! You're damn lucky to have somebody who'll put up with you, and you know it!"

"Is that a fact?"

"Yes! It is!"

"Drive the car, Skip. And don't hit the bus—"

"Don't tell me how to drive!"

"Somebody's got to."

"I told you not to start with me! Didn't I tell you that?"

"You told me, Skip. You told me."

"Garth!" a patrolman yelled as soon as he hit the front doors at the station house. "Sid's got some kid tying up the 911 line. He won't tell anybody what's wrong—he just keeps asking for you."

"What kid?" Garth asked.

"I don't know—the kid won't say. He's crying a lot and—"

Garth could see Sidney hunched over the telephone. He caught sight of Garth and motioned for him to hurry.

"Here you go, son," Sidney said kindly into the receiver as Garth approached. "Detective Garth's here to speak to you."

"Where's the call coming from?" he asked Sidney as he took the phone. "This is Garth," he said into the receiver.

"Saint Xavier's," Sidney said.

"Hello?" Garth said, because no one answered. He made hand motions for the people gathered around him to cut the noise. "This is Garth," he said again, holding his other ear so he could hear better.

He heard a long sniff. "How do I know that, sucker? You could be anybody."

"Hernando?" Garth said.

"How come you know my name?"

"Hernando, I told you the other day. I know who you are. What's the matter?"

"Are you Garth?"

"Yeah, kid, it's me. What—"

"You got to come over here, Garth! You got to bring your gun!"

"Hernando, what's the matter?"

"*He's* here, man! He's going to hurt Miss Jenna! Bring your gun, Garth!"

"Who, Hernando! Who's there?"

Hernando was crying, and Garth was wasting time.

"Hernando, I'm coming. Now you get out of there! You hear me? Hernando!"

Hernando said something and dropped the phone.

"Hernando!" Garth called, but he knew he wouldn't get an answer. He understood the last thing Hernando said:

"Tony's coming!"

"Skip," Garth said, hanging up the phone. "Call home and see where Debbie is."

It only took him a second. Garth could see the relief flood Skip's face when his wife answered. Skip covered the receiver with his hand. "Jenna stayed late, Garth."

Jenna heard the crying distinctly. And so did Tony Zaccato.

"Who is that!" he hissed in her ear, the arm he had around her neck tightening.

"I don't know."

"Who else is here!"

"Nobody else is supposed to be here."

"Hey!" Zaccato yelled. "Who's there!"

He dragged her along with him, and Jenna couldn't keep from crying out in pain.

"Don't you hurt Miss Jenna!" a small voice called from the far end of the hall. She recognized it immediately.

"Hernando, get out of here!" she cried, and Tony Zaccato made sure she suffered for it.

"Don't you hurt Miss Jenna!" Hernando yelled again. "You're going to be sorry, man, when 911 gets here. You'll be sorry!"

Tony Zaccato chuckled to himself. "Little dummy thinks 911 is a person. Yeah, I'm scared to death, kid!" he yelled at Hernando.

"Garth's going to bring his gun!" Hernando warned him, and Jenna closed her eyes.

"What did he say?" Zaccato demanded. She shook her head, pretending she didn't understand him.

"Hey, kid! You know my friend Garth?"

"He ain't your friend! He's *my* friend, sucker. And he's coming to shoot you!"

Tony Zaccato laughed. "Well, well. Looks like we'd better be going, Mrs. Gallagher, before your hero gets here. Hey, thanks for the tip, kid!"

But Hernando's tip came too late. Zaccato forced her down the long hall, and by the time they reached the end door, there was no traffic going by Saint Xavier's. The street should have had cars bumper-to-bumper at this time of day, and Tony Zaccato knew it. He stood cautiously in the doorway, then pressed forward just enough to still hold the door open, keeping her in front of him, the gun pressed under her chin and forcing her head back. She couldn't see where she was going, and she stumbled on the raised weather stripping on the threshold. She didn't have her coat, and the cold wind—and the fear—made her shiver.

She couldn't see anyone—no police, no patrol cars anywhere. Everything was so quiet. Too quiet.

"Where are the bastards?" Tony muttered to himself. "I know they're out there—where are they!"

A nondescript car pulled in at the end of the block. And then another. And another.

Tony Zaccato swore under his breath and dragged her back inside.

"What did you see?" Garth asked. He jerked off his jacket and put on the bullet-proof vest, standing outside the car in the biting wind. His hands were shaking, but he wasn't worried about it. His hands always shook at the beginning of an operation, but once he was into it, he was calm. He was always calm.

"The guy's in there. He's got the woman. He brought her to the door with him, but he didn't come all the way out." The patrolman's voice had a quaver in it. He wasn't used to this.

"How did she look?" Garth asked.

"Scared—he's got a .45 automatic under her chin."

"Did you make him?"

"Nah, I don't know him."

"Six feet tall?" Garth said. "A hundred and eighty pounds? Black hair, combed straight back? Probably wearing a big cashmere coat—gray?"

"Yeah, that's him."

"Did he say anything?"

"Nah, I don't think he knows for sure if we're out here."

"He knows," Garth said. He put his jacket back on and stuffed extra clips into his pockets.

Another car pulled up, and the lieutenant got out.

"This is your call, Garth," he said immediately. "How do you want to handle it?"

"I want to go in. Alone."

"He's not going to let you just walk in there, Garth."

"Yes, he will. Tony's been waiting a long time to get his revenge. And he'll want me there to see it."

The lieutenant stared at him, clearly understanding what Garth *didn't* say. "You go in ahead of the others—but not alone. That's all I'm going to give you."

Garth nodded, and he listened while the lieutenant said what he wanted done. Skip and Rosie Madden would go in with him, but not close. Garth took a slip of paper and rapidly sketched the layout of the building, indicating the two doors that were in most of the classrooms.

"I'm not looking to make an arrest," he said under his breath to Skip, and Rosie heard him. "If that bothers either of you, you better jump off now." He picked up the bullhorn. "Tony!" he said over it. "It's Garth! I'm coming in."

Jenna made a small sound of protest, and Tony Zaccato laughed.

"Looks like he thinks you're worth the trouble, Mrs. Gallagher. That's good. That's real good. Ah! Pretty lady! You going to cry about it? That's good, too. You let Garth see you cry—"

He jerked her around and made her sit on a kitchen bar stool someone had just donated to the kindergarten. She and Debbie had laughed earlier that day about what to do with it, dunce corners no longer being in vogue. It put her at just the right height to shield Zaccato, just at the right height so he could keep the gun under her chin. She struggled to stop crying. She didn't want to distract Garth in any way.

She heard running footsteps, but it wasn't Garth she heard. The footsteps were too quick and light.

"Hernando!" Garth whispered fiercely, reaching out to grab him up as he went flying past. "I told you to get out of here! I could have shot you, man!"

"You got your gun, Garth!" Hernando said, clearly more pleased than intimidated.

Garth wanted to shake the child until his teeth rattled, but he gave him a brief, hard hug instead. "Where are they?"

"Down in my class. You got to get Miss Jenna."

"I will. But you take your butt out of here."

Garth could tell by the look on Hernando's face that there was no way in hell the boy was going to do that. He didn't waste time arguing. He scooped Hernando up and hurried back toward the end doors, keeping an eye on the classroom where Tony was supposed to be, as he went.

"Hey!" Hernando bellowed. "Hey!"

The patrolmen on backup were on the ball, and the door swung open before Garth got to it.

"Handcuff him to something," Garth said, slinging Hernando into a pair of waiting arms. He couldn't help but smile at the elegant convolution of street names Hernando called him. "And wash his mouth out with soap while you're at it."

Garth stood for a moment and stared down the long hallway, listening intently. He could hear a murmur of voices, much as he had on other occasions.

He took a deep breath and walked forward, trying not to think about Jenna and how scared she must be. A noise in another direction made him stop. Rosie and Skip were supposed to be coming in, but he didn't know exactly where they were now. Hernando had said Tony was in the classroom—but then, Hernando was only five years old.

He listened. Everything was quiet.

He tried not to make any sound as he approached the classroom door.

"Please!"

The word stopped him; it was Jenna. He hugged the wall, willing himself not to be stampeded. He didn't want to do anything stupid; he had to forget that she wasn't a name-less civilian.

"He's not going to care!" Jenna said next. "You can't threaten him with what you might do to me!"

"Oh, I can threaten him, pretty lady. You're going to see how I can threaten him—Garth!" Tony suddenly yelled. "You're not saying anything, Garth! You think I don't hear you out there?"

"I didn't come to talk, Tony. I came to kill you."

Zaccato laughed. "Now, how are you going to do that, Garth?" he asked, his voice patronizing, as if he were speaking to a naïve child. "I got something you want here. I got something you want real bad."

Garth's heart contracted at the small noise Jenna made. From where he stood, he could just see her. He couldn't see Zaccato, at least no more than his hand and arm and the gun under her chin. He couldn't see his other hand at all. He moved back a little.

"Yeah, but she understands, Tony," he called.

"Understands what?" Tony snapped, his jovial manner sliding away.

"She understands that first things come first. She understands that I owe you. For Roy Lee. For Mary."

"You don't talk about Mary! Mary is dead because of you!"

Garth wiped at his eyes. He was sweating. The vest was heavy and cumbersome. But he didn't take it off.

"An eye for an eye, Garth! You ever hear of that? Mary is dead because of you, Garth! You knew there was a drug bust going down, but you didn't tell Mary!"

"Who told you that? Hugh Gallagher? I wasn't working narcotics, Tony. *He* was. You think he didn't know the bust was going down? You're the one who sent Mary to make the drop for you. *You* sent her in there!"

"She always made the drop for me! They don't trust me if she doesn't go!"

"Oh, well, then, Tony, why didn't you *say* so? That makes everything all right. Business is business, right?"

"You shut up! I'm going to show you *business*, Garth! You move where I can see you—where *you* can see *me*. I want you to watch when I do this pretty lady of yours. We'll keep it in the family. I took care of her cop husband, I'll take care of her, too."

"What's this, Tony? You down to taking credit for some kid's nickel hit?"

"Nickel hit! What do you know!"

"I know Joey Malaga whacked Patrick Gallagher."

"Not Joey, Garth. Me. *I* pull Joey Malaga's strings. Patrick Gallagher wouldn't stay where he belonged. He started sniffing here, sniffing there. Hugh said he could handle him, but I don't get where I am waiting for somebody to be 'handled.' Anybody bothers me, I want him taken out so he don't bother me no more. You think it was a nickel hit? No! Joey owes me, so he does his cop friend—for nothing! Ah, Garth!" Tony said. "See what you did? You made the pretty lady cry again."

"Jenna!" Garth called, his heart twisting at what she must be feeling now. He caught a glimpse of Skip crossing the hall at the other door of the classroom and slipping inside. "Jenna!" he called again to keep Tony's attention focused in the other direction.

"Garth!" Jenna cried, her voice strong. "I want you to do what you have to do, Garth! For me! For Mary! Don't you let him walk out of here!"

She suddenly stopped as Tony grabbed her by the hair and yanked her head back.

"I told you, Garth!" Tony yelled. "An eye for an eye!"

"Yeah, right, Tony! Hugh took Mary. But you didn't even know he did it, you dumb bastard! You took Patrick on a whim—not for *her*, not for Mary. Mary's in her grave, still waiting for you to catch on.''

"You shut up!"

"Mary's dead because of *you*, Tony, not me."

"I said shut up!"

"You're right about what this is, Tony. It's an eye for an eye!"

With that, Garth abruptly stepped into the doorway, showing himself, counting on Tony's anger to be at a fever pitch.

"For Mary, Tony!" he yelled at him, and Skip was quick and deadly, Annie Oakley all the way—but not quick enough to keep the shot Tony got off from hitting Garth midchest.

Chapter Sixteen

He opened his eyes. He could see the blue sky, and he was very cold. He turned his head slightly, trying to focus on the face that suddenly peered down at him. *Jenna,* he decided. She was wearing that dark green sweater he liked so much. Or was it the way she filled the sweater that he liked?

"What's the matter?" he asked, because she was obviously very upset.

"What's the *matter*? I thought you were too much of a damned hardhead to wear a vest, that's what's the matter!" Her voice was on the verge of cracking.

"No, I've got it on," he said, because she was about to cry and he didn't want her to. "I told you I'd be careful. Didn't I tell you I'd be careful?"

She nodded, but she was going to cry anyway. She suddenly bowed her head.

"Hey," he said softly, reaching up to touch her cheek. "You're not going to bawl, are you?"

"Yes!" she informed him, wiping furiously at her eyes.

He tried to sit up. The effort made him cry out in pain.

"Lie still, for God's sake!" Jenna said, putting her hands on his shoulders. He struggled briefly, then lay back against the parking lot pavement. It wasn't at all comfortable.

He looked up at the sky again. "How did I get out here?"

"You walked, you big dummy!"

He managed a grin. "Tell me something, Jenna. When you call me a big dummy, do you do that because you like me, or what?"

"Garth . . ." she said in exasperation.

"I was only wondering," he said. "God, my chest hurts."

He suddenly remembered. "Tony—"

"Skip shot him, Garth."

"Is he dead?"

"I don't know. Rosie jerked me out of there. I didn't have time to find out—and you were going for your walk."

He reached up to touch the center of his vest. "Damn thing works, doesn't it?"

"It works," she said, putting her hand on his. "But you've probably got some broken ribs."

He tried to sit up again.

"Garth, don't!" Jenna pleaded. "Don't. If you love me, please just lie still. I can't—take anymore." Her voice had gotten all teary again.

"Hey, Garth, how are you doing?" a patrolman said, squatting down beside him.

"Down but not out, Russo," he said.

"The bomber pilot's giving us a fit. Can I kick him loose?"

"Yeah," Garth said. "Let him come over here."

He could hear Hernando's running approach and the skidding halt his shoes made on the asphalt.

"Garth!" Hernando said. "Garth! You ain't killed, are you?"

"No, Hernando."

"Hey, man! You had me arrested! Them suckers put me in a car, and I couldn't get out. You can't have me arrested! I'm only five years old!"

"I'll remember that," Garth promised him. He closed his eyes against the pain in his chest.

"Garth," Jenna said. "Garth!"

He forced his eyes open. "Yeah, baby, what?"

But she didn't tell him what. She just looked stricken. But by then the paramedics had arrived.

"I can walk," he said to the one who began listening to his chest with a stethoscope.

"Maybe you *can*, but you *ain't*, got it? You're going to be wearing the print of that vest on your chest for a month. Brace yourself, macho man, you're going for a ride," he said as his associate rolled the stretcher up close.

Garth suffered the indignity of being lifted onto the stretcher, fighting down the wave of dizziness and pain that suggested that perhaps he couldn't walk after all.

"Jenna?" he called, or thought he called—his chest hurt so bad!

But he couldn't see her. Anywhere.

"Where—?"

"Officer, if you don't keep your butt still, you and me are going to tangle, you understand me?" the paramedic said. "You got broken ribs and a bruised heart, and I ain't having you bouncing around. So far you ain't got no holes in you, and I mean to keep it that way."

"What is it I've got?" he asked weakly as the pain threatened to overwhelm him again.

"Broken ribs. Bruised heart."

No, he thought. It was the other way around.

Jenna . . .

* * *

He opened his eyes. No blue sky this time. Blue ceiling. And he wasn't cold anymore. His chest, however, still talked to him with every breath.

He turned his head. Someone was asleep in the chair by the bed. He watched for a moment—Skip again, he decided. Every time he'd opened his eyes, it seemed that Skip had been here. The kid was a good partner, took all his duties seriously, even the bedside vigil.

"Hey," he said, or tried to. His throat was dry, and he wanted desperately to cough. But he knew what kind of havoc that would wreak, and he fought it down until his eyes watered. After a moment, he tried again. "Hey, Skip!"

"What!" Skip said, jerking awake. "What—"

"Can't you sleep at home, Carver?"

Skip grinned. "Yes, I can sleep at home. But I decided I'd hang out here for a while."

"How long is 'a while'?"

"Oh . . ." he said airily. "About two days."

"Two—" He had to stop, because he was going to cough again.

"Maybe three. You had some trouble with your heart. Fluid and swelling from the trauma of being hit in the chest so hard. And you were exhausted, I guess. You've been asleep a long time."

"Where's . . . Jenna?"

Skip didn't answer him.

"I know you heard me," Garth said. "Where is she?"

"She's—I'm not sure—well, I know where she *is*, I just don't know why . . . she's not here," he finished lamely. "Well, I do know why—or I think I do. . . ."

"Will you make up your mind and tell me?" The outburst caused him to cough in earnest; there was no holding back this one. Excruciating pain shot through his chest, making his breath catch and his eyes water.

"Go ahead," Garth said when he could.

"Garth . . ."

"Go. Ahead."

Skip sighed heavily. "I think hearing what Tony said about having Patrick killed has really thrown her, Garth. I think it's been like having him die all over again. And then *you*—"

"Okay," he said abruptly. He didn't want to hear after all. "She's all right?"

"She's all right, Garth. Tony didn't get the chance to really hurt her."

"Well, that's good. That's good."

Skip suffered for a moment in the awkward silence that followed.

"Well . . . can I get you anything?"

"No. Nothing."

"Hazel and Luigi will be here later."

"That's good," he said again, because the words seemed to fit and he didn't feel like thinking up any others.

"Well, I guess I'll go on then."

"Yeah," Garth said. He waited until Skip had reached the door. "Skip. How good was the shot you made?"

They stared at each other across the room.

"You got what you wanted, Garth," Skip said quietly. "No arrest."

Garth nodded, the relief he felt knowing Tony Zaccato was dead nearly as acute as the sorrow he felt knowing he'd lost Jenna.

"Thanks, Skip," he said, turning his face away. He heard Skip leave and quietly close the door.

Now what? he thought. But there was only one thing he could do. Think. Whether he wanted to or not. About Roy Lee. About Mary. About Tony. About Patrick Gallagher. About Patrick Gallagher's widow.

* * *

He closed his eyes. Maybe he slept again. He didn't know. Maybe he dreamed. The face he saw in his half-waking state was Jenna's—smiling, angry, stormy with passion.

I need you, baby!

But he couldn't tell her that. He'd told her he loved her. Twice. And that was as far as he would go.

Someone was in the room. He braced himself to have to deal with a worried Hazel and Luigi. They'd both be wringing their hands, and how was he going to cope with that when he already felt like bawling?

He turned his head; Jenna stood at the foot of the bed. His heart, bruised and battered as it was, lurched.

He forced himself to look away; he'd been working hard to get used to the idea that she wouldn't be coming, and now here she stood.

"What are you doing here?" he asked, his misery making him less than kind.

"Where else would I be?" she asked.

"You don't have to come here and be nice to me."

"Well, that's good, because I can see already what a chore *that* would be."

He looked back at her, and he made a grand effort at small talk.

"Find an apartment yet?"

"No," she said. "I . . . haven't been up to looking for an apartment."

It was suddenly clear to him. She was only here because she wasn't going to duck the issue. She was an honorable person. She'd tell him to his face that she didn't want any more to do with him. He wondered if the lawyer was still waiting in the wings somewhere, and that thought left him more depressed than ever. He lapsed into silence, dreading what he was sure she would tell him.

"Are you upset because I wasn't here sooner?" she asked.

"No. Why should I be upset?"

"*I* would be. I . . . wanted to come, Garth, but I—I guess things just sort of caught up with me." She tried to smile. "I'm . . . better now, though."

"Glad to hear it," he said, sounding cold and petulant even to himself.

She looked at him thoughtfully. "Rosie told me something once, Garth. I was worried because I hadn't heard from you. She told me when I *did* see you, not to give you any grief about why you weren't there sooner. She said I should just be glad you were there *now*. I thought it was good advice."

He considered this, wondering if he dared to hope what it might mean. He decided to behave like an adult.

"What? You couldn't pick up the telephone? Send me a card?" he said in spite of his decision.

"You were asleep for a long time, Garth. They didn't want you disturbed. And the card's in the mail. All the children at Saint Xavier's signed it. They all write big, so we had to get a really *big* card—"

"Okay. Okay. I understand how bad you must have felt going through everything you did with Tony, and with Roy Lee. I understand how hard it must have been hearing about Patrick. I know it's hard for you to go into a hospital, but—"

"But what?" she asked when he didn't continue.

"But my feelings are hurt! It ticks me off, Jenna!"

"Oh," she said. "Do you want me to go?"

"No, I don't want you to go!" he said, alarmed.

"Well, what do you want?" she said in exasperation.

"I want to . . . pout, okay? And you can't pout unless somebody's there to see it."

He glanced at her. She was trying not to smile.

"That sounds reasonable." She came and sat on the side of the bed. "You pout. I'll wait."

She made herself comfortable, careful not to jar him. And she looked into his eyes. *Her* eyes were full of mischief, and she was humming, of all things. In a moment, he recognized the song.

He couldn't keep from smiling. "'Some Kind of Wonderful,'" he said.

She smiled in return, and she began to softly sing the words.

"I'm not as good as The Drifters," she said after a moment.

"Well, it's the thought that counts," he answered, smiling still. The smile slid away. He could feel his eyes welling up. "Isn't it?"

"Yes," she answered.

He reached up to touch her cheek, finally, and she turned her face to press a kiss into his palm.

"You shouldn't be here. You hate hospitals."

"I know," she agreed. "But I *love* you."

Epilogue

She wouldn't move in with him. It was the perfect solution, *he'd* thought. She was homeless; he was needy. In his whole life, he'd never been so needy. And, God knows, he had the room. He had talked to her—explained, discussed, argued and, yes, even pouted. Roy Lee had said that Garth should teach her to fight, but Roy Lee should have seen her, determined to do what she had to do and not let anyone push her around, not even Garth.

"I love you!" Garth had been reduced to shouting.

"I love you," she'd countered with maddening calm.

But she wouldn't move in with him.

And it wasn't that he hadn't understood. He understood perfectly. Why she hadn't come to him at first when he was in the hospital, and why she had needed more time afterward. She had her panic attacks in hand, but she had still had a lot of loose ends to tie up. She loved Garth, whether she'd wanted to or not. But she had to get used to that, and she had to put Patrick to rest once and for all. And she had to try to make some kind of peace with Mrs. Gallagher. With *both* Mrs. Gallaghers. Patrick's mother—and Patrick's widow. She even had to stand with her in-laws during Hugh's trial, all the while knowing that Hugh's association with Tony Zaccato had likely cost Patrick his life.

That had been hard for Garth. Even if it was harder still for Jenna.

"If I'm not there, people will think it's because I know he's guilty," Jenna had said.

"You do, and he is!"

"I know that, Garth! But he should be tried by the court, not by the media. You know how it will go—'Martyred brother's widow refuses to attend trial.' I have to do this—for Patrick's mother, if nothing else."

And he began to understand a little what it cost a woman, what it cost Jenna, to wed a policeman. To wed herself to The Job.

Garth had understood, but it hadn't helped. He wasn't a patient man, and he'd been afraid. He was still afraid. Happiness—life—was so precarious. He'd learned that the hard way. And Jenna had, too. She *knew* firsthand, just as he did, how easily everything could slip away. But she was still willing to risk it all. It ticked him off—even if he *did* understand.

"Everything has to be right for us," she kept telling him. "As right as I can make it. I'm not going to hide anymore. I'm going to deal with my problems head-on."

He agreed. He didn't like it—he hated having his own words come back to haunt him—but he agreed. And he'd worked hard to help her get everything settled. By keeping his mouth shut about the Gallaghers—even when Hugh was convicted. By *not* keeping his mouth shut about The Job. By sharing the good times—and the bad. By doing everything in his power to allay Jenna's fears, especially her worry that perhaps she wouldn't be able to have his baby. It hadn't been easy to convince her once and for all that she wasn't a means to an end to him, or a reparation for Mary, or an adjunct to The Job, or anything remotely peripheral to his life, that she simply *was* his life. *She* was his life, with children or without.

And so, here he stood, all these months later, a nervous wreck.

"Garth?" Skip said behind him—again. "Oh, Garth," he said, when Garth didn't turn around.

"What!" he snapped.

"Are you . . . all right?"

"Yeah, fine," he said, and he didn't miss the looks Skip and Luigi exchanged. "I'm fine!"

"You don't look fine. Does he, Luigi? Maybe if you could just blink your eyes now and then so we could tell you're not in a coma—"

"Look! I'm nervous, all right? I'm getting married, and I'm nervous! Weren't you nervous when you married Debbie?"

"Who, me? All I had to worry about was whether or not my mother was going to crash the ceremony with a bunch of men in white coats and a court order. Why would I have been nervous?"

"Yeah, well, at least you were sure the bride wouldn't back out," he said.

"Garth, Jenna isn't going to back out. How many times do I have to tell you? She's here—Luigi's seen her. Tell him you've seen her, Luigi."

"I see her, Giovanni," Luigi told him earnestly. "I see her. I even give her a little kiss on the cheek. I say it's from you."

Garth suddenly laughed. "You want to go around kissing brides, old man, you get one of your own and leave mine alone." He boxed Luigi once on the arm. "God! How much longer before this thing starts?"

"Minute, thirty-seven seconds," Skip said without looking at his watch. He cracked the door so he could see out into the congregation. "The church is full," he noted.

"Thanks a lot, Skip! That's all I needed to know—the church is full!"

"Take it easy, Garth! People have to come see this miraculous event, don't they? Hazel finally getting old Garth married? How else are they going to believe it?"

"Very funny," Garth said.

"A miracle is a miracle," Luigi said philosophically.

And you don't know how close to the truth that is, Garth thought. It was a miracle all right—not that he'd asked Jenna to marry him, but that, with all their problems, she had finally agreed.

"No Mrs. Gallagher," Skip said, still peeping out the door.

"What?" Garth said in alarm.

"Not Jenna, Garth! The old lady. She didn't come. Jenna said she wouldn't, but I think she was hoping— you *are* in bad shape."

Luigi came and put his arm around Garth's shoulders. "Giovanni, you listen to this," he said, squeezing hard. "You *love* Jenna. You want her to be your wife. So all you got to do now is say so—to God and to the people. What is so hard about that?"

"God and the people," Garth echoed vaguely. "What's so hard?" he exhaled sharply.

The organ music started in earnest.

"Now!" Luigi said. "You go and do it, right?"

"Right," Garth said, hoping this was like all the other times he'd had the jitters—shaky at first, but then, once he got into it, everything settled down and he was all right. "You got the ring?"

"I got it! I got it! Don't ask me that no more!" Luigi said. "And if I don't got it, Skip's got a spare one for me to use. So go on! We go get you married!"

In spite of Luigi's shoving, Garth took a deep breath before he stepped out into the church proper. Then he walked purposefully to stand where he'd practiced standing just the night before.

It was even worse than he had imagined. He wasn't used to being stared at, and there wasn't a damn thing for all these people—many of them police personnel—to look at but him. Garth, held captive before them and actually wearing a suit.

And Hazel was bawling her head off. She gave him a little wave, which in no way interfered with her crying. Jenna's mother stood at a pew on the opposite side. She wasn't crying, and she didn't wave. She did, however, look at him kindly. They were both holding up well, Garth thought, for two mothers who had had their dreams for their children dashed the way they had. Jenna wasn't a blueblood with money, and Garth didn't work for IBM. He smiled briefly at them both.

Ah, God, he thought, resigned and trying to endure. His tie was choking him to death. It was all he could do not to tug at it—he might even die up here. Of suffocation. But he kept his eyes on the back of the church, looking—waiting—for Jenna. No matter what Skip and Luigi said, he wouldn't be surprised if she didn't appear. He wasn't much of a catch, and he knew it. He was mortally afraid that, as the time for the ceremony drew near, she'd suddenly know it, too.

The music changed; the bridespersons were coming— Rosie Madden and her braids, and Debbie and all of Saint Xavier's kindergarten. He couldn't keep from grinning. The children had on their school uniforms, but in honor of the occasion, all the girls wore flowers in their hair, and all the boys had boutonnieres. He could see Hernando marching along, taking big steps and grinning from ear to ear. Just as he was supposed to file into the front row, he broke away and dashed to where Garth stood, giving him "five" before Debbie shooed him back to where he was supposed to be. The congregation loved it.

Jenna was standing at the back of the church.

Oh, baby, he thought. *You are so beautiful.*

So beautiful. She was dressed in pale pink lace, and she had flowers in her hair, the same kind of flowers she carried in her arms. Her eyes held his all the way down the aisle. When she was close enough, he gave her a wink so she'd know that no matter how rattled and choked he looked, he wasn't going to break and run for it.

Jenna smiled and took his arm, and as it always was with him, his nervousness vanished the moment the action began. His voice was strong and clear, his hands steady and warm as he made his promises to her.

"Love . . . Honor . . . So long as you both shall live?"

No problem. Piece of cake. I love you, Jenna.

Suddenly it was all over.

". . . man and wife."

The words rang in his mind, in his heart. He kissed her, hugged her, kissed her again.

"So," he whispered in her ear before they turned to face the congregation. *"Now* will you move in with me?"

*   *   *   *   *

The tradition continues in November as Silhouette
presents its fifth annual
Christmas collection

SILHOUETTE

Christmas

STORIES
1990

The romance of Christmas sparkles in four
enchanting stories written by some of your
favorite Silhouette authors:

Ann Major * SANTA'S SPECIAL MIRACLE
Rita Rainville * LIGHTS OUT!
Lindsay McKenna * ALWAYS AND FOREVER
Kathleen Creighton * THE MYSTERIOUS GIFT

Spend the holidays with Silhouette and discover
the special magic of falling in love in this
heartwarming Christmas collection.

PASSPORT TO ROMANCE VACATION SWEEPSTAKES

OFFICIAL RULES

SWEEPSTAKES RULES AND REGULATIONS. NO PURCHASE NECESSARY.
HOW TO ENTER:

1. To enter, complete this official entry form and return with your invoice in the envelope provided, or print your name, address, telephone number and age on a plain piece of paper and mail to: Passport to Romance, P.O. Box #1397, Buffalo, N.Y. 14269-1397. No mechanically reproduced entries accepted.
2. All entries must be received by the Contest Closing Date, midnight, December 31, 1990 to be eligible.
3. Prizes: There will be ten (10) Grand Prizes awarded, each consisting of a choice of a trip for two people to: i) London, England (approximate retail value $5,050 U.S.); ii) England, Wales and Scotland (approximate retail value $6,400 U.S.); iii) Caribbean Cruise (approximate retail value $7,300 U.S.); iv) Hawaii (approximate retail value $ 9,550 U.S.); v) Greek Island Cruise in the Mediterranean (approximate retail value $12,250 U.S.); vi) France (approximate retail value $7,300 U.S.).
4. Any winner may choose to receive any trip or a cash alternative prize of $5,000.00 U.S. in lieu of the trip.
5. Odds of winning depend on number of entries received.
6. A random draw will be made by Nielsen Promotion Services, an independent judging organization on January 29, 1991, in Buffalo, N.Y., at 11:30 a.m. from all eligible entries received on or before the Contest Closing Date. Any Canadian entrants who are selected must correctly answer a time-limited, mathematical skill-testing question in order to win. Quebec residents may submit any litigation respecting the conduct and awarding of a prize in this contest to the Régie des loteries et courses du Quebec.
7. Full contest rules may be obtained by sending a stamped, self-addressed envelope to: "Passport to Romance Rules Request", P.O. Box 9998, Saint John, New Brunswick, E2L 4N4.
8. Payment of taxes other than air and hotel taxes is the sole responsibility of the winner.
9. Void where prohibited by law.

PASSPORT TO ROMANCE VACATION SWEEPSTAKES

OFFICIAL RULES

SWEEPSTAKES RULES AND REGULATIONS. NO PURCHASE NECESSARY.
HOW TO ENTER:

1. To enter, complete this official entry form and return with your invoice in the envelope provided, or print your name, address, telephone number and age on a plain piece of paper and mail to: Passport to Romance, P.O. Box #1397, Buffalo, N.Y. 14269-1397. No mechanically reproduced entries accepted.
2. All entries must be received by the Contest Closing Date, midnight, December 31, 1990 to be eligible.
3. Prizes: There will be ten (10) Grand Prizes awarded, each consisting of a choice of a trip for two people to: i) London, England (approximate retail value $5,050 U.S.); ii) England, Wales and Scotland (approximate retail value $6,400 U.S.); iii) Caribbean Cruise (approximate retail value $7,300 U.S.); iv) Hawaii (approximate retail value $ 9,550 U.S.); v) Greek Island Cruise in the Mediterranean (approximate retail value $12,250 U.S.); vi) France (approximate retail value $7,300 U.S.).
4. Any winner may choose to receive any trip or a cash alternative prize of $5,000.00 U.S. in lieu of the trip.
5. Odds of winning depend on number of entries received.
6. A random draw will be made by Nielsen Promotion Services, an independent judging organization on January 29, 1991, in Buffalo, N.Y., at 11:30 a.m. from all eligible entries received on or before the Contest Closing Date. Any Canadian entrants who are selected must correctly answer a time-limited, mathematical skill-testing question in order to win. Quebec residents may submit any litigation respecting the conduct and awarding of a prize in this contest to the Régie des loteries et courses du Quebec.
7. Full contest rules may be obtained by sending a stamped, self-addressed envelope to: "Passport to Romance Rules Request", P.O. Box 9998, Saint John, New Brunswick, E2L 4N4.
8. Payment of taxes other than air and hotel taxes is the sole responsibility of the winner
9. Void where prohibited by law.

RLS-DIR

PASSPORT
WIN
1 of 10 Vacations
SEE INSIDE
TO ROMANCE

VACATION SWEEPSTAKES

MONTH 2 ENTRY

Official Entry Form

Yes, enter me in the drawing for one of ten Vacations-for-Two! If I'm a winner, I'll get my choice of any of the six different destinations being offered — and I won't have to decide until after I'm notified!

Return entries with invoice in envelope provided along with Daily Travel Allowance Voucher. Each book in your shipment has two entry forms — and the more you enter, the better your chance of winning!

Name _____

Address _____ Apt. _____

City _____ State/Prov. _____ Zip/Postal Code _____

Daytime phone number _____
Area Code

☐ I am enclosing a Daily Travel Allowance Voucher in the amount of $_____ Write in amount revealed beneath scratch-off

© 1990 HARLEQUIN ENTERPRISES LTD

PASSPORT
WIN
1 of 10 Vacations
SEE INSIDE
TO ROMANCE

VACATION SWEEPSTAKES

MONTH 2 ENTRY

Official Entry Form

Yes, enter me in the drawing for one of ten Vacations-for-Two! If I'm a winner, I'll get my choice of any of the six different destinations being offered — and I won't have to decide until after I'm notified!

Return entries with invoice in envelope provided along with Daily Travel Allowance Voucher. Each book in your shipment has two entry forms — and the more you enter, the better your chance of winning!

Name _____

Address _____ Apt. _____

City _____ State/Prov. _____ Zip/Postal Code _____

Daytime phone number _____
Area Code

☐ I am enclosing a Daily Travel Allowance Voucher in the amount of $_____ Write in amount revealed beneath scratch-off

CPS-TWO